BEREN AND LÚTHIEN

BY
J.R.R. Tolkien

Edited by Christopher Tolkien

With illustrations by Alan Lee

HarperCollins*Publishers*

HarperCollins*Publishers*
1 London Bridge Street,
London SE1 9GF
www.tolkien.co.uk

www.tolkienestate.com

Published by HarperCollins*Publishers* 2018

1

A CIP catalogue record for this book is available
from the British Library

ISBN 978 0 00 821422 7

Printed and bound in Great Britain by
CPI Group (UK) Ltd, Croydon CR0 4YY

For Baillie

CONTENTS

PLATES

PREFACE

After the publication of *The Silmarillion* in 1977 I spent several years investigating the earlier history of the work, and writing a book which I called *The History of The Silmarillion*. Later this became the (somewhat shortened) basis of the earlier volumes of *The History of Middle-earth*.

In 1981 I wrote at length to Rayner Unwin, the chairman of Allen and Unwin, giving him an account of what I had been, and was still, doing. At that time, as I informed him, the book was 1,968 pages long and sixteen and a half inches across, and obviously not for publication. I said to him: 'If and/or when you see this book, you will perceive immediately why I have said that it is in no conceivable way publishable. The textual and other discussions are far too detailed and minute; the size of it is (and will become progressively more so) prohibitive. It is done partly for my own satisfaction in getting things right, and because I wanted to know how the whole conception did in reality evolve from the earliest origins. . . .

'If there is a future for such enquiries, I want to make as sure as I can that any later research into JRRT's "literary history" is not turned into a nonsense by mistaking the actual course of its evolution. The chaos and intrinsic difficulty of many of the papers (the layer upon layer of changes in a single manuscript page, the vital clues on scattered scraps found anywhere in the archive, the texts written on the backs of other works, the disordering and separation of manuscripts, the near or total illegibility in places, is simply inexaggerable. . . .

'In theory, I could produce a lot of books out of the *History*, and there are many possibilities and combinations of possibilities. For example, I could do "Beren", with the original Lost Tale*, *The Lay of Leithian*, and an essay on the development of the legend. My preference, if it came to anything so positive, would probably be for the treating of one legend as a developing entity, rather than to give all the Lost Tales at one go; but the difficulties of exposition in detail would in such a case be great, because one would have to explain so often what was happening elsewhere, in other unpublished writings.'

I said that I would enjoy writing a book called 'Beren' on the lines I suggested: but 'the problem would be its organisation, so that the matter was comprehensible without the editor becoming overpowering.'

When I wrote this I meant what I said about publication: I had no thought of its possibility, other than my idea of

---

* 'The Lost Tales' is the name of the original versions of the legends of *The Silmarillion*.

selecting a single legend 'as a developing entity'. I seem now to have done precisely that – though with no thought of what I had said in my letter to Rayner Unwin thirty-five years ago: I had altogether forgotten it, until I came on it by chance when this book was all but completed.

There is however a substantial difference between it and my original idea, which is a difference of context. Since then, a large part of the immense store of manuscripts pertaining to the First Age, or Elder Days, has been published, in close and detailed editions: chiefly in volumes of *The History of Middle-earth*. The idea of a book devoted to the evolving story of 'Beren' that I ventured to mention to Rayner Unwin as a possible publication would have brought to light much hitherto unknown and unavailable writing. But this book does not offer a single page of original and unpublished work. What then is the need, now, for such a book?

I will attempt to provide an (inevitably complex) answer, or several answers. In the first place, an aspect of those editions was the presentation of the texts in a way that adequately displayed my father's apparently eccentric mode of composition (often in fact imposed by external pressures), and so to discover the sequence of stages in the development of a narrative, and to justify my interpretation of the evidence.

At the same time, the First Age in *The History of Middle-earth* was in those books conceived as a *history* in two senses. It was indeed a history – a chronicle of lives and events in Middle-earth; but it was also a history of the changing literary conceptions in the passing years; and therefore the story of Beren and Lúthien is spread over many years and several books. Moreover, since that story became entangled with the slowly evolving 'Silmarillion', and ultimately an essential part of it, its developments are recorded in successive manuscripts primarily concerned with the whole history of the Elder Days.

To follow the story of Beren and Lúthien, as a single and well-defined narrative, in *The History of Middle-earth* is therefore not easy.

In an often quoted letter of 1951 my father called it 'the chief of the stories of the *Silmarillion*', and he said of Beren that he is 'the outlawed mortal who succeeds (with the help of Lúthien, a mere maiden even if an elf of royalty) where all the armies and warriors have failed: he penetrates the stronghold of the Enemy and wrests one of the Silmarilli from the Iron Crown. Thus he wins the hand of Lúthien and the first marriage of mortal and immortal is achieved.

'As such the story is (I think a beautiful and powerful) heroic-fairy-romance, receivable in itself with only a very general vague knowledge of the background. But it is also a fundamental link in the cycle, deprived of its full significance out of its place therein.'

In the second place, my purpose in this book is twofold. On the one hand I have tried to separate the story of Beren and Tinúviel (Lúthien) so that it stands alone, so far as that can be done (in my opinion) without distortion. On the other hand, I have wished to show how this fundamental story evolved over the years. In my foreword to the first volume of *The Book of Lost Tales* I said of the changes in the stories:

In the history of the history of Middle-earth the development was seldom by outright rejection – far more often it was by subtle transformation in stages, so that the growth of the legends (the process, for instance, by which the Nargothrond story made contact with that of Beren and Lúthien, a contact not even hinted at in the *Lost Tales*, though both elements were present) can seem like the growth of legends among peoples, the product of many minds and generations.

It is an essential feature of this book that these developments in the legend of Beren and Lúthien are shown in my father's own words, for the method that I have employed is the extraction of passages from much longer manuscripts in prose or verse written over many years.

In this way, also, there are brought to light passages of close description or dramatic immediacy that are lost in the summary, condensed manner characteristic of so much *Silmarillion* narrative writing; there are even to be discovered elements in the story that were later altogether lost. Thus, for example, the cross-examination of Beren and Felagund and their companions, disguised as Orcs, by Thû the Necromancer (the first appearance of Sauron), or the entry into the story of the appalling Tevildo, Prince of Cats, who clearly deserves to be remembered, short as was his literary life.

Lastly, I will cite another of my prefaces, that to *The Children of Húrin* (2007):

It is undeniable that there are a very great many readers of *The Lord of the Rings* for whom the legends of the Elder Days are altogether unknown, unless by their repute as strange and inaccessible in mode and manner.

It is also undeniable that the volumes of *The History of Middle-earth* in question may well present a deterrent aspect. This is because my father's mode of composition was intrinsically difficult: and a primary purpose of the *History* was to try to disentangle it: thereby (it may seem) exhibiting the tales of the Elder Days as a creation of unceasing fluidity.

I believe that he might have said, in explanation of some rejected element in a tale: I came to see that it was not like that; or, I realised that that was not the right name. The fluidity should not be exaggerated: there were nonetheless great, essential, permanences. But it was certainly my hope, in composing this book, that it would show how the creation of an ancient legend of Middle-earth, changing and growing over many years, reflected the search of the author for a presentation of the myth nearer to his desire.

In my letter to Rayner Unwin of 1981 I observed that in the event of my restricting myself to a single legend from among the legends that make up the *Lost Tales* 'the difficulties of exposition in detail would in such a case be great, because one would have to explain so often what was happening elsewhere, in other unpublished writings'. This has proved an accurate prediction in the case of *Beren and Lúthien*. A solution of some sort must be achieved, for Beren and Lúthien did not live, love, and die, with their friends and foes, on an empty stage, alone and with no past. I have therefore followed my own solution in *The Children of Húrin*. In my preface to that book I wrote:

> It seems unquestionable, from my father's own words, that if he could achieve final and finished narratives on the scale he desired, he saw the three 'Great Tales' of the Elder Days (Beren and Lúthien, the Children of Húrin, and the Fall of Gondolin) as works sufficiently complete in themselves as not to demand knowledge of the great body of legend known as *The Silmarillion*. On the other hand . . . the tale of the Children of Húrin is integral to the history of Elves and Men in the Elder Days, and there are necessarily a good many references to events and circumstances in that larger story.

I therefore gave 'a very brief sketch of Beleriand and its peoples near the end of the Elder Days', and I included 'a list of all names occurring in the text with very concise indications concerning each.' In this book I have adopted from *The Children of Húrin* that brief sketch, adapting and shortening it, and I have likewise provided a list of all names occurring in the texts, in this case with explanatory indications of a very varied nature. None of this ancillary matter is essential, but is intended merely as an assistance if desired.

A further problem which I should mention arose from the very frequent changes of names. To follow with exactness and consistency the succession of names in texts of different dates would not serve the purpose of this book. I have therefore observed no rule in this respect, but distinguished old and new in some cases but not in others, for various reasons. In a great many cases my father would alter a name in a manuscript at some later, or even much later, time, but not consistently: for example, *Elfin* to *Elven*. In such cases I have made *Elven* the sole form, or *Beleriand* for earlier *Broseliand*; but in others I have retained both, as in *Tinwelint/Thingol*, *Artanor/Doriath*.

The purpose of this book, then, is altogether different from that of the volumes of *The History of Middle-earth* from which it is derived. It is emphatically not intended as an adjunct to those books. It is an attempt to extract one narrative element from a vast work of extraordinary richness and complexity; but that narrative, the story of Beren and Lúthien, was itself continually evolving, and developing new associations as it became more embedded in the wider history. The decision of what to include and what to exclude of that ancient world 'at large' could only be a matter of personal and often question-able judgement: in such an attempt there can be no attainable 'correct way'. In general, however, I have erred on the side of clarity, and resisted the urge to explain, for fear of undermin-ing the primary purpose and method of the book.

In my ninety-third year this is (presumptively) my last book in the long series of editions of my father's writings, very largely previously unpublished, and is of a somewhat curious nature. This tale is chosen *in memoriam* because of its deeply-rooted presence in his own life, and his intense thought on the union of Lúthien, whom he called 'the greatest of the Eldar', and of Beren the mortal man, of their fates, and of their second lives.

It goes back a long way in my life, for it is my earliest actual recollection of some element in a story that was being told to me – not simply a remembered image of the scene of the storytelling. My father told it to me, or parts of it, speaking it without any writing, in the early 1930s.

The element in the story that I recall, in my mind's eye, is that of the eyes of the wolves as they appeared one by one in the darkness of the dungeon of Thû.

In a letter to me on the subject of my mother, written in the year after her death, which was also the year before his own, he wrote of his overwhelming sense of bereavement, and of his wish to have *Lúthien* inscribed beneath her name on the grave. He returned in that letter, as in that cited on p. 29 of this book, to the origin of the tale of Beren and Lúthien in a small woodland glade filled with hemlock flowers near Roos in Yorkshire, where she danced; and he said: 'But the story has gone crooked, and I am left, and *I* cannot plead before the inexorable Mandos.'

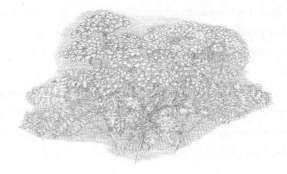

NOTES ON THE ELDER DAYS

The depth in time to which this story reaches back was memorably conveyed in a passage in *The Lord of the Rings*. At the great council in Rivendell Elrond spoke of the Last Alliance of Elves and Men and the defeat of Sauron at the end of the Second Age, more than three thousand years before:

Thereupon Elrond paused a while and sighed. 'I remember well the splendour of their banners,' he said. 'It recalled to me the glory of the Elder Days and the hosts of Beleriand, so many great princes and captains were assembled. And yet not so many, nor so fair, as when Thangorodrim was broken, and the Elves deemed that evil was ended for ever, and it was not so.'

'You remember?' said Frodo, speaking his thought aloud in his astonishment. 'But I thought,' he stammered as Elrond turned towards him, 'I thought that the fall of Gil-galad was a long age ago.'

'So it was indeed,' answered Elrond gravely. 'But my memory reaches back even to the Elder Days. Eärendil was my sire, who was born in Gondolin before its fall; and my mother was Elwing, daughter of Dior, son of Lúthien of Doriath. I have seen three ages in the West of the world, and many defeats, and many fruitless victories.'

Of Morgoth

Morgoth, the Black Enemy, as he came to be called, was in his origin, as he declared to Húrin brought captive before him, 'Melkor, first and mightiest of the Valar, who was before the world.' Now become permanently incarnate, in form a gigantic and majestic, but terrible, King in the north-west of Middle-earth, he was physically present in his huge fortress of Angband, the Hells of Iron: the black reek that issued from the summits of Thangorodrim, the mountains that he piled above Angband, could be seen far off staining the northern sky. It is said in the *Annals of Beleriand* that 'the gates of Morgoth were but one hundred and fifty leagues from the bridge of Menegroth; far and yet all too near.' These words refer to the bridge leading to the dwellings of the Elvish king Thingol; they were called Menegroth, the Thousand Caves.

But being incarnate Morgoth was afraid. My father wrote of him:

'As he grew in malice, and sent forth from himself the evil that he conceived in lies and creatures of wickedness, his power passed into them and was dispersed, and he himself became ever more earth-bound, unwilling to issue from his dark strongholds.' Thus when Fingolfin, High King of the Noldorin Elves rode alone to Angband to challenge Morgoth to combat, he cried at the gate: Come forth, thou coward king, to fight with thine own hand! Den-dweller, wielder of thralls, liar and lurker, foe of Gods and Elves, come! For I would see thy craven face. Then (it is told) Morgoth came. For he could not refuse such a challenge before the face of his captains. He fought with the great hammer Grond, which at each blow made a great pit, and he beat Fingolfin to the ground; but as he died he pinned the great foot of Morgoth to the earth, and the black blood gushed forth and filled the pits of Grond. Morgoth went ever halt thereafter. So also, when Beren and Lúthien made their way into the deepest hall in Angband where Morgoth sat, Lúthien cast a spell on him; and suddenly he fell, as a hill sliding in avalanche, and hurled like thunder from his throne lay prone upon the floors of hell.

Of Beleriand

When Treebeard strode through the forest of Fangorn carrying Merry and Pippin each in the crook of his arm he sang to them of ancient forests in the great country of Beleriand, which was destroyed in the tumults of the Great Battle at the end of the Elder Days. The Great Sea poured in and drowned all the lands west of the Blue Mountains, called Ered Luin and Ered Lindon; so that the map accompanying *The Silmarillion* ends in the east with that mountain-chain, whereas the map accompanying *The Lord of the Rings* ends in the west, also with the Blue Mountains. The coastal lands beyond them on their western sides were all that remained in the Third Age of that country, called Ossiriand, Land of Seven Rivers, in which Treebeard once walked:

> *I wandered in Summer in the elm-woods of Ossiriand.*
> *Ah! the light and the music in the Summer by the Seven*
> *   Rivers of Ossir!*
> *And I thought that was best.*

It was over the passes of the Blue Mountains that Men entered Beleriand; in those mountains were the cities of the Dwarves, Nogrod and Belegost; and it was in Ossiriand that Beren and Lúthien dwelt after they were permitted by Mandos to return to Middle-earth (p. 235).

Treebeard walked also among the pine-trees of Dorthonion ('Land of Pines'):

> *To the pine-trees upon the highland of Dorthonion I climbed*
> *   in the Winter.*
> *Ah! the wind and the whiteness and the black branches of*
> *   Winter upon Orod-na-Thôn!*
> *My voice went up and sang in the sky.*

That country came afterwards to be called Taur-nu-Fuin, 'the Forest under Night', when Morgoth turned it into 'a region of dread and dark enchantment, of wandering and despair' (see p. 107).

Of the Elves

The Elves appeared on earth far off in a distant land (Palisor) beside a lake named Cuiviénen, the Water of Awakening; and thence they were summoned by the Valar to leave Middle-earth, and passing over the Great Sea to come to the 'Blessed Realm' of Aman in the west of the world, the land of the Gods. Those who accepted the summons were led on a great march across Middle-earth by the Vala Oromë, the Hunter, and they are called the Eldar, the Elves of the Great Journey, the High Elves, distinct from those who, refusing the summons, chose Middle-earth for their land and their destiny.

But not all the Eldar, though they had crossed the Blue Mountains, departed over the sea; and those who remained in Beleriand are named the Sindar, the Grey Elves. Their high king was Thingol (which means 'Grey-cloak'), who ruled from Menegroth, the Thousand Caves in Doriath (Artanor). And not all the Eldar who crossed the Great Sea remained in the land of the Valar; for one of their great kindreds, the Noldor (the 'Loremasters'), returned to Middle-earth, and they are called the Exiles.

The prime mover in their rebellion against the Valar was Fëanor, maker of the Silmarils; he was the eldest son of Finwë, who had led the host of the Noldor from Cuiviénen, but was now dead. In my father's words:

> The Jewels were coveted by Morgoth the Enemy, who stole them and, after destroying the Trees, took them to Middle-earth, and guarded them in his great fortress of

Thangorodrim. Against the will of the Valar Fëanor forsook the Blessed Realm and went in exile to Middle-earth, leading with him a great part of his people, for in his pride he purposed to recover the Jewels from Morgoth by force.

Thereafter followed the hopeless war of the Eldar and the Edain [the Men of the Three Houses of the Elf-friends] against Thangorodrim, in which they were at last utterly defeated.

Before their departure from Valinor there took place the dreadful event that marred the history of the Noldor in Middle-earth. Fëanor demanded of those Teleri, the third host of the Eldar on the Great Journey, who dwelt now on the coast of Aman, that they give up to the Noldor their fleet of ships, their great pride, for without ships the crossing to Middle-earth by such a host would not be possible. This the Teleri refused utterly.

Then Fëanor and his people attacked the Teleri in their city of Alqualondë, the Haven of the Swans, and took the fleet by force. In that battle, which was known as The Kinslaying, many of the Teleri were slain. This is referred to in *The Tale of Tinúviel* (p. 42): 'the evil deeds of the Gnomes at the Haven of the Swans', and see p. 130, lines 514–19.

Fëanor was slain in battle soon after the return of the Noldor to Middle-earth, and his seven sons held wide lands in the east of Beleriand, between Dorthonion (Taur-na-fuin) and the Blue Mountains.

The second son of Finwë was Fingolfin (the half-brother of Fëanor), who was held the overlord of all the Noldor; and he with his son Fingon ruled Hithlum, which lay to the north and west of the great chain of Ered Wethrin, the Mountains of Shadow. Fingolfin died in single combat with Morgoth. The second son of Fingolfin, the brother of Fingon, was Turgon, the founder and ruler of the hidden city of Gondolin.

The third son of Finwë, the brother of Fingolfin and half-brother of Fëanor, was in earlier texts Finrod, later Finarfin (see p. 104). The eldest son of Finrod/Finarfin was in earlier texts Felagund, but later Finrod; he, inspired by the magnificence and beauty of Menegroth in Doriath, founded the underground fortress-city of Nargothrond, for which he was named Felagund, 'Lord of Caves': thus earlier Felagund = later Finrod Felagund.

The doors of Nargothrond opened onto the gorge of the river Narog in West Beleriand; but Felagund's realm extended far and wide, east to the river Sirion and west to the river Nenning that reached the sea at the haven of Eglarest. But Felagund was slain in the dungeons of Thû the Necromancer, later Sauron; and Orodreth, the second son of Finarfin, took the crown of Nargothrond, as told in this book (pp. 109, 120).

The other sons of Finarfin, Angrod and Egnor, vassals of their brother Finrod Felagund, dwelt on Dorthonion, looking northwards over the vast plain of Ard-galen. Galadriel, the sister of Finrod Felagund, dwelt long in Doriath with Melian the Queen. Melian (in early texts Gwendeling and other forms) was a Maia, a spirit of great power who took human form and dwelt in the forests of Beleriand with King Thingol: she was the mother of Lúthien and the foremother of Elrond.

In the sixtieth year after the return of the Noldor, ending many years of peace, a great host of Orcs came down from Angband, but was utterly defeated and destroyed by the Noldor. This was called *Dagor Aglareb*, the Glorious Battle; but the Elvish lords took warning from it, and set the Siege of Angband, which lasted for almost four hundred years.

The Siege of Angband ended with a terrible suddenness (though long prepared) on a night of midwinter. Morgoth released rivers of fire that ran down from Thangorodrim, and the great grassy plain of Ard-galen that lay to the north of Dorthonion was transformed into a parched and arid waste, known thereafter by a changed name, *Anfauglith*, the Gasping Dust.

This catastrophic assault was called *Dagor Bragollach*, the Battle of Sudden Flame (p. 106). Glaurung Father of Dragons emerged from Angband now for the first time in his full might; vast armies of Orcs poured southwards; the Elvish lords of Dorthonion were slain, and a great part of the warriors of Bëor's people (pp. 105–6). King Fingolfin and his son Fingon were driven back with the warriors of Hithlum to the fortress of Eithel Sirion (Sirion's Well), where the great river rose in the east face of the Mountains of Shadow. The torrents of fire were stopped by the Mountains of Shadow, and Hithlum and Dor-lómin remained unconquered.

It was in the year after the *Bragollach* that Fingolfin, in a fury of despair, rode to Angband and challenged Morgoth.

*

BEREN AND LÚTHIEN

IN A LETTER of my father's written on the 16th of July 1964 he said:

> The germ of my attempt to write legends of my own to fit my private languages was the tragic tale of the hapless Kullervo in the Finnish *Kalevala*. It remains a major matter in the legends of the First Age (which I hope to publish as *The Silmarillion*), though as 'The Children of Húrin' it is entirely changed except in the tragic ending. The second point was the writing, 'out of my head', of 'The Fall of Gondolin', the story of Idril and Earendel, during sick-leave from the army in 1917; and by the original version of the 'Tale of Lúthien Tinúviel and Beren' later in the same year. That was founded on a small wood with a great undergrowth of 'hemlock' (no doubt many other related plants were also there) near Roos in Holderness, where I was for a while on the Humber Garrison.

My father and mother were married in March 1916, when he was twenty-four and she was twenty-seven. They lived at first in the village of Great Haywood in Staffordshire; but he

embarked for France and the Battle of the Somme early in
June of that year. Taken ill, he was sent back to England at the
beginning of November 1916; and in the spring of 1917 he
was posted to Yorkshire.

This primary version of *The Tale of Tinúviel*, as he called
it, written in 1917, does not exist – or more precisely, exists
only in the ghostly form of a manuscript in pencil that he all
but entirely erased for most of its length; over this he wrote
the text that is for us the earliest version. *The Tale of Tinúviel*
was one of the constituent stories of my father's major early
work of his 'mythology', *The Book of Lost Tales*, an exceed-
ingly complex work which I edited in the first two volumes
of *The History of Middle-earth*, 1983–4. But since the present
book is expressly devoted to the evolution of the legend of
Beren and Lúthien I will here very largely pass by the strange
setting and audience of the *Lost Tales*, for *The Tale of Tinúviel*
is in itself almost entirely independent of that setting.

Central to *The Book of Lost Tales* was the story of an
English mariner of the 'Anglo-Saxon' period named Eriol or
Ælfwine who, sailing far westwards over the ocean, came at
last to Tol Eressëa, the Lonely Isle, where dwelt Elves who had
departed from 'the Great Lands', afterwards 'Middle-Earth'
(a term not used in the *Lost Tales*). During his sojourn in Tol
Eressëa he learned from them the true and ancient history of
the Creation, of the Gods, of the Elves, and of England. This
history is 'The Lost Tales of Elfinesse'.

The work is extant in a number of battered little 'exercise
books' in ink and pencil, often formidably difficult to read,

though after many hours of peering at the manuscript with a lens I was able, many years ago, to elucidate all the texts with only occasional unsolved words. *The Tale of Tinúviel* is one of the stories that was told to Eriol by the Elves in the Lonely Isle, in this case by a maiden named Vëannë: there were many children present at these story-tellings. Sharply observant of detail (a striking feature), it is told in an extremely individual style, with some archaisms of word and construction, altogether unlike my father's later styles, intense, poetic, at times deeply 'elvish-mysterious'. There is also an undercurrent of sardonic humour in the expression here and there (in the terrible confrontation with the demonic wolf Karkaras as she fled with Beren from Melko's hall Tinúviel enquires 'Wherefore this surliness, Karkaras?').

Rather than awaiting the conclusion of the *Tale* I think it may be helpful to draw attention here to certain aspects of this earliest version of the legend, and to give brief explanations of some names important in the narrative (which are also to be found in the List of Names at the end of the book).

The Tale of Tinúviel in its rewritten form, which is the earliest form for us, was by no means the earliest of the *Lost Tales*, and light is shed on it by features in other *Tales*. To speak only of narrative structure, some of them, such as the tale of Túrin, are not very far removed from the version in the published *Silmarillion*; some, notably the Fall of Gondolin, the first to be written, is present in the published work only in a severely compressed form; and some, most remarkably the present Tale, are strikingly different in certain aspects.

A fundamental change in the evolution of the legend of Beren and Tinúviel (Lúthien) was the entry into it later of the story of Felagund of Nargothrond and the sons of Fëanor; but equally significant, in a different aspect, was the alteration in the identity of Beren. In the later versions of the legend it was an altogether essential element that Beren was a mortal man, whereas Lúthien was an immortal Elf; but this was not present in the *Lost Tale*: Beren, also, was an Elf. (It is seen, however, from my father's notes to other Tales, that he was originally a Man; and it is clear that this was true also in the erased manuscript of *The Tale of Tinúviel.*) Beren the Elf was of the Elvish people named the Noldoli (later Noldor), which in the *Lost Tales* (and later) is translated 'Gnomes': Beren was a Gnome. This translation later became a problem for my father. He was using another word *Gnome*, wholly distinct in origin and meaning from those Gnomes who nowadays are small figures specially associated with gardens. This other *Gnome* was derived from a Greek word gnōmē 'thought, intelligence'; it barely survives in modern English, with the meaning 'aphorism, maxim', together with the adjective *gnomic.*

In a draft for Appendix F of *The Lord of the Rings* he wrote:

I have sometimes (not in this book) used 'Gnomes' for *Noldor* and 'Gnomish' for *Noldorin.* This I did, for to some 'Gnome' will still suggest knowledge. Now the High-elven name of this people, Noldor, signifies Those who Know; for of the three kindreds of the Eldar from

their beginning the Noldor were ever distinguished, both by their knowledge of the things that are and were in this world, and by their desire to know more. Yet they in no way resembled the Gnomes either of learned theory or popular fancy; and I have now abandoned this rendering as too misleading.

(In passing, I would mention that he said also [in a letter of 1954] that he greatly regretted having used the word 'Elves', which has become 'overloaded with regrettable tones' that are 'too much to overcome'.)

The hostility shown to Beren, as an Elf, is explained thus in the old Tale (p. 42): 'all the Elves of the woodland thought of the Gnomes of Dor-lómin as treacherous creatures, cruel and faithless'.

It may well seem somewhat puzzling that the word 'fairy, fairies' is frequently used of Elves. Thus, of the white moths that flew in the woods 'Tinúviel being a fairy minded them not' (p. 41); she names herself 'Princess of Fairies' (p. 64); it is said of her (p. 72) that she 'put forth her skill and fairy-magic'. In the first place, the word *fairies* in the *Lost Tales* is synonymous with *Elves*; and in those tales there are several references to the relative physical stature of Men and Elves. In those early days my father's conceptions on such matters were somewhat fluctuating, but it is clear that he conceived a changing relation as the ages passed. Thus he wrote:

Men were almost of a stature at first with Elves, the fairies being far greater and Men smaller than now.

But the evolution of Elves was greatly influenced by the coming of Men:

Ever as Men wax more powerful and numerous so the fairies fade and grow small and tenuous, filmy and transparent, but Men larger and more dense and gross. At last Men, or almost all, can no longer see the fairies.

There is thus no need to suppose, on account of the word, that my father thought of the 'Fairies' of this tale as filmy and transparent; and of course years later, when the Elves of the Third Age had entered the history of Middle-earth, there was nothing 'fairylike', in the modern sense, about them.

The word *fay* is more obscure. In *The Tale of Tinúviel* it is used frequently of Melian (the mother of Lúthien), who came from Valinor (and is called [p. 40] 'a daughter of the Gods'), but also of Tevildo, who was said to be 'an evil fay in beastlike shape' (p. 69). Elsewhere in the *Tales* there are references to 'the wisdom of fays and of Eldar', to 'Orcs and dragons and evil fays', and to 'a fay of the woods and dells'. Most notable perhaps is the following passage from the *Tale of the Coming of the Valar*:

About them fared a great host who are the sprites [spirits] of trees and woods, of dale and forest and mountain-side, or those that sing amid the grass at morning and chant among the standing corn at eve. These are the Nermir and the Tavari, Nandini and Orossi [fays (?) of the meads, of the woods, of the valleys, of the mountains], fays, pixies, leprawns, and what else are they not called, for their number is very great; yet must they not be confused with the Eldar [Elves], for they were born before the world, and are older than its oldest, and are not of it.

Another puzzling feature, appearing not only in *The Tale of Tinúviel*, of which I have found no explanation, nor any more general observation, concerns the power that the Valar possess over the affairs of Men and Elves, and indeed over their minds and hearts, in the far distant Great Lands (Middle-earth). To give examples: on p. 78 'the Valar brought [Huan] to a glade' where Beren and Lúthien were lying on the ground in their flight from Angband; and she said to her father (p. 82): 'The Valar alone saved [Beren] from a bitter death'. Or again, in the account of Lúthien's flight from Doriath (p. 57), 'she entered not that dark region, and regaining heart pressed on' was later changed to 'she entered not that dark region, and the Valar set a new hope in her heart, so that she pressed on once more.'

As regards the names that appear in the Tale, I will note here that *Artanor* corresponds to later *Doriath* and was also called *The Land Beyond*; to the north lay the barrier of the *Iron Mountains*, also called the *Bitter Hills*, over which Beren came: afterwards they became *Ered Wethrin, the Mountains of Shadow*. Beyond the mountains lay *Hisilómë* (*Hithlum*)

the Land of Shadow, also called *Dor-lómin*. *Palisor* (p. 37) is
the land where the Elves awoke.

The Valar are often referred to as the Gods, and are called
also the *Ainur* (singular *Ainu*). *Melko* (later *Melkor*) is the
great evil Vala, called *Morgoth*, the Black Foe, after his theft
of the Silmarils. *Mandos* is the name both of the Vala and the
place of his abode. He is the keeper of the Houses of the Dead.

Manwë is the lord of the Valar; Varda, maker of the stars, is
the spouse of Manwë and dwells with him on the summit of
Taniquetil, the highest mountain of Arda. The Two Trees are
the great trees whose flowers gave light to Valinor, destroyed
by Morgoth and the monstrous spider Ungoliant.

Lastly, this is a convenient place to say something of the
Silmarils, fundamental to the legend of Beren and Lúthien:
they were the work of Fëanor, greatest of the Noldor: 'the
mightiest in skill of word and of hand'; his name means 'Spirit
of Fire'. I will quote here a passage from the later (1930)
'Silmarillion' text entitled *Quenta Noldorinwa*, on which see
p. 103.

In those far days Fëanor began on a time a long and marvellous labour, and all his power and all his subtle magic he
called upon, for he purposed to make a thing more fair than
any of the Eldar yet had made, that should last beyond the
end of all. Three jewels he made, and named them Silmarils.
A living fire burned within them that was blended of the light
of the Two Trees; of their own radiance they shone even in
the dark; no mortal flesh impure could touch them, but was

withered and was scorched. These jewels the Elves prized beyond all the works of their hands, and Manwë hallowed them, and Varda said: 'The fate of the Elves is locked herein, and the fate of many things beside.' The heart of Fëanor was wound about the things he himself had made.

A terrible and deeply destructive oath was sworn by Fëanor and his seven sons in assertion of their sole and inviolable right to the Silmarils, which were stolen by Morgoth.

Vëannë's tale was expressly addressed to Eriol (Ælfwine), who had never heard of Tinúviel, but as she tells it there is no formal opening: she begins with an account of Tinwelint and Gwendeling (afterwards known as Thingol and Melian). I will however turn again to the *Quenta Noldorinwa* for this essential element in the legend. In the *Tale* the formidable Tinwelint (Thingol) is a central figure: the king of the Elves who dwelt in the deep woodlands of Artanor, ruling from his vast cavern in the heart of the forest. But the queen was also a personage of great significance, although seldom seen, and I give here the account of her given in the *Quenta Noldorinwa.*

In this it is told that on the Great Journey of the Elves from far off Palisor, the place of their awakening, with the ultimate goal of reaching Valinor in the far West beyond the great Ocean

[many Elves] were lost upon the long dark roads, and they wandered in the woods and mountains of the world, and never came to Valinor, nor saw the light of the Two Trees.

Therefore they are called Ilkorindi, the Elves that dwelt never in Kôr, the city of the Eldar [Elves] in the land of the Gods. The Dark-elves are they, and many are their scattered tribes, and many are their tongues.

Of the Dark-elves the chief in renown was Thingol. For this reason he came never to Valinor. Melian was a fay. In the gardens of [the Vala] Lórien she dwelt, and among all his fair folk none were there that surpassed her beauty, nor none more wise, nor none more skilled in magical and enchanting song. It is told that the Gods would leave their business and the birds of Valinor their mirth, that Valmar's bells were silent, and the fountains ceased to flow, when at the mingling of the light Melian sang in the gardens of the God of Dreams. Nightingales went always with her, and their song she taught them. But she loved deep shadow, and often strayed on long journeys into the Outer Lands [Middle-earth], and there filled the silence of the dawning world with her voice and the voices of her birds.

The nightingales of Melian Thingol heard and was enchanted and left his folk. Melian he found beneath the trees and was cast into a dream and a great slumber, so that his people sought him in vain.

In Vëannë's account, when Tinwelint awoke from his mythically long sleep 'he thought no more of his people (and indeed it had been vain, for long now had those reached Valinor)', but desired only to see the lady of the twilight. She was not far off, for she had watched over him as he slept. 'But more of their story I know not, O Eriol, save that in the end she became his wife, for Tinwelint and Gwendeling very long indeed were king and queen of the Lost Elves of Artanor or the Land Beyond, or so it is said here.'

Vëannë said further that the dwelling of Tinwelint 'was hidden from the vision and knowledge of Melko by the magics of Gwendeling the fay, and she wove spells about the paths thereto that none but the Eldar [Elves] might tread them easily, and so was the king secured from all dangers save it be treachery alone. Now his halls were built in a deep cavern of great size, and they were nonetheless a kingly and a fair abode. This cavern was in the heart of the mighty forest of Artanor that is the mightiest of forests, and a stream ran before its doors, but none could enter that portal save across the stream, and a bridge spanned it narrow and well guarded.' Then Vëannë exclaimed: 'Lo, now I will tell you of things that happened in the halls of Tinwelint'; and this seems to be the point at which the tale proper can be said to begin.

THE TALE OF TINÚVIEL

Two children had Tinwelint then, Dairon and Tinúviel, and Tinúviel was a maiden, and the most beautiful of all the maidens of the hidden Elves, and indeed few have been so fair, for her mother was a fay, a daughter of the Gods; but Dairon was then a boy strong and merry, and above all things he delighted to play upon a pipe of reeds or other woodland instruments, and he is named now among the three most magic players of the Elves, and the others are Tinfang Warble and Ivárë who plays beside the sea. But Tinúviel's joy was rather in the dance, and no names are set with hers for the beauty and subtlety of her twinkling feet.

Now it was the delight of Dairon and Tinúviel to fare away from the cavernous palace of Tinwelint their father and together spend long times amid the trees. There often would Dairon sit upon a tussock or a tree-root and make music while Tinúviel danced thereto, and when she danced to the playing of Dairon more lissom was she than Gwendeling, more magical than Tinfang Warble neath the moon, nor may any see such lilting save be it only in the rose gardens of Valinor where Nessa dances on the lawns of never-fading green.

Even at night when the moon shone pale still would they play and dance, and they were not afraid as I should be, for the rule of Tinwelint and of Gwendeling held evil from the woods and Melko troubled them not as yet, and Men were hemmed beyond the hills.

Now the place that they loved the most was a shady spot, and elms grew there, and beech too, but these were not very tall, and some chestnut trees there were with white flowers, but the ground was moist and a great misty growth of hemlocks rose beneath the trees. On a time of June they were playing there, and the white umbels of the hemlocks were like a cloud about the boles of the trees, and there Tinúviel danced until the evening faded late, and there were many white moths abroad. Tinúviel being a fairy minded them not as many of the children of Men do, although she loved not beetles, and spiders will none of the Eldar touch because of Ungweliantë – but now the white moths flittered about her head and Dairon trilled an eerie tune, when suddenly that strange thing befell.

Never have I heard how Beren came thither over the hills; yet was he braver than most, as thou shalt hear, and 'twas the love of wandering maybe alone that had sped him through the terrors of the Iron Mountains until he reached the Lands Beyond.

Now Beren was a Gnome, son of Egnor the forester who hunted in the darker places in the north of Hisilómë. Dread and suspicion was between the Eldar and those of their kindred that had tasted the slavery of Melko, and in this did the evil deeds of the Gnomes at the Haven of the Swans revenge itself. Now the lies of Melko ran among Beren's folk so that they believed evil things of the secret Elves, yet now did he see Tinúviel dancing in the twilight, and Tinúviel was in a silver-pearly dress, and her bare white feet were twinkling among the hemlock-stems. Then Beren cared not whether she were Vala or Elf or child of Men and crept near to see; and he leant against a young elm that grew upon a mound so that he might look down into the little glade where she was dancing, for the enchantment made him faint. So slender was she and so fair that at length he stood heedlessly in the open the better to gaze upon her, and at that moment the full moon came brightly through the boughs and Dairon caught sight of Beren's face. Straightway did he perceive that he was none of their folk, and all the Elves of the woodland thought of the Gnomes of Dor-lómin as treacherous creatures, cruel and faithless, wherefore Dairon dropped his instrument and crying 'Flee, flee, O Tinúviel, an enemy walks this wood' he was gone swiftly through the trees. Then Tinúviel in her amaze followed not straightway, for she understood not his words at once, and knowing she could not run or leap so hardily as her brother she slipped suddenly down among the white hemlocks and hid herself beneath a very tall flower with many spreading leaves; and here she looked in her white raiment like a spatter of moonlight shimmering through the leaves upon the floor.

Then Beren was sad, for he was lonely and was grieved at their fright, and he looked for Tinúviel everywhere about, thinking her not fled. Thus suddenly did he lay his hand upon her slender arm beneath the leaves, and with a cry she started away from him and flitted as fast as she could in the wan light, darting and wavering in the moonbeams as only the Eldar can, in and about the tree-trunks and the hemlock-stalks. The tender touch of her arm made Beren yet more eager than before to find her, and he followed swiftly and yet not swiftly enough, for in the end she escaped him, and reached the dwellings of her father in fear; nor did she dance alone in the woods for many a day after.

This was a great sorrow to Beren, who would not leave those places, hoping to see that fair elven maiden dance yet again, and he wandered in the wood growing wild and lonely for many a day and searching for Tinúviel. By dawn and dusk he sought her, but ever more hopefully when the moon shone bright. At last one night he caught a sparkle afar off, and lo, there she was dancing alone on a little treeless knoll and Dairon was not there. Often and often she came there after and danced and sang to herself, and sometimes Dairon would be nigh, and then Beren watched from the wood's edge afar, and sometimes he was away and Beren crept then closer. Indeed for long Tinúviel knew of his coming and feigned otherwise, and for long her fear had departed by reason of the wistful hunger of his face lit by the moonlight; and she saw that he was kind and in love with her beautiful dancing.

Then Beren took to following Tinúviel secretly through the woods even to the entrance of the cave and the bridge's head, and when she was gone in he would cry across the stream, softly saying 'Tinúviel', for he had caught the name from Dairon's lips; and although he knew it not Tinúviel often hearkened from within the shadows of the cavernous doors and laughed softly or smiled. At length one day as she danced alone he stepped out more boldly and said to her: 'Tinúviel, teach me to dance.' 'Who art thou?' said she. 'Beren. I am from across the Bitter Hills.' 'Then if thou wouldst dance, follow me,' said the maiden, and she danced before Beren away, and away into the woods, nimbly and yet not so fast that he could not follow, and ever and anon she would look back and laugh at him stumbling after, saying 'Dance, Beren, dance! as they dance beyond the Bitter Hills!' In this way they came by winding paths to the abode of Tinwelint, and Tinúviel beckoned Beren beyond the stream, and he followed her wondering down into the cave and the deep halls of her home.

When however Beren found himself before the king he was abashed, and of the stateliness of Queen Gwendeling he was in great awe, and behold when the king said: 'Who art thou that stumbleth into my halls unbidden?' he had nought to say. Tinúviel answered therefore for him, saying: 'This, my father, is Beren, a wanderer from beyond the hills, and he would learn to dance as the elves of Artanor can dance,' and she laughed, but the king frowned when he heard whence Beren came, and he said: 'Put away thy light words, my child, and say has this wild Elf of the shadows sought to do thee any harm?'

'Nay, father,' said she, 'and I think there is not evil in his heart at all, and be thou not harsh with him, unless thou desirest to see thy daughter Tinúviel weep, for more wonder has he at my dancing than any that I have known.' Therefore said Tinwelint now: 'O Beren son of the Noldoli, what does thou desire of the Elves of the wood ere thou returnest whence thou camest?'

So great was the amazed joy of Beren's heart when Tinúviel spake thus for him to her father that his courage rose within him, and his adventurous spirit that had brought him out of Hisilómë and over the Mountains of Iron awoke again, and looking boldly upon Tinwelint he said: 'Why, O king, I desire thy daughter Tinúviel, for she is the fairest and most sweet of all maidens I have seen or dreamed of.'

Then was there a silence in the hall, save that Dairon laughed, and all who heard were astounded, but Tinúviel cast down her eyes, and the king glancing at the wild and rugged aspect of Beren burst also into laughter, whereat Beren flushed for shame, and Tinúviel's heart was sore for him. 'Why! wed my Tinúviel fairest of the maidens of the world, and become a prince of the woodland Elves – 'tis but a little boon for a stranger to ask,' quoth Tinwelint. 'Haply I may with right ask somewhat in return. Nothing great shall it be, a token only of thy esteem. Bring me a Silmaril from the Crown of Melko, and that day Tinúviel weds thee, an she will.'

Then all in that place knew that the king treated the matter as an uncouth jest, having pity on the Gnome, and they smiled, for the fame of the Silmarils of Fëanor was now great throughout the world, and the Noldoli had told tales of them, and many that had escaped from Angamandi had seen them now blazing lustrous in the iron crown of Melko.

Never did this crown leave his head, and he treasured those
jewels as his eyes, and no one in the world, or fay or elf or
man, could hope ever to set finger even on them and live. This
indeed did Beren know, and he guessed the meaning of their
mocking smiles, and aflame with anger he cried; 'Nay, but
'tis too small a gift to the father of so sweet a bride. Strange
nonetheless seem to me the customs of the woodland Elves,
like to the rude laws of the folk of Men, that thou shouldst
name the gift unoffered, yet lo! I Beren, a huntsman of the
Noldoli, will fulfil thy small desire,' and with that he burst
from the hall while all stood astonished; but Tinúviel wept
suddenly. ''Twas ill done, O my father,' she cried, 'to send one
to his death with thy sorry jesting – for now methinks he will
attempt the deed, being maddened by thy scorn, and Melko
will slay him, and none will look ever again with such love
upon my dancing.'

Then said the king: ''Twill not be the first of Gnomes that
Melko has slain and for less reason. It is well for him that
he lies not bound here in grievous spells for his trespass in
my halls and for his insolent speech'; yet Gwendeling said
nought, neither did she chide Tinúviel or question her sudden
weeping for this unknown wanderer.

Beren however going from before the face of Tinwelint
was carried by his wrath far through the woods, until he
drew nigh to the lower hills and treeless lands that warned of
the approach of the bleak Iron Mountains. Only then did he
feel his weariness and stay his march, and thereafter did his
greater travails begin. Nights of deep despondency were his
and he saw no hope whatever in his quest, and indeed there

was little, and soon, as he followed the Iron Mountains till he drew nigh to the terrible regions of Melko's abode, the greatest fears assailed him. Many poisonous snakes were in those places and wolves roamed about, and more fearsome still were the wandering bands of the goblins and the Orcs – foul broodlings of Melko who fared abroad doing his evil work, snaring and capturing beasts, and Men, and Elves, and dragging them to their lord.

Many times was Beren near to capture by the Orcs, and once he escaped the jaws of a great wolf only after a combat wherein he was armed but with an ashen club, and other perils and adventures did he know each day of his wandering to Angamandi. Hunger and thirst too tortured him often, and often he would have turned back had not that been well nigh as perilous as going on; but the voice of Tinúviel pleading with Tinwelint echoed in his heart, and at night time it seemed to him that his heart heard her sometimes weeping softly for him far away in the woodlands of her home: and this was indeed true.

One day he was driven by great hunger to search amid a deserted camping of some Orcs for scraps of food, but some of these returned unawares and took him prisoner, and they tormented him but did not slay him, for their captain seeing his strength, worn though he was with hardships, thought that Melko might perchance be pleasured if he was brought before him and might set him to some heavy thrall-work in his mines or in his smithies. So came it that Beren was dragged before Melko, and he bore a stout heart within him nonetheless, for it was a belief among his father's kindred that the power of

Melko would not abide for ever, but the Valar would hearken at last to the tears of the Noldoli, and would arise and bind Melko and open Valinor once more to the weary Elves, and great joy should come back upon Earth.

Melko however looking upon him was wroth, asking how a Gnome, a thrall by birth of his, had dared to fare away into the woods unbidden, but Beren answered that he was no runagate but came of a kindred of Gnomes that dwelt in Aryador and mingled much there among the folk of Men. Then was Melko yet more angry, for he sought ever to destroy the friendship and intercourse of Elves and Men, and said that evidently here was a plotter of deep treacheries against Melko's lordship, and one worthy of the tortures of the Balrogs; but Beren seeing his peril answered: 'Think not, O most mighty Ainu Melko, Lord of the World, that this can be true, for if it were then should I not be here unaided and alone. No friendship has Beren son of Egnor for the kindred of Men; nay indeed, wearying utterly of the lands infested by that folk he has wandered out of Aryador. Many a great tale has my father made to me aforetime of thy splendour and glory, wherefore, albeit I am no renegade thrall, I do desire nothing so much as to serve thee in what small manner I may,' and Beren said therewith that he was a great trapper of small animals and a snarer of birds, and had become lost in the hills in these pursuits until after much wandering he had come into strange lands, and even had not the Orcs seized him he would indeed have had no other rede of safety but to approach the majesty of Ainu Melko and beg him to grant him some humble office – as a winner of meats for his table perchance.

Now the Valar must have inspired that speech, or perchance it was a spell of cunning words cast on him in compassion by Gwendeling, for indeed it saved his life, and Melko marking his hardy frame believed him, and was willing to accept him as a thrall of his kitchens. Flattery savoured ever sweet in the nostrils of that Ainu, and for all his unfathomed wisdom many a lie of those whom he despised deceived him, were they clothed sweetly in words of praise; therefore now he gave orders for Beren to be made a thrall of Tevildo Prince of Cats. Now Tevildo was a mighty cat – the mightiest of all – and possessed of an evil sprite, as some say, and he was in Melko's constant following; and that cat had all cats subject to him, and he and his subjects were the chasers and getters of meat for Melko's table and for his frequent feasts. Wherefore is it that there is hatred still between the Elves and all cats even now when Melko rules no more, and his beasts are become of little account.

When therefore Beren was led away to the halls of Tevildo, and these were not utterly distant from the place of Melko's throne, he was much afraid, for he had not looked for such a turn in things, and those halls were ill-lighted and were full of growling and of monstrous purrings in the dark.

All about shone cats' eyes glowing like green lamps or red or yellow where Tevildo's thanes sat waving and lashing their beautiful tails, but Tevildo himself sat at their head and he was a mighty cat and coal-black and evil to look upon. His eyes were long and very narrow and slanted, and gleamed both red and green, but his great grey whiskers were as stout and as sharp as needles. His purr was like the roll of drums and his growl like thunder, but when he yelled in wrath it turned the blood cold, and indeed small beasts and birds were frozen as to stone, or dropped lifeless often at the very sound. Now Tevildo seeing Beren narrowed his eyes until they seemed to shut, and said: 'I smell dog', and he took dislike to Beren from that moment. Now Beren had been a lover of hounds in his own wild home.

'Why,' said Tevildo, 'do ye dare to bring such a creature before me, unless perchance it is to make meat of him?' But those who led Beren said: 'Nay, 'twas the word of Melko that this unhappy Elf wear out his life as a catcher of beasts and birds in Tevildo's employ.' Then indeed did Tevildo screech in scorn and said: 'Then in sooth was my lord asleep or his thoughts were settled elsewhere, for what use think ye is a child of the Eldar to aid the Prince of Cats and his thanes in the catching of birds or of beasts – as well had ye brought some clumsy-footed Man, for none are there either of Elves or Men that can vie with us in our pursuit.' Nonetheless he set Beren to a test, and he bade him go catch three mice, 'for my hall is infested with them,' said he. This indeed was not true, as might be imagined, yet a certain few there were – a very wild, evil, and magic kind that dared to dwell there in dark holes, but they were larger than rats and very fierce, and Tevildo harboured them for his own private sport and suffered not their numbers to dwindle.

Three days did Beren hunt them, but having nothing wherewith to devise a trap (and indeed he did not lie to Melko saying that he had cunning in such contrivances) he hunted in vain getting nothing better than a bitten finger for all his labour. Then was Tevildo scornful and in great anger, but Beren got no harm of him or his thanes at that time because of Melko's bidding other than a few scratches. Evil however were his days thereafter in the dwellings of Tevildo. They made him a scullion, and his days passed miserably in the washing of floors and vessels, in the scrubbing of tables and the hewing of wood and the drawing of water. Often too he would be set to the turning of spits whereon birds and fat mice were daintily roasted for the cats, yet seldom did he get food or sleep himself, and he became haggard and unkempt, and wished often that never straying out of Hisilómë he had not even caught sight of the vision of Tinúviel.

Now that fair maiden wept for a very great while after Beren's departure and danced no more about the woods, and Dairon grew angry and could not understand her, but she had grown to love the face of Beren peeping through the branches and the crackle of his feet as they followed her through the wood; and his voice that called wistfully 'Tinúviel, Tinúviel' across the stream before her father's doors she longed to hear again, and she would not now dance when Beren was fled to the evil halls of Melko and maybe had already perished. So bitter did this thought become at last that that most tender maiden went to her mother, for to her father she dared not go nor even suffer him to see her weep.

'O Gwendeling, my mother,' said she, 'tell me of thy magic, if thou canst, how doth Beren fare. Is all yet well with him?' 'Nay,' said Gwendeling. 'He lives indeed, but in an evil captivity, and hope is dead in his heart, for behold, he is a slave in the power of Tevildo Prince of Cats.'

'Then,' said Tinúviel, 'I must go and succour him, for none else do I know that will.'

Now Gwendeling laughed not, for in many matters she was wise, and forewise, yet it was a thing unthought in a mad dream that any Elf, still less a maiden, the daughter of the king, should fare untended to the halls of Melko, even in those earlier days before the Battle of Tears when Melko's power had not grown great and he veiled his designs and spread his net of lies. Wherefore did Gwendeling softly bid her not to speak such folly; but Tinúviel said: 'Then must thou plead with my father for aid, that he send warriors to Angamandi and demand the freedom of Beren from Ainu Melko.'

This indeed did Gwendeling do, of love for her daughter, and so wroth was Tinwelint that Tinúviel wished that never had her desire been made known; and Tinwelint bade her nor speak nor think of Beren more, and swore he would slay him an he trod those halls again. Now then Tinúviel pondered much what she might do, and going to Dairon she begged him to aid her, or indeed to fare away with her to Angamandi an he would; but Dairon thought with little love of Beren, and he said: 'Wherefore should I go into the direst peril that there is in the world for the sake of a wandering Gnome of the woods? Indeed I have no love for him, for he has destroyed our play together, our music and our dancing.' But Dairon moreover told the king of what Tinúviel had desired of him – and this he did not of ill intent but fearing lest Tinúviel fare away to her death in the madness of her heart.

Now when Tinwelint heard this he called Tinúviel and said: 'Wherefore, O maiden of mine, does thou not put this folly away from thee, and seek to do my bidding?' But Tinúviel would not answer, and the king bade her promise him that neither would she think more on Beren, nor would she seek in her folly to follow after him to the evil lands whether alone or tempting any of his folk with her. But Tinúviel said that the first she would not promise and the second only in part, for she would not tempt any of the folk of the woodlands to go with her.

Then was her father mightily angry, and beneath his anger not a little amazed and afraid, for he loved Tinúviel; but this was the plan he devised, for he might not shut his daughter for ever in the caverns where only a dim and flickering light ever came. Now above the portals of his cavernous hall was a steep slope falling to the river, and there grew mighty beeches; and one there was that was named Hirilorn, the Queen of Trees, for she was very mighty, and so deeply cloven was her bole that it seemed as if three shafts sprang from the ground together and they were of like size, round and straight, and their grey rind was smooth as silk, unbroken by branch or twig for a very great height above men's heads.

Now Tinwelint let build high up in that strange tree, as high as men could fashion their longest ladders to reach, a little house of wood, and it was above the first branches and was sweetly veiled in leaves. Now that house had three corners and three windows in each wall, and at each corner was one of the shafts of Hirilorn. There then did Tinwelint bid Tinúviel dwell until she would consent to be wise, and when she fared up the ladders of tall pine these were taken from beneath and no way had she to get down again. All that she required was brought to her, and folk would scale the ladders and give her food or whatever else she wished for, and then descending again take away the ladders, and the king promised death to any who left one leaning against the tree or who should try by stealth to place one there at night. A guard therefore was set nigh the tree's foot, and yet came Dairon often thither in sorrow at what he had brought to pass, for he was lonely without Tinúviel; but Tinúviel had at first much pleasure in her house among the leaves, and would gaze out of her little window while Dairon made his sweetest melodies beneath.

But one night a dream of the Valar came to Tinúviel and she dreamt of Beren, and her heart said: 'Let me be gone to seek him whom all others have forgot'; and waking, the moon was shining through the trees, and she pondered very deeply how she might escape. Now Tinúviel daughter of Gwendeling was not ignorant of magics or of spells, as may well be believed, and after much thought she devised a plan. The next day she asked those who came to her to bring, if they would, some of the clearest water of the stream below, 'but this,' she said, 'must be drawn at midnight in a silver bowl, and brought to my hand with no word spoken,' and after that she desired wine to be brought, 'but this,' she said, 'must be borne hither in a flagon of gold at noon, and he who brings it must sing as he comes,' and they did as they were bid, but Tinwelint was not told.

Then said Tinúviel, 'Go now to my mother and say to her that her daughter desires a spinning wheel to pass her weary hours,' but Dairon secretly she begged fashion her a tiny loom, and he did this even in the little house of Tinúviel in the tree. 'But wherewith will you spin and wherewith weave?' said he; and Tinúviel answered: 'With spells and magics,' but Dairon knew not her design, nor said more to the king or to Gwendeling.

Now Tinúviel took the wine and water when she was alone, and singing a very magical song the while, she mingled them together, and as they lay in the bowl of gold she sang a song of growth, and as they lay in the bowl of silver she sang another song, and the names of all the tallest and longest things upon Earth were set in that song; the beards of the Indravangs, the tail of Karkaras, the body of Glorund, the bole of Hirilorn, and the sword of Nan she named, nor did she forget the chain Angainu that Aulë and Tulkas made or the neck of Gilim the giant, and last and longest of all she spake of the hair of Uinen the lady of the sea that is spread through all the waters. Then did she lave her head with the mingled water and wine, and as she did so she sang a third song, a song of uttermost sleep, and the hair of Tinúviel which was dark and finer than the most delicate threads of twilight began suddenly to grow very fast indeed, and after twelve hours had passed it nigh filled the little room, and then Tinúviel was very pleased and she lay down to rest; and when she awoke the room was full as with a black mist and she was deep hidden under it, and lo! her hair was trailing out of the windows and blowing about the tree boles in the morning. Then with difficulty she found her little shears and cut the threads of that growth nigh to her head, and after that her hair grew only as it was wont before.

Then was the labour of Tinúviel begun, and though she

laboured with the deftness of an Elf long was the spinning and longer weaving still, and did any come and hail her from below she bid them be gone, saying: 'I am abed, and desire only to sleep,' and Dairon was much amazed, and called often up to her, but she did not answer.

Now of that cloudy hair Tinúviel wove a robe of misty black soaked with drowsiness more magical far than even that one that her mother had worn and danced in long ago, and therewith she covered her garments of shimmering white, and magic slumbers filled the air about her; but of what remained she twisted a mighty strand, and this she fastened to the bole of the tree within her house, and then was her labour ended, and she looked out of her window westward to the river. Already the sunlight was fading in the trees, and as dusk filled the woods she began a song very soft and low, and as she sang she cast out her long hair from the window so that its slumbrous mist touched the heads and faces of the guards below, and they listening to her voice fell suddenly into a fathomless sleep. Then did Tinúviel clad in her garments of darkness slip down that rope of hair light as a squirrel, and away she danced to the bridge, and before the bridgewards could cry out she was among them dancing; and as the hem of her black robe touched them they fell asleep, and Tinúviel fled very far away as fast as her dancing feet would flit.

Now when the escape of Tinúviel reached the ears of Tinwelint great was his mingled grief and wrath, and all his court was in uproar, and all the woods ringing with the search, but Tinúviel was already far away drawing nigh to the gloomy foothills where the Mountains of Night begin; and 'tis said that Dairon following after her became utterly lost, and came never back to Elfinesse, but turned towards Palisor, and there plays subtle magic musics still, wistful and lonely in the woods and forests of the south.

Yet ere long as Tinúviel went forward a sudden dread overtook her at the thought of what she had dared to do and what lay before; then did she turn back for a while, and she wept, wishing Dairon were with her, and it is said that he indeed was not far off, but was wandering lost in the great pines, the Forest of Night, where afterward Túrin slew Beleg by mishap.

Nigh was Tinúviel now to those places, but she entered not that dark region, and regaining heart pressed on, and by reason of the greater magic of her being and because of the spell of wonder and of sleep that fared about her no such dangers assailed her as did Beren before; yet was it a long and evil and weary journey for a maiden to tread.

Now is it to be told that in those days Tevildo had but one trouble in the world, and that was the kindred of the Dogs. Many indeed of these were neither friends nor foes of the Cats, for they had become subject to Melko and were as savage and cruel as any of his animals; indeed from the most cruel and most savage he bred the race of wolves, and they were very dear indeed to him. Was it not the great grey wolf Karkaras Knife-fang, father of wolves, who guarded the gates of Angamandi in those days and long had done so? Many were there however who would neither bow to Melko nor live wholly in fear of him, but dwelt either in the dwellings of Men and guarded them from much evil that had otherwise befallen them, or roamed the woods of Hisilómë or passing the mountainous places fared even at times into the region of Artanor and the lands beyond and to the south.

Did ever any of these view Tevildo or any of his thanes or subjects, then there was a great baying and a mighty chase, and albeit seldom was any cat slain by reason of their skill in climbing and in hiding and because of the protecting might of Melko, yet was great enmity between them, and some of those hounds were held in dread among the cats. None however did Tevildo fear, for he was as strong as any among them, and more agile and more swift save only than Huan Captain of Dogs. So swift was Huan that on a time he had tasted the fur of Tevildo, and though Tevildo had paid him for that with a gash from his great claws, yet was the pride of the Prince of Cats unappeased and he lusted to do a great harm to Huan of the Dogs.

Great therefore was the good fortune that befell Tinúviel in meeting with Huan in the woods, although at first she was mortally afraid and fled. But Huan overtook her in two leaps, and speaking soft and deep the tongue of the Lost Elves he bid her be not afraid, and 'Wherefore,' said he, 'do I see an Elven maiden, and one most fair, wandering alone so nigh to the abodes of the Ainu of Evil? Knowest thou not that these are very evil places to be in, little one, even with a companion, and they are death to the lonely?'

'That know I,' said she, 'and I am not here for the love of wayfaring, but I seek only Beren.'

'What knowest thou then,' said Huan, 'of Beren – or indeed meanest thou Beren son of the huntsman of the Elves, Egnor bo-Rimion, a friend of mine since very ancient days?'

'Nay, I know not even whether my Beren be thy friend, for I seek only Beren from beyond the Bitter Hills, whom I knew in the woods near to my father's home. Now is he gone, and my mother Gwendeling says of her wisdom that he is a thrall in the cruel house of Tevildo Prince of Cats; and whether this be true or yet worse be now befallen him I do not know, and I go to discover him – though plan I have none.'

'Then will I make thee one,' said Huan, 'but do thou trust in me, for I am Huan of the Dogs, chief foe of Tevildo. Rest thee now with me a while within the shadows of the wood, and I will think deeply.'

Then Tinúviel did as he said, and indeed she slept long while Huan watched, for she was very weary. But after a while awakening she said: 'Lo, I have tarried over long. Come, what is thy thought, O Huan?'

And Huan said: 'A dark and difficult matter is this, and no other rede can I devise but this. Creep now if thou hast the heart to the abiding place of that Prince while the sun is high, and Tevildo and the most of his household drowze upon the terraces before his gates. There discover in what manner thou mayst whether Beren be indeed within, as thy mother said to thee. Now I will lie not far hence in the woods, and thou wilt do me a pleasure and aid thy own desires if going before Tevildo, be Beren there or be he not, thou tellest him how thou hast stumbled upon Huan of the Dogs lying sick in the woods at this place. Do not indeed direct him hither, for thou must guide him, if it may be, thyself. Then wilt thou see what I contrive for thee and for Tevildo. Methinks that bearing such tidings Tevildo will not entreat thee ill within his halls nor seek to hold thee there.'

In this way did Huan design both to do Tevildo a hurt, or perchance if it might so be to slay him, and to aid Beren whom he guessed in truth to be that Beren son of Egnor whom the hounds of Hisilómë loved. Indeed hearing the name of Gwendeling and knowing thereby that this maiden was a princess of the woodland fairies he was eager to aid her, and his heart warmed to her sweetness.

Now Tinúviel taking heart stole near to the halls of Tevildo, and Huan wondered much at her courage, following unknown to her, as far as he might for the success of his design. At length however she passed beyond his sight, and leaving the shelter of the trees came to a region of long grass dotted with bushes that sloped ever upward toward a shoulder of the hills. Now upon that rocky spur the sun shone, but over all the hills and mountains at its back a black cloud brooded, for there was Angamandi; and Tinúviel fared on not daring to look up at that gloom, for fear oppressed her, and as she went the ground rose and the grass grew more scant and rock-strewn until it came even to a cliff, sheer of one side, and there upon a stony shelf was the castle of Tevildo. No pathway led thereto, and the place where it stood fell towards the woods in terrace after terrace so that none might reach its gates save by many great leaps, and those became ever steeper as the castle drew more nigh. Few were the windows of that house and upon the ground there were none – indeed the very gate was in the air where in the dwellings of Men are wont to be the windows of the upper floor; but the roof had many wide and flat spaces open to the sun.

Now does Tinúviel wander disconsolate upon the lowest terrace and look in dread at the dark house upon the hill, when behold, she came at a bend in the rock upon a lone cat lying in the sun and seemingly asleep. As she approached he opened a yellow eye and blinked at her, and thereupon rising and stretching he stepped up to her and said: 'Whither away, little maid – dost not know that you trespass on the sunning ground of his highness Tevildo and his thanes?'

Now Tinúviel was very much afraid, but she made as bold an answer as she was able, saying: 'That know I, my lord' – and this pleased the old cat greatly, for he was in truth only Tevildo's doorkeeper – 'but I would indeed of your goodness be brought to Tevildo's presence now – nay, even if he sleeps,' said she, for the doorkeeper lashed his tail in astonished refusal.

'I have words of immediate import for his private ear. Lead me to him, my lord,' she pleaded, and thereat the cat purred so loudly that she dared to stroke his ugly head, and this was much larger than her own, being greater than that of any dog that is now on Earth. Thus entreated, Umuiyan, for such was his name, said: 'Come then with me,' and seizing Tinúviel suddenly by her garments at the shoulder to her great terror he tossed her upon his back and leaped upon the second terrace. There he stopped, and as Tinúviel scrambled from his back he said: 'Well is it for thee that this afternoon my lord Tevildo lieth upon this lowly terrace far from his house, for a great weariness and a desire for sleep has come upon me, so that I fear me I should not be willing to carry thee much farther'; now Tinúviel was robed in her robe of sable mist.

So saying Umuiyan yawned mightily and stretched himself before he led her along that terrace to an open space, where upon a wide couch of baking stones lay the horrible form of Tevildo himself, and both his evil eyes were shut. Going up to him the door-cat Umuiyan spoke in his ear softly, saying: 'A maiden awaits thy pleasure, my lord, who hath news of importance to deliver to thee, nor would she take my refusal.' Then did Tevildo angrily lash his tail, half opening an eye – 'What is it – be swift,' said he, 'for this is no hour to come desiring audience of Tevildo Prince of Cats.'

'Nay, lord,' said Tinúviel trembling, 'be not angry; nor do I think that thou wilt when thou hearest, yet is the matter such that it were better not even whispered here where the breezes blow,' and Tinúviel cast a glance as it were of apprehension toward the woods.

'Nay, get thee gone,' said Tevildo, 'thou smellest of dog, and what news of good came ever to a cat from a fairy that had had dealings with the dogs?'

'Why, sir, that I smell of dogs is no matter of wonder, for I have just escaped from one – and it is indeed of a certain very mighty dog whose name thou knowest that I would speak.' Then up sat Tevildo and opened his eyes, and he looked all about him, and stretched three times, and at last bade the door-cat lead Tinúviel within; and Umuiyan caught her upon his back as before. Now was Tinúviel in the sorest dread, for having gained what she desired, a chance of entering Tevildo's stronghold and maybe of discovering whether

Beren were there, she had no plan more, and knew not what would become of her – indeed had she been able she would have fled; yet now do those cats begin to ascend the terraces towards the castle, and one leap does Umuiyan make bearing Tinúviel upwards and then another, and at the third he stumbled so that Tinúviel cried out in fear, and Tevildo said: 'What ails thee, Umuiyan, thou clumsy-foot? It is time that thou left my employ if age creeps on thee so swiftly.' But Umuiyan said: 'Nay, lord, I know not what it is, but a mist is before my eyes and my head is heavy,' and he staggered as one drunk, so that Tinúviel slid from his back, and thereupon he laid him down as if in a dead sleep; but Tevildo was wroth and seized Tinúviel and none too gently, and himself bore her to the gates. Then with a mighty leap he sprang within, and bidding that maiden alight he set up a yell that echoed fearsomely in the dark ways and passages. Forthwith they hastened to him from within, and some he bid descend to Umuiyan and bind him and cast him from the rocks 'on the northern side where they fall most sheer, for he is of no use more to me,' he said, 'for age has robbed him of his sureness of foot'; and Tinúviel quaked to hear the ruthlessness of this beast. But even as he spoke he himself yawned and stumbled as with a sudden drowziness, and he bid others to lead Tinúviel away to a certain chamber within, and that was the one where Tevildo was accustomed to sit at meat with his greatest thanes. It was full of bones and smelt evilly; no windows were there and but one door; but a hatchway gave from it upon the great kitchens, and a red light crept thence and dimly lit the place.

Now so adread was Tinúviel when those catfolk left her

there that she stood a moment unable to stir, but soon becoming used to the darkness she looked about and espying the hatchway that had a wide sill she sprang thereto, for it was not over high and she was a nimble Elf. Now gazing therethrough, for it was ajar, she saw the wide vaulted kitchens and the great fires that burnt there, and those that toiled always within, and the most were cats – but behold, there by a great fire stooped Beren, and he was grimed with labour, and Tinúviel sat and wept, but as yet dared nothing. Indeed even as she sat the harsh voice of Tevildo sounded suddenly within that chamber: 'Nay, where then in Melko's name has that mad Elf fled,' and Tinúviel hearing shrank against the wall, but Tevildo caught sight of her where she was perched and cried: 'Then the little bird sings not any more; come down or I must fetch thee, for behold, I will not encourage the Elves to seek audience of me in mockery.'

Then partly in fear, and part in hope that her clear voice might carry even to Beren, Tinúviel began suddenly to speak very loud and to tell her tale so that the chambers rang; but 'Hush, dear maiden,' said Tevildo, 'if the matter were secret without it is not one for bawling within.' Then said Tinúviel: 'Speak not thus to me, O cat, mighty Lord of Cats though thou be, for am I not Tinúviel Princess of Fairies that have stepped out of my way to do thee a pleasure?' Now at those words, and she had shouted them even louder than before, a great crash was heard in the kitchens as of a number of vessels of metal and earthenware let suddenly fall, but Tevildo snarled: 'There trippeth that fool Beren the Elf. Melko rid me of such folk' – yet Tinúviel, guessing that Beren had heard

and been smitten with astonishment, put aside her fears and repented her daring no longer. Tevildo nonetheless was very wroth at her haughty words, and had he not been minded first to discover what good he might get from her tale, it had fared ill with Tinúviel straightway. Indeed from that moment she was in great peril, for Melko and all his vassals held Tinwelint and his folk as outlaws, and great was their joy to ensnare them and cruelly entreat them, so that much favour would Tevildo have gained had he taken Tinúviel before his lord. Indeed, so soon as she named herself, this did he purpose to do when his own business had been done, but of a truth his wits were drowzed that day, and he forgot to marvel more why Tinúviel sat perched upon the sill of the hatchway; nor did he think more of Beren, for his mind was bent only to the tale Tinúviel bore to him. Wherefore said he, dissembling his evil mood, 'Nay, Lady, be not angry, but come, delay whetteth my desire – what is it that thou hast for my ears, for they twitch already.'

But Tinúviel said: 'There is a great beast, rude and violent, and his name is Huan' – and at that name, Tevildo's back curved, and his hair bristled and crackled, and the light of his eyes was red – 'and', she went on, 'it seems to me a shame that such a brute be suffered to infest the woods so nigh even to the abode of the powerful Prince of Cats, my lord Tevildo'; but Tevildo said: 'Nor is he suffered, and cometh never there save it be by stealth.'

'Howso that may be,' said Tinúviel, 'there he is now, yet methinks that at last may his life be brought utterly to an end; for lo, as I was going through the woods I saw where a great animal lay upon the ground moaning as in sickness – and behold, it was Huan, and some evil spell or malady has him in its grip, and still he lies helpless in a dale not a mile westward in the woods from this hall. Now with this perhaps I would not have troubled your ears, had not the brute when I approached to succour him snarled upon me and essayed to bite me, and meseems that such a creature deserves whatever come to him.'

Now all this that Tinúviel spake was a great lie in whose devising Huan had guided her, and maidens of the Eldar are not wont to fashion lies; yet have I never heard that any of the Eldar blamed her therein nor Beren afterward, and neither do I, for Tevildo was an evil cat and Melko the wickedest of all beings, and Tinúviel was in dire peril at their hands. Tevildo however, himself a great and skilled liar, was so deeply versed in the lies and subtleties of all the beasts and creatures that he seldom knew whether to believe what was said to him or not, and was wont to disbelieve all things save those he wished to believe true, and so was he often deceived by the more honest. Now the story of Huan and his helplessness so pleased him that he was fain to believe it true, and determined at least to test it; yet at first he feigned indifference, saying this was a small matter for such secrecy and might have been spoken outside without further ado. But Tinúviel said she had not thought that Tevildo Prince of Cats needed to learn that the ears of Huan heard the slightest sounds a league away, and the voice of a cat further than any sound else.

Now therefore Tevildo sought to discover from Tinúviel under pretence of mistrusting her tale where exactly Huan might be found, but she made only vague answers, seeing in this her only hope of escaping from the castle, and at length Tevildo, overcome by curiosity and threatening evil things if she should prove false, summoned two of his thanes to him, and one was Oikeroi, a fierce and warlike cat. Then did the three set out with Tinúviel from that place, but Tinúviel took off her magical garment of black and folded it, so that for all its size and density it appeared no more than the smallest kerchief (for so was she able), and thus was she borne down the terraces upon the back of Oikeroi without mishap, and no drowziness assailed her bearer. Now crept they through the woods in the direction she had named, and soon does Tevildo smell dog and bristles and lashes his great tail, but after he climbs a lofty tree and looks down from thence into that dale that Tinúviel had shown to them. There he does indeed see the great form of Huan lying prostrate groaning and moaning, and he comes down in much glee and haste, and indeed in his eagerness he forgets Tinúviel, who now in great fear for Huan lies hidden in a bank of fern. The design of Tevildo and his two companions was to enter that dale silently from different quarters and so come all suddenly upon Huan unawares and slay him, or if he were too stricken to make fight to make sport of him and torment him. This did they now, but even as they leapt out upon him Huan sprang up into the air with a mighty baying, and his jaws closed in the back close to the neck of that cat Oikeroi, and Oikeroi died; but the other thane fled howling up a great tree, and so was Tevildo left alone face to face with Huan, and such an encounter was not much to his mind, yet was Huan upon him too swiftly for flight, and they fought fiercely in that glade, and the noise that Tevildo made was very hideous; but at length Huan had him by the throat, and that cat might well have perished had not his claws as he struck out blindly pierced Huan's eye. Then did Huan give tongue, and Tevildo screeching fearsomely got himself loose with a great wrench and leapt up a tall and smooth tree that stood by, even as his companion had done. Despite his grievous hurt Huan now leaps beneath that tree baying mightily, and Tevildo curses him and casts evil words upon him from above.

Then said Huan: 'Lo, Tevildo, these are the words of Huan whom thou thoughtest to catch and slay helpless as the miserable mice it is thy wont to hunt – stay for ever up thy lonely tree and bleed to death of thy wounds, or come down and feel again my teeth. But if neither are to thy liking, then tell me where is Tinúviel Princess of Fairies and Beren son of Egnor, for these are my friends. Now these shall be set as ransom against thee – though it be valuing thee far over thy worth.'

'As for that cursed Elf, she lies whimpering in the ferns yonder, an my ears mistake not,' said Tevildo, 'and Beren methinks is being soundly scratched by Miaulë my cook in the kitchens of my castle for his clumsiness there an hour ago.'

'Then let them be given to me in safety,' said Huan, 'and thou mayest return thyself to thy halls and lick thyself unharmed.'

'Of a surety my thane who is here with me shall fetch them for thee,' said Tevildo, but growled Huan: 'Ay, and fetch also all thy tribe and the hosts of the Orcs and the plagues of

68

Melko. Nay, I am no fool; rather shalt thou give Tinúviel a token and she shall fetch Beren, or thou shalt stay here if thou likest not the other way.' Then was Tevildo forced to cast down his golden collar – a token no cat dare dishonour, but Huan said: 'Nay, more yet is needed, for this will arouse all thy folk to seek thee,' and this Tevildo knew and had hoped. So was it that in the end weariness and hunger and fear prevailed upon that proud cat, a prince of the service of Melko, to reveal the secret of the cats and the spell that Melko had entrusted to him; and those were words of magic whereby the stones of his evil house were held together, and whereby he held all beasts of the catfolk under his sway, filling them with an evil power beyond their nature; for long has it been said that Tevildo was an evil fay in beastlike shape. When therefore he had told it Huan laughed till the woods rang, for he knew that the days of the power of the cats were over.

Now sped Tinúviel with the golden collar of Tevildo back to the lowest terrace before the gates, and standing she spake the spell in her clear voice. Then behold, the air was filled with the voices of cats and the house of Tevildo shook; and there came therefrom a host of indwellers and they were shrunk to puny size and were afeared of Tinúviel, who waving the collar of Tevildo spake before them certain of the words that Tevildo had said in her hearing to Huan, and they cowered before her. But she said: 'Lo, let all those of the folk of the Elves or of the children of Men that are bound within these halls be brought forth,' and behold, Beren was brought forth, but of other thralls there were none, save only Gimli, an aged Gnome, bent in thraldom and grown blind, but whose hearing was the keenest that has been in the world, as all songs say. Gimli came leaning upon a stick and Beren aided him, but Beren was clad in rags and haggard, and he had in his hand a great knife he had caught up in the kitchen, fearing some new ill when the house shook and all the voices of the cats were heard; but when he beheld Tinúviel standing amid the host of cats that shrank from her and saw the great collar of Tevildo, then was he amazed utterly, and knew not what to think. But Tinúviel was very glad, and spoke saying: 'O Beren from beyond the Bitter Hills, wilt thou now dance with me – but let it not be here.' And she led Beren far away, and all those cats set up a howling and wailing, so that Huan and Tevildo heard it in the woods, but none followed or molested them, for they were afraid, and the magic of Melko was fallen from them.

This indeed they rued afterward when Tevildo returned home followed by his trembling comrade, for Tevildo's wrath was terrible, and he lashed his tail and dealt blows at all who stood nigh. Now Huan of the dogs, though it might seem a folly, when Beren and Tinúviel came to that glade had suffered that evil Prince to return without further war, but the great collar of gold he had set about his own neck, and at this was Tevildo more angry than all else, for a great magic of strength and power lay therein. Little to Huan's liking was it that Tevildo lived still, but now no longer did he fear the cats, and that tribe has fled before the dogs ever since, and the dogs hold them still in scorn since the humbling of Tevildo in the woods nigh Angamandi; and Huan has not done any greater deed. Indeed afterward Melko heard all and he cursed Tevildo and his folk and banished them, nor have they since that day had lord or master or any friend, and their voices wail and screech for their hearts are very lonely and bitter and full of loss, yet there is only darkness therein and no kindliness.

At the time however whereof the tale tells it was Tevildo's chief desire to recapture Beren and Tinúviel and to slay Huan, that he might regain the spell and magic he had lost, for he was in great fear of Melko, and he dared not seek his master's aid and reveal his defeat and the betrayal of his spell. Unwitting of this Huan feared those places, and was in great dread lest those doings come swiftly to Melko's ear, as did most things that came to pass in the world; wherefore now Tinúviel and Beren wandered far away with Huan, and they became great in friendship with him, and in that life Beren grew strong again and his thraldom fell from him, and Tinúviel loved him.

Yet wild and rugged and very lonely were those days, for never a face of Elf or of Man did they see, and Tinúviel grew at last to long sorely for Gwendeling her mother and the songs of sweet magic she was used to sing to her children as twilight fell in the woodlands by their ancient halls. Often she half fancied she heard the flute of Dairon her brother, in pleasant glades wherein they sojourned, and her heart grew heavy. At length she said to Beren and to Huan: 'I must return home,' and now is it Beren's heart that is overcast with sorrow, for he loved that life in the woods with the dogs (for by now many others had become joined to Huan), yet not if Tinúviel were not there.

Nonetheless said he: 'Never may I go back with thee to the land of Artanor – nor come there ever after to seek thee,

71

sweet Tinúviel, save only bearing a Silmaril; nor may that ever
now be achieved, for am I not a fugitive from the very halls
of Melko, and in danger of the most evil pains do any of his
servants spy me.' Now this he said in the grief of his heart
at parting with Tinúviel, and she was torn in mind, abiding
not the thought of leaving Beren nor yet of living ever thus
in exile. So sat she a great while in sad thought and she spoke
not, but Beren sat nigh and at length said: 'Tinúviel, one thing
only can we do – go get a Silmaril'; and she sought thereupon
Huan, asking his aid and advice, but he was very grave and
saw nothing but folly in the matter. Yet in the end Tinúviel
begged of him the fell of Oikeroi that he slew in the affray
of the glade; now Oikeroi was a very mighty cat and Huan
carried that fell with him as a trophy.

Now doth Tinúviel put forth her skill and fairy-magic, and
she sews Beren into this fell and makes him to the likeness of
a great cat, and she teaches him how to sit and sprawl, to step
and bound and trot in the semblance of a cat, till Huan's very
whiskers bristled at the sight, and thereat Beren and Tinúviel
laughed. Never however could Beren learn to screech or wail
or to purr like any cat that ever walked, nor could Tinúviel
awaken a glow in the dead eyes of the catskin – 'but we must
put up with that,' said she, 'and thou hast the air of a very
noble cat if thou but hold thy tongue.'

Then did they bid farewell to Huan and set out for the
halls of Melko by easy journeys, for Beren was in great dis-
comfort and heat within the fur of Oikeroi, and Tinúviel's
heart became lighter awhile than it had been for long, and she
stroked Beren or pulled his tail, and Beren was angry because

he could not lash it in answer as fiercely as he wished. At length however they drew near to Angamandi, as indeed the rumblings and deep noises, and the sound of mighty hammerings of ten thousand smiths labouring unceasingly, declared to them. Nigh were the sad chambers where the thrall-Noldoli laboured bitterly under the Orcs and goblins of the hills, and here the gloom and darkness was great so that their hearts fell, but Tinúviel arrayed her once more in her dark garment of deep sleep. Now the gates of Angamandi were of iron wrought hideously and set with knives and spikes, and before them lay the greatest wolf the world has ever seen, even Karkaras Knife-fang who had never slept; and Karkaras growled when he saw Tinúviel approach, but of the cat he took not much heed, for he thought little of cats and they were ever passing in and out.

'Growl not, O Karkaras,' said she, 'for I go to seek my lord Melko, and this thane of Tevildo goeth with me as escort.' Now the dark robe veiled all her shimmering beauty, and Karkaras was not much troubled in mind, yet nonetheless he approached as was his wont to snuff the air of her, and the sweet fragrance of the Eldar that garment might not hide. Therefore straightway did Tinúviel begin a magic dance, and the black strands of her dark veil she cast in his eyes so that his legs shook with a drowziness and he rolled over and was asleep. But not until he was fast in dreams of great chases in the woods of Hisilómë when he was yet a whelp did Tinúviel cease, and then did those twain enter that black portal, and winding down many shadowy ways they stumbled at length into the very presence of Melko.

In that gloom Beren passed well enough as a very thane of Tevildo, and indeed Oikeroi had aforetime been much about the halls of Melko, so that none heeded him and he slunk under the very chair of the Ainu unseen, but the adders and evil things there lying set him in great fear so that he durst not move.

Now all this fell out most fortunately, for had Tevildo been with Melko their deceit would have been discovered – and indeed of that danger they had thought, not knowing that Tevildo sat now in his halls and knew not what to do should his discomfiture become noised in Angamandi; but behold, Melko espieth Tinúviel and saith: 'Who art thou that flittest about my halls like a bat? How camest thou in, for of a surety thou dost not belong here?'

'Nay, that I do not yet,' saith Tinúviel, 'though I may perchance hereafter, of thy goodness, my lord Melko. Knowest thou not that I am Tinúviel daughter of Tinwelint the outlaw, and he hath driven me from his halls, for he is an overbearing Elf and I give not my love at his command.'

Now in truth was Melko amazed that the daughter of Tinwelint came thus of her free will to his dwelling, Angamandi the terrible, and suspecting something untoward he asked what was her desire: 'for knowest thou not,' saith he, 'that there is no love here for thy father or his folk, nor needest thou hope for soft words and good cheer from me.'

'So hath my father said,' saith she, 'but wherefore need I believe him? Behold, I have a skill of subtle dances, and I would dance now before you, my lord, for then methinks I might readily be granted some humble corner of your halls wherein to dwell until such times as you should call for the little dancer Tinúviel to lighten your cares.'

'Nay,' saith Melko, 'such things are little to my mind; but as thou hast come thus far to dance, dance, and after we will see,' and with that he leered horribly, for his dark mind pondered some evil.

Then did Tinúviel begin such a dance as neither she nor any other sprite or fay or elf danced ever before or has done since, and after a while even Melko's gaze was held in wonder. Round the hall she fared, swift as a swallow, noiseless as a bat, magically beautiful as only Tinúviel ever was, and now she was at Melko's side, now before him, now behind, and her misty draperies touched his face and waved before his eyes, and the folk that sat about the walls or stood in that place were whelmed one by one in sleep, falling down into deep dreams of all that their ill hearts desired.

Beneath his chair the adders lay like stones, and the wolves before his feet yawned and slumbered, and Melko gazed on enchanted, but he did not sleep. Then began Tinúviel to dance a yet swifter dance before his eyes, and even as she danced she sang in a voice very low and wonderful a song which Gwendeling had taught her long ago, a song that the youths and maidens sang beneath the cypresses of the gardens of Lórien when the Tree of Gold had waned and Silpion was gleaming. The voices of nightingales were in it, and many subtle odours seemed to fill the air of that noisome place as she trod the floor lightly as a feather in the wind; nor has any voice or sight of such beauty ever again been seen there, and Ainu Melko for all his power and majesty succumbed to the magic of that Elf-maid, and indeed even the eyelids of Lórien had grown heavy had he been there to see. Then did Melko fall forward drowzed, and sank at last in utter sleep down from his chair upon the floor, and his iron crown rolled away.

Suddenly Tinúviel ceased. In the hall no sound was heard save of slumbrous breath; even Beren slept beneath the very seat of Melko, but Tinúviel shook him so that he awoke at last. Then in fear and trembling he tore asunder his disguise and freeing himself from it leapt to his feet. Now does he draw that knife that he had from Tevildo's kitchens and he seizes the mighty iron crown, but Tinúviel could not move it and scarcely might the thews of Beren avail to turn it. Great is the frenzy of their fear as in that dark hall of sleeping evil Beren labours as noiselessly as may be to prise out a Silmaril with his knife. Now does he loosen the great central jewel and the sweat pours from his brow, but even as he forces it from the crown lo! his knife snaps with a loud crack.

Tinúviel smothers a cry thereat and Beren springs away with the one Silmaril in his hand, and the sleepers stir and Melko groans as though ill thoughts disturbed his dreams, and a black look comes upon his sleeping face. Content now with that one flashing gem those twain fled desperately from the hall, stumbling wildly down many dark passages till from the glimmering of grey light they knew they neared the gates – and behold! Karkaras lies across the threshold, awake once more and watchful.

Straightway Beren thrust himself before Tinúviel although she said him nay, and this proved in the end ill, for Tinúviel had not time to cast her spell of slumber over the beast again, ere seeing Beren he bared his teeth and growled angrily. 'Wherefore this surliness, Karkaras?' said Tinúviel. 'Wherefore this Gnome who entered not and yet now issueth in haste?' quoth Knife-fang, and with that he leapt upon Beren, who struck straight between the wolf's eyes with his fist, catching for his throat with the other hand.

Then Karkaras seized that hand in his dreadful jaws, and it was the hand wherein Beren clasped the blazing Silmaril, and both hand and jewel Karkaras bit off and took into his red maw. Great was the agony of Beren and the fear and anguish of Tinúviel, yet even as they expect to feel the teeth of the wolf a new thing strange and terrible comes to pass. Behold now that Silmaril blazeth with a white and hidden fire of its own nature and is possessed of a fierce and holy magic – for did it not come from Valinor and the blessed realms, being fashioned with spells of the Gods and Gnomes before evil came there; and it doth not tolerate the touch of evil flesh or of unholy hand. Now cometh it into the foul body of Karkaras, and suddenly that beast is burnt with a terrible anguish and the howling of his pain is ghastly to hear as it echoeth in those rocky ways, so that all the sleeping court within awakes. Then did Tinúviel and Beren flee like the wind from the gates, yet was Karkaras far before them raging and in madness as a beast pursued by Balrogs; and after when they might draw breath Tinúviel wept over the maimed arm of Beren kissing it often, so that behold it bled not, and pain left it, and was healed by the tender healing of her love; yet was Beren ever after surnamed among all folk Ermabwed the One-handed, which in the language of the Lonely Isle is Elmavoitë.

Now however must they bethink them of escape – if such may be their fortune, and Tinúviel wrapped part of her dark mantle about Beren, and so for a while flitting by dusk and dark amid the hills they were seen by none, albeit Melko had raised all his Orcs of terror against them; and his fury at the rape of that jewel was greater than the Elves had ever seen it yet.

Even so it seems soon to them that the net of the hunters drew ever more tightly upon them, and though they had reached the edge of the more familiar woods and passed the glooms of the forest of Taurfuin, still were there many leagues of peril yet to pass between them and the caverns of the king, and even did they reach ever there it seemed like they would but draw the chase behind them thither and Melko's hate upon all that woodland folk. So great indeed was the hue and cry that Huan learnt of it far away, and he marvelled much at the daring of those twain, and still more that ever they had escaped from Angamandi.

Now goes he with many dogs through the woods hunting Orcs and thanes of Tevildo, and many hurts he got thus, and many of them he slew or put to fear and flight, until one even at dusk the Valar brought him to a glade in that northward region of Artanor that was called afterward Nan Dumgorthin, the land of the dark idols, but that is a matter that concerns not this tale. Howbeit it was even then a dark land and gloomy and foreboding, and dread wandered beneath its lowering trees no less even than in Taurfuin; and those two Elves Tinúviel and Beren were lying therein weary and without hope, and Tinúviel wept but Beren was fingering his knife.

Now when Huan saw them he would not suffer them to speak or to tell any of their tale, but straightway took Tinúviel upon his mighty back and bade Beren run as best he could beside him, 'for,' said he, 'a great company of the Orcs are drawing swiftly hither, and wolves are their trackers and their scouts.' Now doth Huan's pack run about them, and they go very swiftly along quick and secret paths towards the homes of the folk of Tinwelint far away. Thus was it that they eluded the host of their enemies, but had nonetheless many an encounter afterward with wandering things of evil, and Beren slew an Orc that came nigh to dragging off Tinúviel, and that was a good deed. Seeing then that the hunt still pressed them close, once more did Huan lead them by winding ways, and dared not yet straightly to bring them to the land of the woodland fairies. So cunning however was his leading that at last after many days the chase fell far away, and no longer did they see or hear anything of the bands of Orcs; no goblins waylaid them nor did the howling of any evil wolves come upon the airs at night, and belike that was because already they had stepped within the circle of Gwendeling's magic that hid the paths from evil things and kept harm from the regions of the woodelves.

Then did Tinúviel breathe freely once more as she had not done since she fled from her father's halls, and Beren rested in the sun far from the glooms of Angband until the last bitterness of thraldom left him. Because of the light falling through green leaves and the whisper of clean winds and the song of birds once more are they wholly unafraid.

At last came there nevertheless a day whereon waking out of a deep slumber Beren started up as one who leaves a dream of happy things coming suddenly to his mind, and he said: 'Farewell, O Huan, most trusty comrade, and thou, little Tinúviel, whom I love, fare thee well. This only I beg of thee, get thee now straight to the safety of thy home, and may good Huan lead thee. But I – lo, I must away into the solitude of the woods, for I have lost that Silmaril which I had, and never dare I draw near to Angamandi more, wherefore neither will I enter the halls of Tinwelint.' Then he wept to himself, but Tinúviel who was nigh and had hearkened to his musing came beside him and said; 'Nay, now is my heart changed, and if thou dwellest in the woods, O Beren Ermabwed, then so will I, and if thou wilt wander in the wild places there will I wander also, or with thee or after thee: – yet never shall my father see me again save only if thou takest me to him.' Then indeed was Beren glad of her sweet words, and fain would he have dwelt with her as a huntsman of the wild, but his heart smote him for all that she had suffered for him, and for her he put away his pride. Indeed she reasoned with him, saying it would be folly to be stubborn, and that her father would greet them with nought but joy, being glad to see his daughter yet alive – 'and maybe,' said she, 'he will have shame that his jesting has given thy fair hand to the jaws of Karkaras.' But Huan also she implored to return with them a space, for 'my father owes thee a very great reward, O Huan,' saith she, 'an he loves his daughter at all.'

So came it that those three set forward once again together, and came at last back to the woodlands that Tinúviel knew and loved nigh to the dwellings of her folk and to the deep halls of her home. Yet even as they approach they find fear and tumult among that people such as had not been for a long age, and asking some that wept before their doors they learned that ever since the day of Tinúviel's secret flight ill-fortune had befallen them. Lo, the king had been distraught with grief and had relaxed his ancient wariness and cunning; indeed his warriors had been sent hither and thither deep into the unwholesome woods searching for that maiden, and many had been slain or lost for ever, and war there was with Melko's servants about all their northern and eastern borders, so that the folk feared mightily lest that Ainu upraise his strength and come utterly to crush them and Gwendeling's magic have not the strength to withhold the numbers of the Orcs. 'Behold,' said they, 'now is the worst of all befallen, for long has Queen Gwendeling sat aloof and smiled not nor spoken, looking as it were to a great distance with haggard eyes, and the web of her magic has blown thin about the woods, and the woods are dreary, for Dairon comes not back, neither is his music heard ever in the glades. Behold now the crown of all our evil tidings, for know that there has broken upon us raging from the halls of Evil a great grey wolf filled with an evil spirit, and he fares as though lashed by some hidden madness, and none are safe. Already has he slain many as he runs wildly snapping and yelling through the woods, so that the very banks of the stream that flows before the king's halls has become a lurking-place of danger. There comes the awful wolf oftentimes to drink, looking as the evil Prince himself with bloodshot eyes and tongue lolling out, and never can he slake his desire for water as though some inward fire devours him.'

Then was Tinúviel sad at the thought of the unhappiness that had come upon her folk, and most of all was her heart bitter at the story of Dairon, for of this she had not heard any murmur before. Yet could she not wish Beren had come never to the lands of Artanor, and together they made haste to Tinwelint; and already to the Elves of the wood it seemed that the evil was at an end now that Tinúviel was come back among them unharmed. Indeed they scarce had hoped for that.

In great gloom do they find King Tinwelint, yet suddenly is his sorrow melted to tears of gladness, and Gwendeling sings again for joy when Tinúviel enters there and casting away her raiment of dark mist she stands before them in her pearly radiance of old. For a while all is mirth and wonder in that hall, and yet at length the king turns his eyes to Beren and says: 'So thou hast returned too – bringing a Silmaril, beyond doubt, in recompense for all the ill thou hast wrought my land; or an thou hast not, I know not wherefore thou art here.'

Then Tinúviel stamped her foot and cried so that the king and all about him wondered at her new and fearless mood: 'For shame, my father – behold, here is Beren the brave whom thy jesting drove into dark places and foul captivity and the Valar alone saved from a bitter death. Methinks 'twould rather befit a king of the Eldar to reward him than revile him.'

'Nay,' said Beren, 'the king thy father hath the right. Lord,' said he, 'I have a Silmaril in my hand even now.'

'Show me then,' said the king in amaze.

'That I cannot,' said Beren, 'for my hand is not here', and he held forth his maimed arm.

Then was the king's heart turned to him by reason of his stout and courteous demeanour, and he bade Beren and Tinúviel relate to him all that had befallen either of them, and he was eager to hearken, for he did not fully comprehend the meaning of Beren's words. When however he had heard all yet more was his heart turned to Beren, and he marvelled at the love that had awakened in the heart of Tinúviel so that she had done greater deeds and more daring than any of the warriors of his folk.

'Never again,' said he, 'O Beren I beg of thee, leave this court nor the side of Tinúviel, for thou art a great Elf and thy name will ever be great among the kindreds.' Yet Beren answered him proudly, and said: 'Nay, O King, I hold to my word and thine, and I will get thee that Silmaril or ever I dwell in peace in thy halls.' And the king entreated him to journey no more into the dark and unknown realms, but Beren said: 'No need is there thereof, for behold that jewel is even now nigh to thy caverns,' and he made clear to Tinwelint that that beast that ravaged his land was none other than Karkaras, the wolfward of Melko's gates – and this was not known to all, but Beren knew it taught by Huan, whose cunning in the reading of track and slot was greatest among all the hounds, and therein are none of them unskilled. Huan indeed was with Beren now in the halls, and when those twain spoke of a chase and a great hunt he begged to be in that deed; and it was granted gladly. Now do those three prepare themselves to harry that beast, that all the folk be rid of the terror of the wolf, and Beren keep his word, bringing a Silmaril to shine once more in Elfinesse. King Tinwelint himself led that chase, and Beren was beside him, and Mablung the heavy-handed, chief of the king's thanes, leaped up and grasped a spear – a mighty weapon captured in battle with the distant Orcs – and with those three stalked Huan mightiest of dogs, but others they would not take according to the desire of the king, who said: 'Four is enough for the slaying even of the Hell-wolf' – but only those who had seen knew how fearsome was that beast, nigh as large as a horse among Men, and so great was the ardour of his breath that it scorched whatsoever it touched. About the hour of sunrise they set forth, and soon after Huan espied a new slot beside the stream, not far from the king's doors, 'and,' quoth he, 'this is the print of Karkaras.' Thereafter they followed that stream all day, and at many places its banks were new-trampled and torn and the water of the pools that lay about it was fouled as though some beasts possessed of madness had rolled and fought there not long before.

Now sinks the sun and fades beyond the western trees and darkness is creeping down from Hisilómë so that the light of the forest dies. Even so they come to a place where the spoor swerves from the stream or perchance is lost in its waters and Huan may no longer follow it; and here therefore they encamp, sleeping in turns beside the stream, and the early night wears away.

Suddenly in Beren's watch a sound of great terror leaped up from far away – a howling as of seventy maddened wolves – then lo! the brushwood cracks and saplings snap as the terror draweth near, and Beren knows that Karkaras is upon them. Scarce had he time to rouse the others, and they were but just sprung up and half-awake, when a great form loomed in the wavering moonlight filtering there, and it was fleeing like one mad, and its course was bent towards the water. Thereat Huan gave tongue, and straightway the beast swerved aside towards them, and foam was dripping from his jaws and a red light shining from his eyes, and his face was marred with mingled terror and with wrath. No sooner did he leave the trees than Huan rushed upon him fearless of heart, but he with a mighty leap sprang right over that great dog, for all his fury was kindled suddenly against Beren whom he recognized as he stood behind, and to his dark mind it seemed that there was the cause of all his agony. Then Beren thrust swiftly upward with a spear into his throat, and Huan leapt again and had him by a hind leg, and Karkaras fell like a stone, for at that same moment the king's spear found his heart, and his evil spirit gushed forth and sped howling faintly as it fared over the dark hills to Mandos; but Beren lay under him crushed beneath his weight. Now they roll back that carcase and fall to cutting it open, but Huan licks Beren's face whence blood is flowing. Soon is the truth of Beren's words made clear, for the vitals of the wolf are half-consumed as though an inner fire had long been smouldering there, and suddenly the night is filled with a wondrous lustre, shot with pale and secret colours, as Mablung draws forth the Silmaril. Then holding it out he said: 'Behold, O King', but Tinwelint said: 'Nay, never will I handle it save only if Beren give it to me.' But Huan said: 'and that seems like never to be, unless ye tend him swiftly, for methinks he is hurt sorely'; and Mablung and the king were ashamed.

Therefore now they raised Beren gently up and tended him and washed him, and he breathed, but he spoke not nor opened his eyes, and when the sun arose and they had rested a little they bore him as softly as might be upon a bier of boughs back through the woodlands; and nigh midday they drew near the homes of the folk again, and then were they deadly weary, and Beren had not moved nor spoken, but groaned thrice.

There did all the people flock to meet them when their approach was noised among them, and some bore them meat and cool drinks and salves and healing things for their hurts, and but for the harm that Beren had met great indeed had been their joy. Now then they covered the leafy boughs whereon he lay with soft raiment, and they bore him away to the halls of the king, and there was Tinúviel awaiting them in great distress; and she fell upon Beren's breast and wept and kissed him, and he awoke and knew her, and after Mablung gave him that Silmaril, and he lifted it above him gazing at its beauty, ere he said slowly and with pain: 'Behold, O King, I give thee the wondrous jewel thou didst desire, and it is but a little thing found by the wayside, for once methinks thou hadst one beyond thought more beautiful, and she is now mine.' Yet even as he spake the shadows of Mandos lay upon his face, and his spirit fled in that hour to the margin of the world, and Tinúviel's tender kisses called him not back.

*

[Here Vëannë suddenly ceased speaking, but she wept, and after a while she said 'Nay, that is not all the tale; but here endeth all that I rightly know'. In the conversation that followed one Ausir said: 'I have heard that the magic of Tinúviel's tender kisses healed Beren, and recalled his spirit from the gates of Mandos, and long time he dwelt among the Lost Elves . . .']

But another said: 'Nay, that was not so, O Ausir, and if thou wilt listen I will tell the true and wondrous tale; for Beren died there in Tinúviel's arms even as Vëannë has said, and Tinúviel crushed with sorrow and finding no comfort or light in all the world followed him swiftly down those dark ways that all must tread alone. Now her beauty and tender loveliness touched even the cold heart of Mandos, so that he suffered her to lead Beren forth once more into the world, nor has this ever been done since to Man or Elf, and many songs and stories are there of the prayer of Tinúviel before the throne of Mandos that I remember not right well. Yet said Mandos to those twain: "Lo, O Elves, it is not to any life of perfect joy that I dismiss you, for such may no longer be found in all the world where sits Melko of the evil heart – and know that ye will become mortal even as Men, and when ye fare hither again it will be for ever, unless the Gods summon you indeed to Valinor." Nonetheless those twain departed hand in hand, and they fared together through the northern woods, and oftentimes were they seen dancing magic dances down the hills, and their name became heard far and wide.'

[Then Vëannë said:] 'Aye, and they did more than dance, for their deeds afterward were very great, and many tales are

87

there thereof that thou must hear, O Eriol Melinon, upon another time of tale-telling. For these twain it is that stories name i-Cuilwarthon, which is to say the dead that live again, and they became mighty fairies in the lands about the north of Sirion. Behold now all is ended – and doth it like thee?'

[Then Eriol said that he had not expected to hear such an astonishing story from one such as Vëannë, to which she answered:]

'Nay, but I fashioned it not with words of myself; but it is dear to me – and indeed all the children know of the deeds that it relates – and I have learned it by heart, reading it in the great books, and I do not comprehend all that is set therein.'

*

DURING THE 1920s my father was engaged in the casting of the Lost Tales of Turambar and Tinúviel into verse. The first of these poems, *The Lay of the Children of Húrin*, in the Old English alliterative metre, was begun in 1918, but when far from completion he abandoned it, very probably when he left the University of Leeds. In the summer of 1925, the year in which he took up his appointment to the professorship of Anglo-Saxon at Oxford, he began 'the poem of Tinúviel', called *The Lay of Leithian*. This he translated 'Release from Bondage', but he never explained the title.

Remarkably and uncharacteristically he inserted dates at many points. The first of these, at line 557 (in the numbering of the poem as a whole) is 23 August 1925; and the last, 17 September 1931, is written against line 4085. Not far beyond this, at line 4223, the poem was abandoned, at the point in the narrative where 'the fangs of Carcharoth crashed together like a trap' on Beren's hand bearing the Silmaril, as he fled from Angband. For the remainder of the poem that was never written there are prose synopses.

In 1926 he sent many of his poems to R.W. Reynolds, who had been his teacher at King Edward's School in Birmingham. In that year he composed a substantial text with the title *Sketch of the mythology with especial reference to The Children of Húrin*, and on the envelope containing this manuscript he wrote later that this text was 'the original Silmarillion', and that he had written it for Mr Reynolds in order to 'explain the background of the "alliterative version" of Túrin and the Dragon.'

This *Sketch of the Mythology* was 'the original Silmarillion' because from it there was a direct line of evolution; whereas there is no stylistic continuity with the Lost Tales. The *Sketch* is what its name implies: it is a synopsis, composed in a terse, present-tense manner. I give here the passage in the text that tells in briefest form the tale of Beren and Lúthien.

A PASSAGE FROM THE
'SKETCH OF THE MYTHOLOGY'

The power of Morgoth begins to spread once more. One by one he overthrows Men and Elves in the North. Of these a famous chieftain of Men was Barahir, who had been a friend of Celegorm of Nargothrond.

Barahir is driven into hiding, his hiding betrayed, and Barahir slain; his son Beren after a life outlawed flees south, crosses the Shadowy Mountains, and after grievous hardships comes to Doriath. Of this and his other adventures is told in *The Lay of Leithian*. He gains the love of Tinúviel 'the nightingale' – his own name for Lúthien – the daughter of Thingol. To win her Thingol, in mockery, requires a Silmaril from the crown of Morgoth. Beren sets out to achieve this, is captured, and set in dungeon in Angband, but conceals his real identity and is given as a slave to Thû the hunter. Lúthien is imprisoned by Thingol, but escapes and goes in search of Beren. With the aid of Huan lord of dogs she rescues Beren, and gains entrance to Angband where Morgoth is enchanted and finally wrapped in slumber by her dancing. They get a Silmaril and escape, but are barred at gates of Angband by Carcaras the Wolf-ward. He bites off Beren's hand which holds the Silmaril, and goes mad with the anguish of its burning within him.

They escape and after many wanderings get back to Doriath. Carcaras ravening through the woods bursts into Doriath. There follows the Wolf-hunt of Doriath, in which Carcaras is slain, and Huan is killed in defence of Beren. Beren is however mortally wounded and dies in Lúthien's arms. Some songs say that Lúthien went even over the Grinding Ice, aided by the power of her divine mother, Melian, to Mandos' halls and won him back; others that Mandos hearing his tale released him. Certain it is that he alone of mortals came back from Mandos and dwelt with Lúthien and never spoke to Men again, living in the woods of Doriath and in the Hunters' Wold, west of Nargothrond.

It will be seen that there have been great changes in the legend, the most immediately evident being that of Beren's captor: here we meet Thû 'the hunter'. At the end of the *Sketch* it is said of Thû that he was the 'great chief' of Morgoth, and that he 'escaped the Last Battle and dwells still in dark places, and perverts Men to his dreadful worship'. In *The Lay of Leithian* Thû emerges as the fearful Necromancer, Lord of Wolves, who dwelt in Tol Sirion, the island in the river Sirion with an Elvish watchtower, which came to be Tol-in-Gaurhoth, the Isle of Werewolves. He is, or will be, Sauron. Tevildo and his realm of cats have disappeared.

But in the background another significant element in the legend had emerged after *The Tale of Tinúviel* was written: this concerns the father of Beren. Egnor the forester, the Gnome 'who hunted in the darker places of Hisilómë' (p.41) has gone. Now, in the passage from the *Sketch* just given, his father is Barahir, 'a famous chieftain of *Men*': driven into hiding by the growing hostile power of Morgoth, his hiding was betrayed, and he was slain. 'His son Beren after a life outlawed flees south, crosses the Shadowy Mountains, and after grievous hardships comes to Doriath. Of this and his other adventures is told in *The Lay of Leithian*.'

A PASSAGE EXTRACTED FROM
THE LAY OF LEITHIAN

I give here the passage in the *Lay* (written in 1925; see p. 88)
that describes the treachery of Gorlim, known as Gorlim
the Unhappy, who betrayed to Morgoth the hiding place of
Barahir and his companions, and the aftermath. I should mention here that the textual detail of the poem is very complex,
but since my (ambitious) purpose in this book is to make a
readily readable text that shows the narrative evolution of the
legend at different stages, I have neglected virtually all detail
of this nature, which could only confuse that purpose. An
account of the textual history of the poem will be found in my
book *The Lays of Beleriand* (*The History of Middle-earth*,
Vol. III, 1985). I have taken the extracts from the *Lay* in the
present book word for word from the text that I prepared for
The Lays of Beleriand. The line-numbers are simply those of
the extracts, and have no relation to those of the whole poem.

The extract that follows is taken from Canto II of the *Lay*.
It is preceded by a description of the ferocious tyranny of

Morgoth over the northern lands at the time of Beren's coming
into Artanor (Doriath), and of the survival in hiding of Barahir
and Beren and ten others, hunted in vain by Morgoth for many
years, until at last 'their feet were caught in Morgoth's snare'.

>   Gorlim it was, who wearying
> of toil and flight and harrying
> one night by chance did turn his feet
> o'er the dark fields by stealth to meet
> with hidden friend within a dale,   5
> and found a homestead looming pale
> against the misty stars, all dark
> save one small window, whence a spark
> of fitful candle strayed without.
> Therein he peeped, and filled with doubt   10
> he saw, as in a dreaming deep
> when longing cheats the heart in sleep,
> his wife beside a dying fire
> lament him lost; her thin attire
> and greying hair and paling cheek   15
> of tears and loneliness did speak.
> 'A! fair and gentle Eilinel,
> whom I had thought in darkling hell
> long since emprisoned! Ere I fled
> I deemed I saw thee slain and dead   20
> upon that night of sudden fear
> when all I lost that I held dear':
> thus thought his heavy heart amazed
> outside in darkness as he gazed.

But ere he dared to call her name,   25
or ask how she escaped and came
to this far vale beneath the hills,
he heard a cry beneath the hills!
There hooted near a hunting owl
with boding voice. He heard the howl   30
of the wild wolves that followed him
and dogged his feet through shadows dim.
Him unrelenting, well he knew,
the hunt of Morgoth did pursue.
Lest Eilinel with him they slay   35
without a word he turned away,
and like a wild thing winding led
his devious ways o'er stony bed
of stream, and over quaking fen,
until far from the homes of men   40
he lay beside his fellows few
in a secret place; and darkness grew,
and waned, and still he watched unsleeping,
and saw the dismal dawn come creeping
in dank heavens above gloomy trees.   45
A sickness held his soul for ease,
and hope, and even thraldom's chain
if he might find his wife again.
But all he thought twixt love of lord
and hatred of the king abhorred   50
and anguish for fair Eilinel
who drooped alone, what tale shall tell?

Yet at the last, when many days
of brooding did his mind amaze,
he found the servants of the king   55
and bade them to their master bring
a rebel who forgiveness sought,
if haply forgiveness might be bought
with tidings of Barahir the bold,
and where his hidings and his hold   60
might best be found by night or day.
And thus sad Gorlim, led away
unto those dark deep-dolven halls,
before the knees of Morgoth falls,
and puts his trust in that cruel heart   65
wherein no truth had ever part.
Quoth Morgoth: 'Eilinel the fair
thou shalt most surely find, and there
where she doth dwell and wait for thee
together shall ye ever be,   70
and sundered shall ye sigh no more.
Thus guerdon shall he have that bore
these tidings sweet, O traitor dear!
For Eilinel she dwells not here,
but in the shades of death doth roam   75
widowed of husband and of home –
a wraith of that which might have been,
methinks, it is that thou hast seen!
Now shalt thou through the gates of pain
the land thou askest grimly gain;   80

thou shalt to the moonless mists of hell
descend and seek thy Eilinel.'

Thus Gorlim died a bitter death
and cursed himself with dying breath,
and Barahir was caught and slain,   85
and all good deeds were made in vain.
But Morgoth's guile for ever failed,
nor wholly o'er his foes prevailed;
and some were ever that still fought
unmaking that which malice wrought.   90
Thus Men believed that Morgoth made
the fiendish phantom that betrayed
the soul of Gorlim, and so brought
the lingering hope forlorn to nought
that lived amid the lonely wood;   95
yet Beren had by fortune good
long hunted far afield that day,
and benighted in strange places lay
far from his fellows. In his sleep
he felt a dreadful darkness creep   100
upon his heart, and thought the trees
were bare and bent in mournful breeze;
no leaves they had, but ravens dark
sat thick as leaves on bough and bark,
and croaked, and as they croaked each neb   105
let fall a gout of blood; a web
unseen entwined him hand and limb,
until worn out, upon the rim

of stagnant pool he lay and shivered.
There saw he that a shadow quivered   110
far out upon the water wan,
and grew to a faint form thereon
that glided o'er the silent lake,
and coming slowly, softly spake
and sadly said; 'Lo! Gorlim here,   115
traitor betrayed, now stands! Nor fear,
but haste! For Morgoth's fingers close
upon thy father's throat. He knows
your secret tryst, your hidden lair',
and all the evil he laid bare   120
that he had done and Morgoth wrought.
Then Beren waking swiftly sought
his sword and bow, and sped like wind
that cuts with knives the branches thinned
of autumn trees. At last he came,   125
his heart afire with burning flame,
where Barahir his father lay;
he came too late. At dawn of day
he found the homes of hunted men,
a wooded island in the fen,   130
and birds rose up in sudden cloud –
no fen-fowl were they crying loud.
The raven and the carrion-crow
sat in the alders all a-row;
one croaked: 'Ha! Beren comes too late',   135
and answered all: 'Too late! Too late!'
There Beren buried his father's bones,

and piled a heap of boulder-stones,
and cursed the name of Morgoth thrice,
but wept not, for his heart was ice.   140

     Then over fen and field and mountain
he followed, till beside a fountain
upgushing hot from fires below
he found the slayers and his foe,
the murderous soldiers of the king.   145
And one there laughed, and showed a ring
he took from Barahir's dead hand.
'This ring in far Beleriand,
now mark ye, mates,' he said, 'was wrought.
Its like with gold could not be bought,   150
for this same Barahir I slew,
this robber fool, they say, did do
a deed of service long ago
for Felagund. It may be so;
for Morgoth bade me bring it back,   155
and yet, methinks, he has no lack
of weightier treasure in his hoard.
Such greed befits not such a lord,
and I am minded to declare
the hand of Barahir was bare!'   160
Yet as he spake an arrow sped;
with riven heart he crumpled dead.
Thus Morgoth loved that his own foe
should in his service deal the blow
that punished the breaking of his word.   165

But Morgoth laughed not when he heard
that Beren like a wolf alone
sprang madly from behind a stone
amid that camp beside the well,
and seized the ring, and ere the yell   170
of wrath and rage had left their throat
had fled his foes. His gleaming coat
was made of rings of steel no shaft
could pierce, a web of dwarvish craft;
and he was lost in rock and thorn,   175
for in charméd hour was Beren born;
their hungry hunting never learned
the way his fearless feet had turned.

    As fearless Beren was renowned,
as man most hardy upon ground,   180
while Barahir yet lived and fought;
but sorrow now his soul had wrought
to dark despair, and robbed his life
of sweetness, that he longed for knife,
or shaft, or sword, to end his pain,   185
and dreaded only thraldom's chain.
Danger he sought and death pursued,
and thus escaped the fate he wooed,
and deeds of breathless wonder dared
whose whispered glory widely fared,   190
and softly songs were sung at eve
of marvels he did once achieve
alone, beleaguered, lost at night

by mist or moon, or neath the light
of the broad eye of day. The woods   195
that northward looked with bitter feuds
he filled and death for Morgoth's folk;
his comrades were the beech and oak,
who failed him not, and many things
with fur and fell and feathered wings;   200
and many spirits, that in stone
in mountains old and wastes alone,
do dwell and wander, were his friends.
Yet seldom well an outlaw ends,
and Morgoth was a king more strong   205
than all the world has since in song
recorded, and his wisdom wide
slow and surely who him defied
did hem and hedge. Thus at the last
must Beren flee the forest fast   210
and lands he loved where lay his sire
by reeds bewailed beneath the mire.
Beneath a heap of mossy stones
now crumble those once mighty bones,
but Beren flees the friendless North   215
one autumn night, and creeps him forth;
the leaguer of his watchful foes
he passes – silently he goes.
No more his hidden bowstring sings,
no more his shaven arrow wings,   220
no more his hunted head doth lie
upon the heath beneath the sky.

The moon that looked amid the mist
upon the pines, the wind that hissed
among the heather and the fern   225
found him no more. The stars that burn
about the North with silver fire
in frosty airs, the Burning Briar
that Men did name in days long gone,
were set behind his back, and shone   230
o'er land and lake and darkened hill,
forsaken fen and mountain rill.

His face was South from the Land of Dread,
whence only evil pathways led,
and only the feet of men most bold   235
might cross the Shadowy Mountains cold.
Their northern slopes were filled with woe,
with evil and with mortal foe;
their southern faces mounted sheer
in rocky pinnacle and pier,   240
whose roots were woven with deceit
and washed with waters bitter-sweet.
There magic lurked in gulf and glen,
for far away beyond the ken
of searching eyes, unless it were   245
from dizzy tower that pricked the air
where only eagles lived and cried,
might grey and gleaming be descried
Beleriand, Beleriand,
the borders of the faëry land.   250

THE *QUENTA NOLDORINWA*

After the *Sketch of the Mythology* this text, which I will refer to as 'the *Quenta*', was the only complete and finished version of 'The Silmarillion' that my father achieved: a typescript that he made in (as seems certain) 1930. No preliminary drafts or outlines, if there were any, survive; but it is plain that for a good part of its length he had the *Sketch* before him. It is longer than the *Sketch,* and the 'Silmarillion style' has clearly appeared, but it remains a compression, a compendious account. In the sub-title it is said that it is 'the brief History of the Noldoli or Gnomes', drawn from the *Book of Lost Tales* which Eriol [Ælfwine] wrote. The long poems were of course now in being, substantial but massively unfinished, and my father was still working on *The Lay of Leithian.*

In the *Quenta* there emerges the major transformation of the legend of Beren and Lúthien by the entry of the Noldorin prince, Felagund, son of Finrod. To explain how this could come about I will give here a passage from this text, but a note on names is needed. The leader of the Noldor in the great journey of the Elves from Cuiviénen, the Water of Awakening in the furthest East, was Finwë; his three sons were Fëanor, Fingolfin, and Finrod, who was the father of Felagund. (Later the names were changed: The third son of Finwë became *Finarfin*, and *Finrod* the name of his son; but Finrod was also *Felagund*. This name meant 'Lord of Caves' or 'Cave-hewer' in the language of the Dwarves, for he was the founder of Nargothrond. The sister of Finrod Felagund was Galadriel.)

A PASSAGE EXTRACTED
FROM THE *QUENTA*

This was the time that songs call the Siege of Angband. The
swords of the Gnomes then fenced the earth from the ruin
of Morgoth, and his power was shut behind the walls of
Angband. The Gnomes boasted that never could he break
their leaguer, and that none of his folk could ever pass to
work evil in the ways of the world. . . .

In those days Men came over the Blue Mountains into
Beleriand, bravest and fairest of their race. Felagund it was
that found them, and he was ever their friend. On a time he
was the guest of Celegorm in the East, and rode a-hunting
with him. But he became separated from the others, and at
a time of night he came upon a dale in the western foothills
of the Blue Mountains. There were lights in the dale and
the sound of rugged song. Then Felagund marvelled, for
the tongue of those songs was not the tongue of Eldar or of
Dwarves. Nor was it the tongue of Orcs, though this at first
he feared. There were camped the people of Bëor, a mighty

warrior of Men, whose son was Barahir the bold. They were the first of Men to come into Beleriand. . . .

That night Felagund went among the sleeping men of Bëor's host and sat by their dying fires where none kept watch, and he took a harp which Bëor had laid aside, and he played music on it such as mortal ear had never heard, having learned the strains of music from the Dark-elves alone. Then men woke and listened and marvelled, for great wisdom was in that song, as well as beauty, and the heart grew wiser that listened to it. Thus came it that Men called Felagund, whom they met first of the Noldoli, Wisdom, and after him they called his race the Wise, whom we call the Gnomes.

Bëor lived till death with Felagund, and Barahir his son was the greatest friend of the sons of Finrod.

Now began the time of the ruin of the Gnomes. It was long before this was achieved, for great was their power grown, and they were very valiant, and their allies were many and bold, Dark-elves and Men.

But the tide of their fortune took a sudden turn. Long had Morgoth prepared his forces in secret. On a time of night at winter he let forth great rivers of flame that poured over all the plain before the Mountains of Iron and burned it to a desolate waste. Many of the Gnomes of Finrod's sons perished in that burning, and the fumes of it wrought darkness and confusion among the foes of Morgoth. In the train of the fire came the black armies of the Orcs in numbers such as the Gnomes had never before seen or imagined. In this way Morgoth broke the leaguer of Angband and slew by the hands of the Orcs a great slaughter of the bravest of the besieging hosts. His enemies were scattered far and wide, Gnomes, Ilkorins and Men. Men he drove for the most part back over the Blue Mountains, save the children of Bëor and of Hador who took refuge in Hithlum beyond the Shadowy Mountains, where as yet the Orcs came not in force. The Dark-elves fled south to Beleriand and beyond, but many went to Doriath, and the kingdom and power of Thingol grew great in that time, till he became a bulwark and a refuge of the Elves. The magics of Melian that were woven about the borders of Doriath fenced evil from his halls and realm.

The pine-forest Morgoth took and turned it into a place of dread, and the watchtower of Sirion he took and made it into a stronghold of evil and of menace. There dwelt Thû the chief servant of Morgoth, a sorcerer of dreadful power, the lord of wolves. Heaviest had the burden of that dreadful battle, the second battle and the first defeat of the Gnomes, fallen upon the sons of Finrod. There were Angrod and Egnor slain. There too would Felagund have been taken or slain, but Barahir came up with all his men and saved the Gnomish king and made a wall of spears about him; and though grievous was their loss they fought their way from the Orcs and fled to the fens of Sirion to the South. There Felagund swore an oath of undying friendship and aid in time of need to Barahir and all his kin and seed, and in token of his vow he gave to Barahir his ring.

Then Felagund went South, and on the banks of Narog established after the manner of Thingol a hidden and cavernous city and a realm. Those deep places were called Nargothrond. There came Orodreth [son of Finrod, brother of Felagund] after a time of breathless flight and perilous wanderings, and with him Celegorm and Curufin, the sons of Fëanor, his friends. The people of Celegorm swelled the strength of Felagund, but it would have been better if they had gone rather to their own kin, who fortified the hill of Himling east of Doriath and filled the Gorge of Aglon with hidden arms. . . .

In these days of doubt and fear, after the [Battle of Sudden Flame], many dreadful things befell of which but few are here told. It is told that Bëor was slain and Barahir yielded not to Morgoth, but all his land was won from him and his people scattered, enslaved or slain, and he himself went in outlawry with his son Beren and ten faithful men. Long they hid and did secret and valiant deeds of war against the Orcs. But in the end, as is told in the beginning of the lay of Lúthien and Beren, the hiding place of Barahir was betrayed, and he was slain and his comrades, all save Beren who by fortune was that day hunting afar. Thereafter Beren lived an outlaw alone, save for the help he had from birds and beasts which he loved; and seeking for death in desperate deeds found it not, but glory and renown in the secret songs of fugitives and hidden enemies of Morgoth, so that the tale of his deeds came even to Beleriand, and was rumoured in Doriath. At length Beren fled south from the ever-closing circle of those that hunted him, and crossed the dreadful Mountains of Shadow, and came at last worn and haggard into Doriath. There in secret he won the love of Lúthien daughter of Thingol, and he named her Tinúviel, the nightingale, because of the beauty of her singing in the twilight beneath the trees; for she was the daughter of Melian.

But Thingol was wroth and he dismissed him in scorn, but did not slay him because he had sworn an oath to his daughter. But he desired nonetheless to send him to his death. And he thought in his heart of a quest that could not be achieved, and he said: If thou bring me a Silmaril from the crown of Morgoth, I will let Lúthien wed thee, if she will. And Beren vowed to achieve this, and went from Doriath to Nargothrond bearing the ring of Barahir. The quest of the Silmaril there aroused the oath from sleep that the sons of Fëanor had sworn, and evil began to grow from it. Felagund, though he knew the quest to be beyond his power, was willing to lend all his aid to Beren, because of his own oath to Barahir. But Celegorm and Curufin dissuaded his people and roused up rebellion against him. And evil thoughts awoke in their hearts, and they thought to usurp the throne of Nargothrond, because they were sons of the eldest line. Rather than a Silmaril should be won and given to Thingol, they would ruin the power of Doriath and Nargothrond.

So Felagund gave his crown to Orodreth and departed from his people with Beren and ten faithful men of his own board. They waylaid an Orc-band and slew them, and disguised themselves by the aid of Felagund's magic as Orcs. But they were seen by Thû from his watchtower, which once had been Felagund's own, and were questioned by him, and their magic was overthrown in a contest between Thû and Felagund. Thus they were revealed as Elves, but the spells of Felagund concealed their names and quest. Long were they tortured in the dungeons of Thû, but none betrayed the other.

The oath referred to at the end of this passage was sworn by Fëanor and his seven sons, in the words of the *Quenta,* 'to pursue with hate and vengeance to the ends of the world Vala, Demon, Elf, or Man, or Orc who hold or take or keep a Silmaril against their will.' See pp. 117–18, lines 171–80.

A SECOND EXTRACT FROM
THE LAY OF LEITHIAN

I give now a further passage of *The Lay of Leithian* (see pp. 91, 93) telling the story that has just been given in its very compressed form in the *Quenta*. I take up the poem where the Siege of Angband was ended in what was later called the Battle of Sudden Flame. According to the dates that my father wrote on the manuscript the whole passage was composed in March–April 1928. At line 246 Canto VI of the *Lay* ends and Canto VII begins.

> An end there came, when fortune turned,
> and flames of Morgoth's vengeance burned,
> and all the might which he prepared
> in secret in his fastness flared
> and poured across the Thirsty Plain;   5
> and armies black were in his train.
> The leaguer of Angband Morgoth broke;
> his enemies in fire and smoke

were scattered, and the Orcs there slew
and slew, until the blood like dew   10
dripped from each cruel and crooked blade.
Then Barahir the bold did aid
with mighty spear, with shield and men,
Felagund wounded. To the fen
escaping, there they bound their troth,   15
and Felagund deeply swore an oath
of friendship to his kin and seed
of love and succour in time of need.
But there of Finrod's children four
were Angrod slain and proud Egnor.   20
Felagund and Orodreth then
gathered the remnant of their men,
their maidens and their children fair;
forsaking war they made their lair
and cavernous hold far in the south.   25
On Narog's towering bank its mouth
was opened; which they hid and veiled,
and mighty doors, that unassailed
till Túrin's day stood vast and grim,
they built by trees o'ershadowed dim.   30
And with them dwelt a long time there
Curufin, and Celegorm the fair;
and a mighty folk grew neath their hands
in Narog's secret halls and lands.

    Thus Felagund in Nargothrond   35
still reigned, a hidden king whose bond

was sworn to Barahir the bold.
And now his son through forests cold
wandered alone as in a dream.
Esgalduin's dark and shrouded stream   40
he followed, till its waters frore
were joined to Sirion, Sirion hoar,
pale silver water wide and free
rolling in splendour to the sea.

    Now Beren came unto the pools,   45
wide shallow meres where Sirion cools
his gathered tide beneath the stars,
ere chafed and sundered by the bars
of reedy banks a mighty fen
he feeds and drenches, plunging then   50
into vast chasms underground,
where many miles his way is wound.
Umboth-Muilin, Twilight Meres,
those great wide waters grey as tears
the Elves then named. Through driving rain   55
from thence across the Guarded Plain
the Hills of the Hunters Beren saw
with bare tops bitten bleak and raw
by western winds, but in the mist
of streaming rains that flashed and hissed   60
into the meres he knew there lay
beneath those hills the cloven way
of Narog, and the watchful halls
of Felagund beside the falls
of Ingwil tumbling from the wold.   65

An everlasting watch they hold,
the Gnomes of Nargothrond renowned,
and every hill is tower-crowned,
where wardens sleepless peer and gaze
guarding the plain and all the ways   70
between Narog swift and Sirion pale;
and archers whose arrows never fail
there range the woods, and secret kill
all who creep thither against their will.

  Yet now he thrusts into that land   75
bearing the gleaming ring on hand
of Felagund, and oft doth cry:
'Here comes no wandering Orc or spy,
but Beren son of Barahir
who once to Felagund was dear.'   80

  So ere he reached the eastward shore
of Narog, that doth foam and roar
o'er boulders black, those archers green
came round him. When the ring was seen
they bowed before him, though his plight   85
was poor and beggarly. Then by night
they led him northward, for no ford
nor bridge was built where Narog poured
before the gates of Nargothrond,
and friend nor foe might pass beyond.   90

  To northward, where that stream yet young
more slender flowed, below the tongue
of foam-splashed land that Ginglith pens
when her brief golden torrent ends

and joins the Narog, there they wade.   95
Now swiftest journey thence they made
to Nargothrond's sheer terraces
and dim gigantic palaces.
   They came beneath a sickle moon
to doors there darkly hung and hewn   100
with posts and lintels of ponderous stone
and timbers huge. Now open thrown
were gaping gates, and in they strode
where Felagund on throne abode.

   Fair were the words of Narog's king   105
to Beren, and his wandering
and all his feuds and bitter wars
recounted soon. Behind closed doors
they sat, while Beren told his tale
of Doriath; and words him fail   110
recalling Lúthien dancing fair
with wild white roses in her hair,
remembering her elven voice that rung
while stars in twilight round her hung.
He spake of Thingol's marvellous halls   115
by enchantment lit, where fountain falls
and ever the nightingale doth sing
to Melian and to her king.
The quest he told that Thingol laid
in scorn on him; how for love of maid   120
more fair than ever was born to Men,
of Tinúviel, of Lúthien,

he must essay the burning waste,
and doubtless death and torment taste.

   This Felagund in wonder heard,   125
and heavily spoke at last this word:
'It seems that Thingol doth desire
thy death. The everlasting fire
of those enchanted jewels all know
is cursed with an oath of endless woe,   130
and Fëanor's sons alone by right
are lords and masters of their light.
He cannot hope within his hoard
to keep this gem, nor is he lord
of all the folk of Elfinesse.   135
And yet thou saist for nothing less
can thy return to Doriath
be purchased? Many a dreadful path
in sooth there lies before thy feet –
and after Morgoth, still a fleet   140
untiring hate, as I know well,
would hunt thee from heaven unto hell.
Fëanor's sons would, if they could,
slay thee or ever thou reached his wood
or laid in Thingol's lap that fire,   145
or gained at least thy sweet desire.
Lo! Celegorm and Curufin
here dwell this very realm within,
and even though I, Finrod's son,
am king, a mighty power have won   150

and many of their own folk lead.
Friendship to me in every need
they yet have shown, but much I fear
that to Beren son of Barahir
mercy or love they will not show   155
if once thy dreadful quest they know.'

True words he spoke. For when the king
to all his people told this thing,
and spake of the oath to Barahir,
and how that mortal shield and spear   160
had saved them from Morgoth and from woe
on Northern battlefields long ago,
then many were kindled in their hearts
once more to battle. But up there starts
amid the throng, and loudly cries   165
for hearing, one with flaming eyes,
proud Celegorm with gleaming hair
and shining sword. Then all men stare
upon his stern unyielding face,
and a great hush falls upon that place.   170

'Be he friend or foe, or demon wild
of Morgoth, Elf, or mortal child,
or any that here on earth may dwell,
no law, nor love, nor league of hell,
no might of Gods, no binding spell,   175
shall him defend from hatred fell
of Fëanor's sons, whoso take or steal

or finding keep a Silmaril.
These we alone do claim by right,
our thrice enchanted jewels bright.'   180

Many wild and potent words he spoke,
and as before in Tûn awoke
his father's voice their hearts to fire,
so now dark fear and brooding ire
he cast on them, foreboding war   185
of friend with friend; and pools of gore
their minds imagined lying red
in Nargothrond about the dead,
did Narog's host with Beren go;
or haply battle, ruin, and woe   190
in Doriath where great Thingol reigned,
if Fëanor's fatal jewel he gained.
And even such as were most true
to Felagund his oath did rue,
and thought with terror and despair   195
of seeking Morgoth in his lair
with force or guile. This Curufin
when his brother ceased did then begin
more to impress upon their minds;
and such a spell he on them binds   200
that never again till Túrin's day
would Gnome of Narog in array
of open battle go to war.
With secrecy, ambush, spies and lore
of wizardry, with silent leaguer   205

of wild things wary, watchful, eager,
of phantom hunters, venomed darts,
and unseen stealthy creeping arts,
with padding hatred that its prey
with feet of velvet all the day   210
followed remorseless out of sight
and slew it unawares at night –
thus they defended Nargothrond,
and forgot their kin and solemn bond
for dread of Morgoth that the art   215
of Curufin set within their heart.

    So would they not that angry day
King Felagund their lord obey,
but sullen murmured that Finrod
nor yet his son were as a god.   220
Then Felagund took off his crown
and at his feet he cast it down,
the silver helm of Nargothrond:
'Yours ye may break, but I my bond
must keep, and kingdom here forsake.   225
If hearts here were that did not quake,
or that to Finrod's son were true,
then I at least should find a few
to go with me, not like a poor
rejected beggar scorn endure,   230
turned from my gates to leave my town,
my people, and my realm and crown!'

Hearing these words there swiftly stood
beside him ten tried warriors good,
men of his house who had ever fought   235
wherever his banners had been brought.
One stooped and lifted up his crown,
and said: 'O king, to leave this town
is now our fate, but not to lose
thy rightful lordship. Thou shalt choose   240
one to be steward in thy stead.'
Then Felagund upon the head
of Orodreth set it: 'Brother mine,
till I return this crown is thine.'
Then Celegorm no more would stay,   245
and Curufin smiled and turned away.

*****

Thus twelve alone there ventured forth
from Nargothrond, and to the North
they turned their silent secret way,
and vanished in the fading day.   250
No trumpet sounds, no voice there sings,
as robed in mail of cunning rings
now blackened dark with helmets grey
and sombre cloaks they steal away.

Far-journeying Narog's leaping course   255
they followed till they found his source,
the flickering falls, whose freshets sheer
a glimmering goblet glassy-clear

with crystal waters fill that shake
and quiver down from Ivrin's lake,   260
from Ivrin's mere that mirrors dim
the pallid faces bare and grim
of Shadowy Mountains neath the moon.

   Now far beyond the realm immune
from Orc and demon and the dread   265
of Morgoth's might their ways had led.
In woods o'ershadowed by the heights
they watched and waited many nights,
till on a time when hurrying cloud
did moon and constellation shroud,   270
and winds of autumn's wild beginning
soughed in the boughs, and leaves went spinning
down the dark eddies rustling soft,
they heard a murmur hoarsely waft
from far, a croaking laughter coming;   275
now louder; now they heard the drumming
of hideous stamping feet that tramp
the weary earth. Then many a lamp
of sullen red they saw draw near,
swinging, and glistening on spear   280
and scimitar. There hidden nigh
they saw a band of Orcs go by
with goblin faces swart and foul.
Bats were about them, and the owl,
the ghostly forsaken night-bird cried   285
from trees above. The voices died,

the laughter like clash of stone and steel
passed and faded. At their heel
the Elves and Beren crept more soft
than foxes stealing through a croft   290
in search of prey. Thus to the camp
lit by flickering fire and lamp
they stole, and counted sitting there
full thirty Orcs in the red flare
of burning wood. Without a sound   295
they one by one stood silent round,
each in the shadow of a tree;
each slowly, grimly, secretly
bent then his bow and drew the string.

  Hark! how they sudden twang and sing,   300
when Felagund lets forth a cry;
and twelve Orcs sudden fall and die.
Then forth they leap casting their bows.
Out their bright swords, and swift their blows!
The stricken Orcs now shriek and yell   305
as lost things deep in lightless hell.
Battle there is beneath the trees
bitter and swift; but no Orc flees;
there left their lives that wandering band
and stained no more the sorrowing land   310
with rape and murder. Yet no song
of joy, or triumph over wrong,
the Elves there sang. In peril sore
they were, for never alone to war

so small an Orc-band went, they knew.   315
Swiftly the raiment off they drew
and cast the corpses in a pit.
This desperate counsel had the wit
of Felagund for them devised:
as Orcs his comrades he disguised.   320

   The poisoned spears, the bows of horn,
the crooked swords their foes had borne
they took; and loathing each him clad
in Angband's raiment foul and sad.
They smeared their hands and faces fair   325
with pigment dark; the matted hair
all lank and black from goblin head
they shore, and joined it thread by thread
with Gnomish skill. As each one leers
at each dismayed, about his ears   330
he hangs it noisome, shuddering.
   Then Felagund a spell did sing
of changing and of shifting shape;
their ears grew hideous, and agape
their mouths did start, and like a fang   335
each tooth became, as slow he sang.
Their Gnomish raiment then they hid,
and one by one behind him slid,
behind a foul and goblin thing
that once was elven-fair and king.   340

Northward they went; and Orcs they met
who passed, nor did their going let,
but hailed them in greeting; and more bold
they grew as past the long miles rolled.
 At length they came with weary feet   345
beyond Beleriand. They found the fleet
young waters, rippling, silver-pale
of Sirion hurrying through that vale
where Taur-na-Fuin, Deadly Night,
the trackless forest's pine-clad height,   350
falls dark forbidding slowly down
upon the east, while westward frown
the northward-bending Mountains grey
and bar the westering light of day.

 An isléd hill there stood alone   355
amid the valley, like a stone
rolled from the mountains vast
when giants in tumult hurtled past.
Around its feet the river looped
a stream divided, that had scooped   360
the hanging edges into caves.
There briefly shuddered Sirion's waves
and ran to other shores more clean.
 An elven watchtower had it been,
and strong it was, and still was fair;   365
but now did grim with menace stare
one way to pale Beleriand,
the other to that mournful land

124

beyond the valley's northern mouth.
Thence could be glimpsed the fields of drouth,   370
the dusty dunes, the desert wide;
and further far could be descried
the brooding cloud that hangs and lowers
on Thangorodrim's thunderous towers.

   Now in that hill was the abode   375
of one most evil; and the road
that from Beleriand thither came
he watched with sleepless eyes of flame.
   Men called him Thû, and as a god
in after days beneath his rod   380
bewildered bowed to him, and made
his ghastly temples in the shade.
Not yet by Men enthralled adored,
now was he Morgoth's mightiest lord,
Master of Wolves, whose shivering howl   385
for ever echoed in the hills, and foul
enchantments and dark sigaldry
did weave and wield. In glamoury
that necromancer held his hosts
of phantoms and of wandering ghosts,   390
of misbegotten or spell-wronged
monsters that about him thronged,
working his bidding dark and vile:
the werewolves of the Wizard's Isle.

From Thû their coming was not hid   395
and though beneath the eaves they slid
of the forest's gloomy-hanging boughs,
he saw them afar, and wolves did rouse:
'Go! fetch me those sneaking Orcs,' he said,
'that fare thus strangely, as if in dread,   400
and do not come, as all Orcs use
and are commanded, to bring me news
of all their deeds, to me, to Thû.'

From his tower he gazed, and in him grew
suspicion and a brooding thought,   405
waiting, leering, till they were brought.
Now ringed about with wolves they stand,
and fear their doom. Alas! the land,
the land of Narog left behind!
Foreboding evil weights their mind,   410
as downcast, halting, they must go
and cross the stony bridge of woe
to Wizard's Isle, and to the throne
there fashioned of blood-darkened stone.

'Where have ye been? What have ye seen?'   415

'In Elfinesse; and tears and distress,
the fire blowing and the blood flowing,
these have we seen, there have we been.
Thirty we slew and their bodies threw

in a dark pit. The ravens sit   420
and the owl cries where our swath lies.'

   'Come, tell me true, O Morgoth's thralls,
what then in Elfinesse befalls?
What of Nargothrond? Who reigneth there?
Into that realm did your feet dare?'   425

   'Only its borders did we dare.
There reigns King Felagund the fair.'

   'Then heard ye not that he is gone,
that Celegorm sits his throne upon?'

   'That is not true! If he is gone,   430
then Orodreth sits his throne upon.'

   'Sharp are your ears, swift have they got
tidings of realms ye entered not!
What are your names, O spearmen bold?
Who your captain, ye have not told.'   435

   'Nereb and Dungalef and warriors ten,
so we are called, and dark our den
under the mountains. Over the waste
we march on an errand of need and haste.
Boldog the captain awaits us there   440
where fires from under smoke and flare.'

'Boldog, I heard, was lately slain
warring on the borders of that domain
where Robber Thingol and outlaw folk
cringe and crawl beneath elm and oak   445
in drear Doriath. Heard ye not then
of that pretty fay, of Lúthien?
Her body is fair, very white and fair.
Morgoth would possess her in his lair.
Boldog he sent, but Boldog was slain: 450
strange ye were not in Boldog's train.

   Nereb looks fierce, his frown is grim.
Little Lúthien! What troubles him?
Why laughs he not to think of his lord
crushing a maiden in his hoard,   455
that foul should be what once was clean,
that dark should be where light has been?

   Whom do ye serve, Light or Mirk?
Who is the maker of mightiest work?
Who is the king of earthly kings,   460
the greatest giver of gold and rings?
Who is the master of the wide earth?
Who despoiled them of their mirth,
the greedy Gods! Repeat your vows,
Orcs of Bauglir! Do not bend your brows!   465
Death to light, to law, to love!
Cursed be moon and stars above!
May darkness everlasting old
that waits outside in surges cold

drown Manwë, Varda, and the sun!   470
May all in hatred be begun
and all in evil ended be,
in the moaning of the endless Sea!'

But no true Man nor Elf yet free
would ever speak that blasphemy,   475
and Beren muttered: 'Who is Thû
to hinder work that is to do?
Him we serve not, nor to him owe
obeisance, and we now would go.'

Thû laughed: 'Patience! Not very long   480
shall ye abide. But first a song
I will sing to you, to ears intent.'
Then his flaming eyes he on them bent,
and darkness black fell round them all.
Only they saw as through a pall   485
of eddying smoke those eyes profound
in which their senses choked and drowned.
  He chanted a song of wizardry,
of piercing, opening, of treachery,
revealing, uncovering, betraying.   490
Then sudden Felagund there swaying
sang in answer a song of staying,
resisting, battling against power,
of secrets kept, strength like a tower,
and trust unbroken, freedom, escape;   500

129

of changing and of shifting shape,
of snares eluded, broken traps,
the prison opening, the chain that snaps.
    Backwards and forwards swayed their song.
Reeling and foundering, as ever more strong   505
Thû's chanting swelled, Felagund fought,
and all the magic and might he brought
of Elfinesse into his words.
Softly in the gloom they heard the birds
singing afar in Nargothrond,   510
the sighing of the sea beyond,
beyond the western world, on sand,
on sand of pearls in Elvenland.

    Then the gloom gathered: darkness growing
in Valinor, the red blood flowing   515
beside the sea, where the Gnomes slew
the Foamriders, and stealing drew
their white ships with their white sails
from lamplit havens. The wind wails.
The wolf howls. The ravens flee.   520
The ice mutters in the mouths of the sea.
The captives sad in Angband mourn.
Thunder rumbles, the fires burn,
a vast smoke gushes out, a roar –
and Felagund swoons upon the floor.   525

    Behold! they are in their own fair shape,
fairskinned, brighteyed. No longer gape

Orclike their mouths; and now they stand
betrayed into the wizard's hand.
Thus came they unhappy into woe,   530
to dungeons no hope nor glimmer know,
where chained in chains that eat the flesh
and woven in webs of strangling mesh
they lay forgotten, in despair.

   Yet not all unavailing were   535
the spells of Felagund; for Thû
neither their names nor purpose knew.
These much he pondered and bethought,
and in their woeful chains them sought,
and threatened all with dreadful death,   540
if one would not with traitor's breath
reveal this knowledge. Wolves should come
and slow devour them one by one
before the others' eyes, and last
should one alone be left aghast,   545
then in a place of horror hung
with anguish should his limbs be wrung,
in the bowels of the earth be slow
endlessly, cruelly, put to woe
and torment, till he all declared.   550

   Even as he threatened, so it fared.
From time to time in the eyeless dark
two eyes would grow, and they would hark
to frightful cries, and then a sound

of rending, a slavering on the ground,   555
and blood flowing they would smell.
But none would yield, and none would tell.

Here Canto VII ends. I return now to the *Quenta*, and take it up from the words 'Long were they tortured in the dungeons of Thû, but none betrayed the other' with which the previous extract ends (p. 110); and as previously I follow the *Quenta* account with the vastly different passage in the *Lay*.

A FURTHER EXTRACT FROM
THE *QUENTA*

In the meanwhile Lúthien, learning by the far sight of Melian
that Beren had fallen into the power of Thû, sought in her
despair to fly from Doriath. This became known to Thingol,
who imprisoned her in a house in the tallest of his mighty
beeches far above the ground. How she escaped and came
into the woods, and was found there by Celegorm as they
hunted on the borders of Doriath, is told in *The Lay of
Leithian*. They took her treacherously to Nargothrond, and
Curufin the crafty became enamoured of her beauty. From
her tale they learned that Felagund was in the hands of Thû;
and they purposed to let him perish there, and keep Lúthien
with them, and force Thingol to wed Lúthien to Curufin,
and so build up their power and usurp Nargothrond and
become the mightiest of the princes of the Gnomes. They
did not think to go in search of the Silmarils, or suffer any
others to do so, until they had all the power of the Elves
beneath themselves and obedient to them. But their designs

came to nought save estrangement and bitterness between the kingdoms of the Elves.

Huan was the name of the chief of the hounds of Celegorm. He was of immortal race from the hunting-lands of Oromë. Oromë gave him to Celegorm long before in Valinor, when Celegorm often rode in the train of the God and followed his horn. He came into the Great Lands with his master, and dart nor weapon, spell nor poison, could harm him, so that he went into battle with his lord and saved him many times from death. His fate had been decreed that he should not meet death save at the hands of the mightiest wolf that should ever walk the world.

Huan was true of heart, and he loved Lúthien from the hour that he first found her in the woods and brought her to Celegorm. His heart was grieved by his master's treachery, and he set Lúthien free and went with her to the North.

There Thû slew his captives one by one, till only Felagund and Beren were left. When the hour for Beren's death came Felagund put forth all his power, and burst his bonds, and wrestled with the werewolf that came to slay Beren; and he killed the wolf, but was himself slain in the dark. There Beren mourned in despair, and waited for death. But Lúthien came and sang outside the dungeons. Thus she beguiled Thû to come forth, for the fame of the loveliness of Lúthien had gone through all lands and the wonder of her song. Even Morgoth desired her, and had promised the greatest reward to any who could capture her. Each wolf that Thû sent Huan slew silently, till Draugluin the greatest of his wolves came. Then there was fierce battle, and Thû knew that Lúthien was not alone. But he remembered the fate of Huan, and he made himself the greatest wolf that had yet walked the world, and came forth. But Huan overthrew him, and won from him the keys and the spells that held together his enchanted walls and towers. So the stronghold was broken and the towers thrown down and the dungeons opened. Many captives were released, but Thû flew in bat's form to Taur-na-Fuin. There Lúthien found Beren mourning beside Felagund. She healed his sorrow and the wasting of his imprisonment, but Felagund they buried on the top of his own island hill, and Thû came there no more.

Then Huan returned to his master, and less was the love between them after. Beren and Lúthien wandered careless in happiness until they came nigh to the borders of Doriath once more. There Beren remembered his vow, and bade Lúthien farewell, but she would not be sundered from him. In Nargothrond there was tumult. For Huan and many of the captives of Thû brought back the tidings of the deeds of Lúthien, and the death of Felagund, and the treachery of Celegorm and Curufin was laid bare. It is said they had sent a secret embassy to Thingol ere Lúthien escaped, but Thingol in wrath had sent their letters back by his own servants to Orodreth. Wherefore now the hearts of the people of Narog turned back to the house of Finrod, and they mourned their king Felagund whom they had forsaken, and they did the bidding of Orodreth.

But he would not suffer them to slay the sons of Fëanor as they wished. Instead he banished them from Nargothrond, and swore that little love should there be between Narog and any of the sons of Fëanor thereafter. And so it was.

Celegorm and Curufin were riding in haste and wrath through the woods to find their way to Himling when they came upon Beren and Lúthien, even as Beren sought to part from his love. They rode down on them, and recognizing them tried to trample Beren under their hooves.

But Curufin lifted Lúthien to his saddle. Then befell the leap of Beren, the greatest leap of mortal Men. For he sprang like a lion right upon the speeding horse of Curufin, and grasped him about the throat, and horse and rider fell in confusion upon the earth, but Lúthien was flung far off and lay dazed upon the ground. There Beren choked Curufin, but his death was very nigh from Celegorm, who rode back with his spear. In that hour Huan forsook the service of Celegorm, and sprang upon him so that his horse swerved aside, and no man for fear of the terror of the great hound dared go nigh. Lúthien forbade the death of Curufin, but Beren despoiled him of his horse and weapons, chief of which was his famous knife, made by the Dwarves. It would cut iron like wood. Then the brothers rode off, but shot back at Huan treacherously and at Lúthien. Huan they did not hurt, but Beren sprang before Lúthien and was wounded, and Men remembered that wound against the sons of Fëanor, when it became known.

Huan stayed with Lúthien, and hearing of their perplexity and the purpose Beren had still to go to Angband, he went and fetched them from the ruined halls of Thû a werewolf's coat and a bat's. Three times only did Huan speak with the tongue of Elves or Men. The first was when he came to Lúthien in Nargothrond. This was the second, when he devised the desperate counsel for their quest. So they rode North, till they could no longer go on horse in safety. Then they put on the garments as of wolf and bat, and Lúthien in guise of evil fay rode upon the werewolf.

In *The Lay of Leithian* is all told how they came to Angband's gate, and found it newly guarded, for rumour of he knew not what design abroad among the Elves had come to Morgoth. Wherefore he fashioned the mightiest of all wolves, Carcharas Knife-fang, to sit at the gates. But Lúthien set him in spells, and they won their way to the presence of Morgoth, and Beren slunk beneath his chair. Then Lúthien dared the most dreadful and most valiant deed that any of the women of the Elves have ever dared; no less than the challenge of Fingolfin is it accounted, and may be greater, save that she was half-divine. She cast off her disguise and named her own name, and feigned that she was brought captive by the wolves of Thû. And she beguiled Morgoth, even as his heart plotted foul evil within him; and she danced before him, and cast all his court in sleep; and she sang to him, and she flung the magic robe she had woven in Doriath in his face, and she set a binding dream upon him – what song can sing the marvel of that deed, or the wrath and humiliation of Morgoth, for even the Orcs laugh in secret when they remember it, telling how Morgoth fell from his chair and his iron crown rolled upon the floor.

Then forth leaped Beren casting aside the wolvish robe, and drew out the knife of Curufin. With that he cut forth a Silmaril. But daring more he essayed to gain them all. Then the knife of the treacherous Dwarves snapped, and the ringing sound of it stirred the sleeping hosts and Morgoth groaned.

Terror seized the hearts of Beren and Lúthien, and they fled
down the dark ways of Angband. The doors were barred by
Carcharas, now aroused from the spell of Lúthien. Beren set
himself before Lúthien, which proved ill; for ere she could
touch the wolf with her robe or speak word of magic, he
sprang upon Beren, who now had no weapon. With his right
he smote at the eyes of Carcharas, but the wolf took the hand
into his jaws and bit it off. Now that hand held the Silmaril.
Then was the maw of Carcharas burned with a fire of anguish
and torment, when the Silmaril touched his evil flesh; and
he fled howling from before them, so that all the mountains
shuddered, and the madness of the wolf of Angband was of
all the horrors that ever came into the North the most dire
and terrible. Hardly did Lúthien and Beren escape, ere all
Angband was aroused.

Of their wanderings and despair, and of the healing of
Beren, who ever since has been called Beren Ermabwed the
One-handed, of their rescue by Huan, who had vanished
suddenly from them ere they came to Angband, and of their
coming to Doriath once more, here there is little to tell. But
in Doriath many things had befallen. Ever things had gone
ill there since Lúthien fled away. Grief had fallen on all the
people and silence on their songs when their hunting found
her not. Long was the search, and in searching Dairon the
piper of Doriath was lost, who loved Lúthien before Beren
came to Doriath. He was the greatest of the musicians of the
Elves, save Maglor son of Fëanor, and Tinfang Warble. But
he came never back to Doriath and strayed into the East of
the world.

Assaults too there were on Doriath's borders, for rumours that Lúthien was astray had reached Angband. Boldog the captain of the Orcs was there slain in battle by Thingol, and his great warriors Beleg the Bowman and Mablung Heavyhand were with Thingol in that battle. Thus Thingol learned that Lúthien was yet free of Morgoth, but that he knew of her wandering; and Thingol was filled with fear. In the midst of his fear came the embassy of Celegorm in secret, and said that Beren was dead, and Felagund, and Lúthien was at Nargothrond. Then Thingol found it in his heart to regret the death of Beren, and his wrath was aroused at the hinted treachery of Celegorm to the house of Finrod, and because he kept Lúthien and did not send her home. Wherefore he sent spies into the land of Nargothrond and prepared for war. But he learned that Lúthien had fled and that Celegorm and his brother were gone to Aglon. So now he sent an embassy to Aglon, since his might was not great enough to fall upon all the seven brothers, nor was his quarrel with others than Celegorm and Curufin. But this embassy journeying in the woods met with the onslaught of Carcharas. That great wolf had run in madness through all the woods of the North, and death and devastation went with him. Mablung alone escaped to bear the news of his coming to Thingol. Of fate, or the magic of the Silmaril that he bore to his torment, he was not stayed by the spells of Melian, but burst into the inviolate woods of Doriath, and far and wide terror and destruction was spread.

Even as the sorrows of Doriath were at their worst came Lúthien and Beren and Huan back to Doriath. Then the heart of Thingol was lightened, but he looked not with love upon Beren in whom he saw the cause of all his woes. When he had learned how Beren had escaped from Thû he was amazed, but he said: 'Mortal, what of thy quest and of thy vow?' Then said Beren: 'Even now I have a Silmaril in my hand.' 'Show it to me,' said Thingol. 'That I cannot,' said Beren, 'for my hand is not here.' And all the tale he told, and made clear the cause of the madness of Carcharas, and Thingol's heart was softened by his brave words, and his forbearance, and the great love that he saw between his daughter and this most valiant Man.

Now therefore did they plan the wolf-hunt of Carcharas. In that hunt was Huan and Thingol and Mablung and Beleg and Beren and no more. And here the sad tale of it must be short, for it is elsewhere told more fully. Lúthien remained behind in foreboding, as they went forth; and well she might, for Carcharas was slain, but Huan died in the same hour, and he died to save Beren. Yet Beren was hurt to the death, but lived to place the Silmaril in the hands of Thingol, when Mablung had cut it from the belly of the wolf. Then he spoke not again, until they had borne him with Huan at his side back to the doors of Thingol's halls. There beneath the beech, wherein before she had been imprisoned, Lúthien met them, and kissed Beren ere his spirit departed to the halls of awaiting. So ended the long tale of Lúthien and Beren. But not yet was *The Lay of Leithian*, release from bondage, told in full. For it has long been said that Lúthien failed and faded swiftly and vanished from the earth, though some songs say that Melian summoned Thorondor, and he bore her living unto Valinor. And she came to the halls of Mandos, and she sang to him a tale of moving love so fair that he was moved to pity, as never has befallen since. Beren he summoned, and thus, as Lúthien had sworn as she kissed him at the hour of death, they met beyond the western sea. And Mandos suffered them to depart, but he said that Lúthien should become mortal even as her lover, and should leave the earth once more in the manner of mortal women, and her beauty become but a memory of song. So it was, but it is said that in recompense Mandos gave to Beren and to Lúthien thereafter a long span of life and joy, and they wandered knowing thirst nor cold in the fair land of Beleriand, and no mortal Man thereafter spoke to Beren or his spouse.

THE NARRATIVE IN *THE LAY OF LEITHIAN* TO ITS TERMINATION

This substantial portion of the poem takes up from the last line of Canto VII in *The Lay of Leithian* ('But none would yield, and none would tell', p. 132), and the opening of Canto VIII corresponds to the very compressed account in the *Quenta* (p. 133) of the confinement of Lúthien in Nargothrond, imposed on her by Celegorm and Curufin and from which she was rescued by Huan, whose origin is told. A line of asterisks in the text of the *Lay* marks the start of a further Canto; Canto IX at line 329; Canto X at line 619; Canto XI at line 1009; Canto XII at line 1301; Canto XIII at line 1603; and Canto XIV, the last, at line 1939.

> Hounds there were in Valinor
> with silver collars. Hart and boar,
> the fox and hare and nimble roe
> there in the forests green did go.
> Oromë was the lord divine   5

of all those woods. The potent wine
went in his halls and hunting song.
The Gnomes anew have named him long
Tavros, the God whose horns did blow
over the mountains long ago;   10
who alone of Gods had loved the world
before the banners were unfurled
of Moon and Sun; and shod with gold
were his great horses. Hounds untold
baying in woods beyond the West   15
of race immortal he possessed:
grey and limber, black and strong
white with silken coats and long,
brown and brindled, swift and true
as arrow from a bow of yew;   20
their voices like the deeptoned bells
that ring in Valmar's citadels,
their eyes like living jewels, their teeth
like ruel-bone. As sword from sheath
they flashed and fled from leash to scent   25
for Tavros' joy and merriment.

    In Tavros' friths and pastures green
had Huan once a young whelp been.
He grew the swiftest of the swift
and Oromë gave him as a gift   30
to Celegorm, who loved to follow
the great god's horn o'er hill and hollow.
    Alone of hounds of the Land of Light,

when sons of Fëanor took to flight
and came into the North, he stayed   35
beside his master. Every raid
and every foray wild he shared,
and into mortal battle dared.
Often he saved his Gnomish lord
from Orc and wolf and leaping sword.   40
A wolf-hound, tireless, grey and fierce
he grew; his gleaming eyes would pierce
all shadows and all mist, the scent
moons old he found through fen and bent,
through rustling leaves and dusty sand;   45
all paths of wide Beleriand
he knew. But wolves, he loved them best;
he loved to find their throats and wrest
their snarling lives and evil breath.
The packs of Thû him feared as Death.   50

   No wizardry, nor spell, nor dart,
no fang, nor venom devil's art
could brew had harmed him; for his weird
was woven. Yet he little feared
that fate decreed and known to all: 55
before the mightiest he should fall,
before the mightiest wolf alone
that ever was whelped in cave of stone.

   Hark! afar in Nargothrond,
far over Sirion and beyond,   60
there are dim cries and horns blowing,

and barking hounds through the trees going.
    The hunt is up, the woods are stirred.
Who rides to-day? Ye have not heard
that Celegorm and Curufin   65
have loosed their dogs? With merry din
they mounted ere the sun arose,
and took their spears and took their bows.
The wolves of Thû of late have dared
both far and wide. Their eyes have glared   70
by night across the roaring stream
of Narog. Doth their master dream,
perchance, of plots and counsels deep,
of secrets that the Elf-lords keep,
of movements in the Gnomish realm   75
and errands under beech and elm?

    Curufin spake: 'Good brother mine,
I like it not. What dark design
doth this portend? These evil things,
we swift must end their wanderings!   80
And more, 'twould please my heart full well
to hunt a while and wolves to fell.'
And then he leaned and whispered low
that Orodreth was a dullard slow;
long time it was since the king had gone,   85
and rumour or tidings came there none.
    'At least thy profit it would be
to know whether dead he is or free;
to gather thy men and thy array.

"I go to hunt" then thou wilt say,   90
and men will think that Narog's good
ever thou heedest. But in the wood
things may be learned; and if by grace,
by some blind fortune he retrace
his footsteps mad, and if he bear   95
a Silmaril – I need declare
no more in words; but one by right
is thine (and ours), the jewel of light;
another may be won – a throne.
The eldest blood our house doth own.'   100

Celegorm listened. Nought he said,
but forth a mighty host he led;
and Huan leaped at the glad sounds,
the chief and captain of his hounds.
Three days they ride by holt and hill   105
the wolves of Thû to hunt and kill,
and many a head and fell of grey
they take, and many drive away,
till nigh to the borders in the West
of Doriath a while they rest.   110

There were dim cries and horns blowing,
and barking dogs through the woods going.
The hunt was up. The woods were stirred,
and one there fled like a startled bird,
and fear was in her dancing feet.   115
She knew not who the woods did beat.

Far from her home, forwandered, pale,
she flitted ghostlike through the vale;
ever her heart bade her up and on
but her limbs were worn, her eyes were wan.   120

  The eyes of Huan saw a shade
wavering, darting down a glade
like a mist of evening snared by day
and hasting fearfully away.
He bayed, and sprang with sinewy limb   125
to chase the shy thing strange and dim.
On terror's wings, like a butterfly
pursued by a sweeping bird on high,
she fluttered hither, darted there,
now poised, now flying through the air –   130
in vain. At last against a tree
she leaned and panted. Up leaped he.
No word of magic gasped with woe,
no elvish mystery she did know
or had entwined in raiment dark   135
availed against that hunter stark,
whose old immortal race and kind
no spells could ever turn or bind.
Huan alone that she ever met
she never in enchantment set   140
nor bound with spells. But loveliness
and gentle voice and pale distress
and eyes like starlight dimmed with tears
tamed him that death nor monster fears.

Lightly he lifted her, light he bore   145
his trembling burden. Never before
had Celegorm beheld such prey:
'What hast thou brought, good Huan say!
Dark-elvish maid, or wraith, or fay?
Not such to hunt we came today.'   150

''Tis Lúthien of Doriath,'
the maiden spake. 'A wandering path
far from the Wood-elves' sunny glades
she sadly winds, where courage fades
and hope grows faint.' And as she spoke   155
down she let slip her shadowy cloak,
and there she stood in silver and white.
Her starry jewels twinkled bright
in the risen sun like morning dew;
the lilies gold on mantle blue   160
gleamed and glistened. Who could gaze
on that fair face without amaze?
Long did Curufin look and stare.
The perfume of her flower-twined hair,
her lissom limbs, her elvish face,   165
smote to his heart, and in that place
enchained he stood. 'O maiden royal,
O lady fair, wherefore in toil
and lonely journey dost thou go?
What tidings dread of war and woe   170
in Doriath have betid? Come tell!
For fortune thee hath guided well;

friends thou hast found,' said Celegorm,
and gazed upon her elvish form.

In his heart him thought her tale unsaid   175
he knew in part, but nought she read
of guile upon his smiling face.
'Who are ye then, the lordly chase
that follow in this perilous wood?'
she asked; and answer seeming-good   180
they gave. 'Thy servants, lady sweet,
lords of Nargothrond thee greet,
and beg that thou wouldst with them go
back to their hills, forgetting woe
a season, seeking hope and rest.   185
And now to hear thy tale were best.'

So Lúthien tells of Beren's deeds
in northern lands, how fate him leads
to Doriath, of Thingol's ire,
the dreadful errand that her sire   190
decreed for Beren. Sign nor word
the brothers gave that aught they heard
that touched them near. Of her escape
and the marvellous mantle she did shape
she lightly tells, but words her fail   195
recalling sunlight in the vale,
moonlight, starlight in Doriath,
ere Beren took the perilous path.
'Need, too, my lords, there is of haste!

No time in ease and rest to waste. 200
For days are gone now since the queen
Melian whose heart hath vision keen,
looking afar me said in fear
that Beren lived in bondage drear.
The Lord of Wolves hath prisons dark, 205
chains and enchantments cruel and stark,
and there entrapped and languishing
doth Beren lie – if direr thing
hath not brought death or wish for death':
then gasping woe bereft her breath. 210

 To Celegorm said Curufin
apart and low: 'Now news we win
of Felagund, and now we know
wherefore Thû's creatures prowling go',
and other whispered counsels spake, 215
and showed him what answer he should make.
 'Lady,' said Celegorm, 'thou seest
we go a-hunting roaming beast,
and though our host is great and bold,
'tis ill prepared the wizard's hold 220
and island fortress to assault.
Deem not our hearts or wills at fault.
Lo! here our chase we now forsake
and home our swiftest road we take,
counsel and aid there to devise 225
for Beren that in anguish lies.'

To Nargothrond they with them bore
Lúthien, whose heart misgave her sore.
Delay she feared; each moment pressed
upon her spirit, yet she guessed   230
they rode not as swiftly as they might.
Ahead leaped Huan day and night,
and ever looking back his thought
was troubled. What his master sought,
and why he rode not like the fire,   235
why Curufin looked with hot desire
on Lúthien, he pondered deep,
and felt some evil shadow creep
of ancient curse o'er Elfinesse.
His heart was torn for the distress   240
of Beren bold, and Lúthien dear,
and Felagund who knew no fear.

In Nargothrond the torches flared
and feast and music were prepared.
Lúthien feasted not but wept.   245
Her ways were trammelled; closely kept
she might not fly. Her magic cloak
was hidden, and no prayer she spoke
was heeded, nor did answer find
her eager questions. Out of mind,   250
it seemed, were those afar that pined
in anguish and in dungeons blind
in prison and in misery.
Too late she knew their treachery.

It was not hid in Nargothrond   255
that Fëanor's sons her held in bond,
who Beren heeded not, and who
had little cause to wrest from Thû
the king they loved not and whose quest
old vows of hatred in their breast   260
had roused from sleep. Orodreth knew
the purpose dark they would pursue:
King Felagund to leave to die,
and with King Thingol's blood ally
the house of Fëanor by force   265
or treaty. But to stay their course
he had no power, for all his folk
the brothers had yet beneath their yoke,
and all yet listened to their word.
Orodreth's counsel no man heard;   270
their shame they crushed, and would not heed
the tale of Felagund's dire need.

   At Lúthien's feet there day by day
and at night beside her couch would stay
Huan the hound of Nargothrond;   275
and words she spoke to him soft and fond:
'O Huan, Huan, swiftest hound
that ever ran on mortal ground,
what evil doth thy lords possess
to heed no tears nor my distress?   280
Once Barahir all men above
good hounds did cherish and did love;

once Beren in the friendless North,
when outlaw wild he wandered forth,
had friends unfailing among things   285
with fur and fell and feathered wings,
and among the spirits that in stone
in mountains old and wastes alone
still dwell. But now nor Elf nor Man,
none save the child of Melian,   290
remembers him who Morgoth fought
and never to thraldom base was brought.'

Nought said Huan; but Curufin
thereafter never near might win
to Lúthien, nor touch that maid,   295
but shrank from Huan's fangs afraid.
Then on a night when autumn damp
was swathed about the glimmering lamp
of the wan moon, and fitful stars
were flying seen between the bars   300
of racing cloud, when winter's horn
already wound in trees forlorn,
lo! Huan was gone. Then Lúthien lay,
fearing new wrong, till just ere day,
when all is dead and breathless still   305
and shapeless fears the sleepless fill,
a shadow came along the wall.
Then something let there softly fall
her magic cloak beside her couch.
Trembling she saw the great hound crouch   310

beside her, heard a deep voice swell
as from a tower a far slow bell.

    Thus Huan spake, who never before
had uttered words, and but twice more
did speak in elven tongue again: 315
'Lady beloved, whom all Men,
whom Elfinesse, and whom all things
with fur and fell and feathered wings
should serve and love – arise! away!
Put on thy cloak! Before the day   320
comes over Nargothrond we fly
to Northern perils, thou and I.'
And ere he ceased he counsel wrought
for achievement of the thing they sought.
There Lúthien listened in amaze,   325
and softly on Huan did she gaze.
Her arms about his neck she cast –
in friendship that to death should last.

*****

In Wizard's Isle still lay forgot
enmeshed and tortured in that grot   330
cold, evil, doorless, without light,
and blank-eyed stared at endless night
two comrades. Now alone they were.
The others lived no more, but bare

their broken bones would lie and tell   335
how ten had served their master well.

    To Felagund then Beren said:
''Twere little loss if I were dead,
and I am minded all to tell,
and thus, perchance, from this dark hell   340
thy life to loose. I set thee free
from thine old oath, for more for me
hast thou endured than e'er was earned.'

    'A! Beren, Beren hast not learned
that promises of Morgoth's folk   345
are frail as breath. From this dark yoke
of pain shall neither ever go,
whether he learn our names or no,
with Thû's consent. Nay more, I think
yet deeper of torment we should drink,   350
knew he that son of Barahir
and Felagund were captive here,
and even worse if he should know
the dreadful errand we did go.'

    A devil's laugh they ringing heard   355
within their pit. 'True, true the word
I hear you speak,' a voice then said.
''Twere little loss if he were dead,
the outlaw mortal. But the king,

the Elf undying, many a thing   360
no man could suffer may endure.
Perchance, when what these walls immure
of dreadful anguish thy folk learn,
their king to ransom they will yearn
with gold and gem and high hearts cowed;   365
or maybe Celegorm the proud
will deem a rival's prison cheap,
and crown and gold himself will keep.
Perchance, the errand I shall know,
ere all is done, that ye did go.   370
The wolf is hungry, the hour is nigh;
no more need Beren wait to die.'

    The slow time passed. Then in the gloom
two eyes there glowed. He saw his doom,
Beren, silent, as his bonds he strained   375
beyond his mortal might enchained.
Lo! sudden there was rending sound
of chains that parted and unwound,
of meshes broken. Forth there leaped
upon the wolvish thing that crept   380
in shadow faithful Felagund,
careless of fang or mortal wound.
There in the dark they wrestled slow,
remorseless, snarling, to and fro,
teeth in flesh, gripe on throat,   385
fingers locked in shaggy coat,
spurning Beren who there lying

heard the werewolf gasping, dying.
Then a voice he heard: 'Farewell!
On earth I need no longer dwell,   390
friend and comrade, Beren bold.
My heart is burst, my limbs are cold.
Here all my power I have spent
to break my bonds, and dreadful rent
of poisoned teeth is in my breast.   395
I now must go to my long rest
neath Timbrenting in timeless halls
where drink the Gods, where the light falls
upon the shining sea.' Thus died the king,
as elvish harpers yet do sing.   400

    There Beren lies. His grief no tear,
his despair no horror has nor fear,
waiting for footsteps, a voice, for doom.
Silences profounder than the tomb
of long-forgotten kings, neath years   405
and sands uncounted laid on biers
and buried everlasting-deep,
slow and unbroken round him creep.

    The silences were sudden shivered
to silver fragments. Faint there quivered   410
a voice in song that walls of rock,
enchanted hill, and bar and lock,
and powers of darkness pierced with light.
He felt about him the soft night

of many stars, and in the air   415
were rustlings and a perfume rare;
the nightingales were in the trees,
slim fingers flute and viol seize
beneath the moon, and one more fair
than all there be or ever were   420
upon a lonely knoll of stone
in shimmering raiment danced alone.

Then in his dream it seemed he sang,
and loud and fierce his chanting rang,
old songs of battle in the North,   425
of breathless deeds, of marching forth
to dare uncounted odds and break
great powers, and towers, and strong walls shake;
and over all the silver fire
that once Men named the Burning Briar,   430
the Seven Stars that Varda set
about the North, were burning yet,
a light in darkness, hope in woe,
the emblem vast of Morgoth's foe.

'Huan, Huan! I hear a song   435
far under welling, far but strong
a song that Beren bore aloft.
I hear his voice, I have heard it oft
in dream and wandering.' Whispering low
thus Lúthien spake. On the bridge of woe   440
in mantle wrapped at dead of night

she sat and sang, and to its height
and to its depth the Wizard's Isle,
rock upon rock and pile on pile,
trembling echoed. The werewolves howled,   445
and Huan hidden lay and growled
watchful listening in the dark,
waiting for battle cruel and stark.

Thû heard that voice, and sudden stood
wrapped in his cloak and sable hood   450
in his high tower. He listened long,
and smiled, and knew that elvish song.
'A! little Lúthien! What brought
the foolish fly to web unsought?
Morgoth! a great and rich reward   455
to me thou wilt owe when to thy hoard
this jewel is added.' Down he went,
and forth his messengers he sent.

Still Lúthien sang. A creeping shape
with bloodred tongue and jaws agape   460
stole on the bridge; but she sang on
with trembling limbs and wide eyes wan.
The creeping shape leaped to her side,
and gasped, and sudden fell and died.
And still they came, still one by one,   465
and each was seized, and there were none
returned with padding feet to tell
that a shadow lurketh fierce and fell

at the bridge's end, and that below
the shuddering waters loathing flow   470
o'er the grey corpses Huan killed.
 A mightier shadow slowly filled
the narrow bridge, a slavering hate,
an awful werewolf fierce and great:
pale Draugluin, the old grey lord   475
of wolves and beasts of blood abhorred,
that fed on flesh of Man and Elf
beneath the chair of Thû himself.

 No more in silence did they fight.
Howling and baying smote the night,   480
till back by the chair where he had fed
to die the werewolf yammering fled.
'Huan is there' he gasped and died,
and Thû was filled with wrath and pride.
'Before the mightiest he shall fall,   485
before the mightiest wolf of all',
so thought he now, and thought he knew
how fate long spoken should come true.
 Now there came slowly forth and glared
into the night a shape long-haired,   490
dank with poison, with awful eyes
wolvish, ravenous; but there lies
a light therein more cruel and dread
than ever wolvish eyes had fed.
More huge were its limbs, its jaws more wide,   495
its fangs more gleaming-sharp, and dyed

with venom, torment, and with death.
The deadly vapour of its breath
swept on before it. Swooning dies
the song of Lúthien, and her eyes   500
are dimmed and darkened with a fear,
cold and poisonous and drear.

Thus came Thû, as wolf more great
than e'er was seen from Angband's gate
to the burning south, than ever lurked   505
in mortal lands or murder worked.
Sudden he sprang, and Huan leaped
aside in shadow. On he swept
to Lúthien lying swooning faint.
To her drowning senses came the taint   510
of his foul breathing, and she stirred;
dizzily she spake a whispered word,
her mantle brushed across his face.
He stumbled staggering in his pace.
Out leaped Huan. Back he sprang.   515
Beneath the stars there shuddering rang
the cry of hunting wolves at bay,
the tongue of hounds that fearless slay.
Backward and forth they leaped and ran
feinting to flee, and round they span,   520
and bit and grappled, and fell and rose.
   Then suddenly Huan holds and throws
his ghastly foe; his throat he rends,
choking his life. Not so it ends.

From shape to shape, from wolf to worm,   525
from monster to his own demon form,
Thû changes, but that desperate grip
he cannot shake, nor from it slip.
No wizardry, nor spell, nor dart,
no fang, nor venom, nor devil's art   530
could harm that hound that hart and boar
had hunted once in Valinor.

Nigh the foul spirit Morgoth made
and bred of evil shuddering strayed
from its dark house, when Lúthien rose   535
and shivering looked upon his throes.

'O demon dark, O phantom vile
of foulness wrought, of lies and guile,
here shalt thou die, thy spirit roam
quaking back to thy master's home   540
his scorn and fury to endure;
thee he will in the bowels immure
of groaning earth, and in a hole
everlastingly thy naked soul
shall wail and gibber – this shall be   545
unless the keys thou render me
of thy black fortress, and the spell
that bindeth stone to stone thou tell,
and speak the words of opening.'

With gasping breath and shuddering   550
he spake, and yielded as he must,
and vanquished betrayed his master's trust.

Lo! by the bridge a gleam of light,
like stars descended from the night
to burn and tremble here below.   555
There wide her arms did Lúthien throw,
and called aloud with voice as clear
as still at whiles may mortal hear
long elvish trumpets o'er the hill
echo, when all the world is still.   560
The dawn peered over mountains wan;
their grey heads silent looked thereon.
The hill trembled; the citadel
crumbled, and all its towers fell;
the rocks yawned and the bridge broke,   565
and Sirion spumed in sudden smoke.
Like ghosts the owls were flying seen
hooting in the dawn, and bats unclean
went skimming dark through the cold airs
shrieking thinly to find new lairs   570
in Deadly Nightshade's branches dread.
The wolves whimpering and yammering fled
like dusky shadows. Out there creep
pale forms and ragged as from sleep,
crawling, and shielding blinded eyes: 575
the captives in fear and in surprise

from dolour long in clinging night
beyond all hope set free to light.

   A vampire shape with pinions vast
screeching leaped from the ground, and passed,   580
its dark blood dripping on the trees;
and Huan neath him lifeless sees
a wolvish corpse – for Thû had flown
to Taur-na-Fuin, a new throne
and darker stronghold there to build.   585
   The captives came and wept and shrilled
their piteous cries of thanks and praise.
But Lúthien anxious-gazing stays.
Beren comes not. At length she said:
'Huan, Huan, among the dead   590
must we then find him whom we sought,
for love of whom we toiled and fought?'
   Then side by side from stone to stone
o'er Sirion they climbed. Alone
unmoving they him found, who mourned   595
by Felagund, and never turned
to see what feet drew halting nigh.

'A! Beren, Beren!' came her cry,
'almost too late have I thee found?
Alas! that here upon the ground   600
the noblest of the noble race
in vain thy anguish doth embrace!
Alas! in tears that we should meet

who once found meeting passing sweet!'
    Her voice such love and longing filled   605
he raised his eyes, his mourning stilled,
and felt his heart new-turned to flame
for her that through peril to him came.

    'O Lúthien, O Lúthien,
more fair than any child of Men,   610
O loveliest maid of Elfinesse,
what might of love did thee possess
to bring thee here to terror's lair!
O lissom limbs and shadowy hair,
O flower-entwinéd brows so white,   615
O slender hands in this new light!'

    She found his arms and swooned away
just at the rising of the day.

*****

Songs have recalled the Elves have sung
in old forgotten elven tongue   620
how Lúthien and Beren strayed
by the banks of Sirion. Many a glade
they filled with joy, and there their feet
passed by lightly, and days were sweet.
Though winter hunted through the wood   625
still flowers lingered where she stood.
Tinúviel! Tinúviel!

the birds are unafraid to dwell
and sing beneath the peaks of snow
where Beren and where Lúthien go.   630

The isle in Sirion they left behind;
but there on hill-top might one find
a green grave, and a stone set,
and there there lie the white bones yet
of Felagund, of Finrod's son –   635
unless that land is changed and gone,
or foundered in unfathomed seas,
while Felagund laughs beneath the trees
in Valinor, and comes no more
to this grey world of tears and war.   640

To Nargothrond no more he came;
but thither swiftly ran the fame,
of their king dead, of Thû o'erthrown,
of the breaking of the towers of stone.
For many now came home at last   645
who long ago to shadow passed;
and like a shadow had returned
Huan the hound, and scant had earned
or praise or thanks of master wroth;
yet loyal he was, though he was loath.   650
The halls of Narog clamours fill
that vainly Celegorm would still.
There men bewailed their fallen king,
crying that a maiden dared that thing

which sons of Fëanor would not do.   655
'Let us slay these faithless lords untrue!'
the fickle folk now loudly cried
with Felagund who would not ride.
Orodreth spake: 'The kingdom now
is mine alone. I will allow   660
no spilling of kindred blood by kin.
But bread nor rest shall find herein
these brothers who have set at nought
the house of Finrod.' They were brought.
Scornful, unbowed, and unashamed   665
stood Celegorm. In his eye there flamed
a light of menace. Curufin
smiled with his crafty mouth and thin.

'Be gone for ever – ere the day
shall fall into the sea. Your way   670
shall never lead you hither more,
nor any son of Fëanor;
nor ever after shall be bond
of love twixt yours and Nargothrond.'

'We will remember it,' they said,   675
and turned upon their heels, and sped,
and took their horses and such folk
as still them followed. Nought they spoke
but sounded horns, and rode like fire,
and went away in anger dire.   680

167

Towards Doriath the wanderers now
were drawing nigh. Though bare the bough,
though cold the wind, and grey the grasses
through which the hiss of winter passes,
they sang beneath the frosty sky   685
uplifted o'er them pale and high.
They came to Mindeb's narrow stream
that from the hills doth leap and gleam
by western borders where begin
the spells of Melian to fence in   690
King Thingol's land, and stranger steps
to wind bewildered in their webs.

There sudden sad grew Beren's heart:
'Alas, Tinúviel, here we part
and our brief song together ends,   695
and sundered ways each lonely wends!'

'Why part we here? What dost thou say,
just at the dawn of brighter day?'

'For safe thou'rt come to borderlands
o'er which in the keeping of the hands   700
of Melian thou wilt walk at ease
and find thy home and well-loved trees.'

'My heart is glad when the fair trees
far off uprising grey it sees
of Doriath inviolate.   705

Yet Doriath my heart did hate,
and Doriath my feet forsook,
my home, my kin. I would not look
on grass nor leaf there evermore
without thee by me. Dark the shore   710
of Esgalduin the deep and strong!
Why there alone forsaking song
by endless waters rolling past
must I then hopeless sit at last,
and gaze at waters pitiless   715
in heartache and in loneliness?'

'For never more to Doriath
can Beren find the winding path,
though Thingol willed it or allowed;
for to thy father there I vowed   720
to come not back save to fulfill
the quest of the shining Silmaril,
and win by valour my desire.
"Not rock nor steel nor Morgoth's fire
nor all the power of Elfinesse,   725
shall keep the gem I would possess":
thus swore I once of Lúthien
more fair than any child of Men.
My word, alas! I must achieve,
though sorrow pierce and parting grieve.'   730

'Then Lúthien will not go home,
but weeping in the woods will roam,

nor peril heed, nor laughter know.
And if she may not by thee go
against thy will thy desperate feet   735
she will pursue, until they meet,
Beren and Lúthien, love once more
on earth or on the shadowy shore.'

'Nay, Lúthien, most brave of heart,
thou makest it more hard to part.   740
Thy love me drew from bondage drear,
but never to that outer fear,
that darkest mansion of all dread,
shall thy most blissful light be led.'

'Never, never!' she shuddering said.   745
But even as in his arms she pled,
a sound came like a hurrying storm.
There Curufin and Celegorm
in sudden tumult like the wind
rode up. The hooves of horses dinned   750
loud on the earth. In rage and haste
madly northward they now raced
the path twixt Doriath to find
and the shadows dreadly dark entwined
of Taur-na-fuin. That was their road   755
most swift to where their kin abode
in the east, where Himling's watchful hill
o'er Aglon's gorge hung tall and still.

They saw the wanderers. With a shout
straight on them swung their hurrying rout   760
as if neath maddened hooves to rend
the lovers and their love to end.
But as they came their horses swerved
with nostrils wide and proud necks curved;
Curufin, stooping, to saddlebow   765
with mighty arm did Lúthien throw,
and laughed. Too soon; for there a spring
fiercer than tawny lion-king
maddened with arrows barbéd smart,
greater than any hornéd hart   770
that hounded to a gulf leaps o'er,
there Beren gave, and with a roar
leaped on Curufin; round his neck
his arms entwined, and all to wreck
both horse and rider fell to ground;   775
and there they fought without a sound.
Dazed in the grass did Lúthien lie
beneath bare branches and the sky;
the Gnome felt Beren's fingers grim
close on his throat and strangle him,   780
and out his eyes did start, and tongue
gasping from his mouth there hung.

    Up rode Celegorm with his spear,
and bitter death was Beren near.
With elvish steel he nigh was slain   785
whom Lúthien won from hopeless chain,
but baying Huan sudden sprang

before his master's face with fang
white-gleaming, and with bristling hair,
as if he on boar or wolf did stare.   790
    The horse in terror leaped aside,
and Celegorm in anger cried:
'Curse thee, thou baseborn dog, to dare
against thy master teeth to bare!'
But dog nor horse nor rider bold   795
would venture near the anger cold
of mighty Huan fierce at bay.
Red were his jaws. They shrank away,
and fearful eyed him from afar:
nor sword nor knife, nor scimitar,   800
no dart of bow, nor cast of spear,
master nor man did Huan fear.

    There Curufin had left his life,
had Lúthien not stayed that strife.
Waking she rose and softly cried   805
standing distressed at Beren's side:
'Forbear thy anger now, my lord!
nor do the work of Orcs abhorred;
for foes there be of Elfinesse,
unnumbered, and they grow not less,   810
while here we war by ancient curse
distraught, and all the world to worse
decays and crumbles. Make thy peace!'

    Then Beren did Curufin release;
but took his horse and coat of mail   815

and took his knife there gleaming pale,
hanging sheathless, wrought of steel.
No flesh could leeches ever heal
that point had pierced; for long ago
the dwarves had made it, singing slow   820
enchantments, where their hammers fell
in Nogrod ringing like a bell.
Iron as tender wood it cleft,
and sundered mail like woollen weft.
But other hands its haft now held;   825
its master lay by mortal felled.
Beren uplifting him, far him flung,
and cried 'Begone!', with stinging tongue;
'Begone! thou renegade and fool,
and let thy lust in exile cool!   830
Arise and go, and no more work
like Morgoth's slaves or curséd Orc;
and deal, proud son of Fëanor,
in deeds more proud than heretofore!'
Then Beren led Lúthien away,   835
while Huan still there stood at bay.

   'Farewell,' cried Celegorm the fair.
'Far get you gone! And better were
to die forhungered in the waste
than wrath of Fëanor's sons to taste,   840
that yet may reach o'er dale and hill.
No gem, nor maid, nor Silmaril
shall ever long in thy grasp lie!

We curse thee under cloud and sky,
we curse thee from rising unto sleep!   845
Farewell!' He swift from horse did leap,
his brother lifted from the ground;
then bow of yew with gold wire bound
he strung, and shaft he shooting sent,
as heedless hand in hand they went;   850
a dwarvish dart and cruelly hooked.
They never turned nor backward looked.
Loud bayed Huan, and leaping caught
the speeding arrow. Quick as thought
another followed deadly singing;   855
but Beren had turned, and sudden springing
defended Lúthien with his breast.
Deep sank the dart in flesh to rest.
He fell to earth. They rode away,
and laughing left him as he lay;   860
yet spurred like wind in fear and dread
of Huan's pursuing anger red.
Though Curufin with bruised mouth laughed,
yet later of that dastard shaft
was tale and rumour in the North,   865
and Men remembered at the Marching Forth,
and Morgoth's will its hatred helped.

    Thereafter never hound was whelped
would follow horn of Celegorm
or Curufin. Though in strife and storm,   870
though all their house in ruin red

174

went down, thereafter laid his head
Huan no more at that lord's feet,
but followed Lúthien, brave and fleet.
Now sank she weeping at the side   875
of Beren, and sought to stem the tide
of welling blood that flowed there fast.
The raiment from his breast she cast;
from shoulder plucked the arrow keen;
his wound with tears she washed it clean.   880
    Then Huan came and bore a leaf,
of all the herbs of healing chief,
that evergreen in woodland glade
there grew with broad and hoary blade.
The powers of all grasses Huan knew,   885
who wide did forest-paths pursue.
Therewith the smart he swift allayed,
while Lúthien murmuring in the shade
the staunching song that Elvish wives
long years had sung in those sad lives   890
of war and weapons, wove o'er him.

    The shadows fell from mountains grim.
Then sprang about the darkened North
the Sickle of the Gods, and forth
each star there stared in stony night   895
radiant, glistering cold and white.
But on the ground there is a glow,
a spark of red that leaps below:
under woven boughs beside a fire

of crackling wood and sputtering briar   900
there Beren lies in drowsing deep,
walking and wandering in sleep.
Watchful bending o'er him wakes
a maiden fair; his thirst she slakes,
his brow caresses, and softly croons   905
a song more potent than in runes
or leeches' lore hath since been writ.
Slowly the nightly watches flit.
The misty morning crawleth grey
from dusk to the reluctant day.   910

Then Beren woke and opened eyes,
and rose and cried: 'Neath other skies,
in lands more awful and unknown,
I wandered long, methought, alone
to the deep shadow where the dead dwell;   915
but ever a voice that I knew well,
like bells, like viols, like harps, like birds,
like music moving without words,
called me, called me through the night,
enchanted drew me back to light!   920
Healed the wound, assuaged the pain!
Now are we come to morn again,
new journeys once more lead us on –
to perils whence may life be won,
hardly for Beren; and for thee   925
a waiting in the wood I see
beneath the trees of Doriath,

while ever follow down my path
the echoes of thine elvish song,
where hills are haggard and roads are long.'   930

'Nay, now no more we have for foe
dark Morgoth only, but in woe,
in wars and feuds of Elfinesse
thy quest is bound; and death, no less,
for thee and me, for Huan bold   935
the end of weird of yore foretold,
all this I bode shall follow swift;
if thou go on. Thy hand shall lift
and lay on Thingol's lap the dire
and flaming jewel, Fëanor's fire,   940
never, never! A why then go?
Why turn we not from fear and woe
beneath the trees to walk and roam
roofless, with all the world as home,
over mountains, beside the seas,   945
 in the sunlight, in the breeze?'

Thus long they spoke with heavy hearts;
and yet not all her elvish arts
nor lissom arms, nor shining eyes
as tremulous stars in rainy skies,   950
nor tender lips, enchanted voice,
his purpose bent or swayed his choice.
Never to Doriath would he fare
save guarded fast to leave her there;

never to Nargothrond would go   955
with her, lest there came war and woe;
and never would in the world untrod
to wander suffer her, worn, unshod
roofless and restless, whom he drew
with love from the hidden realms she knew.   960
'For Morgoth's power is now awake;
already hill and dale doth shake,
the hunt is up, the prey is wild:
a maiden lost, an elven child.
Now Orcs and phantoms prowl and peer   965
from tree to tree, and fill with fear
each shade and hollow. Thee they seek!
At thought thereof my hope grows weak,
my heart is chilled. I curse mine oath,
I curse the fate that joined us both   970
and snared thy feet in my sad doom
of flight and wandering in the gloom!
Now let us haste, and ere the day
be fallen, take our swiftest way,
till o'er the marches of thy land   975
beneath the beech and oak we stand,
in Doriath, fair Doriath
whither no evil finds the path,
powerless to pass the listening leaves
that droop upon those forest-eaves.'   980

  Then to his will she seeming bent.
Swiftly to Doriath they went,
and crossed its borders. There they stayed

resting in deep and mossy glade;
there lay they sheltered from the wind   985
under mighty beeches silken-skinned,
and sang of love that still shall be,
though earth be foundered under sea,
and sundered here for evermore
shall meet upon the Western Shore.   990

One morning as asleep she lay
upon the moss, as though the day
too bitter were for gentle flower
to open in a sunless hour,
Beren arose and kissed her hair,   995
and wept, and softly left her there.
  'Good Huan,' said he, 'guard her well!
In leafless field no asphodel,
in thorny thicket never a rose
forlorn, so frail and fragrant blows.   1000
Guard her from wind and frost, and hide
from hands that seize and cast aside;
keep her from wandering and woe,
for pride and fate now make me go.'

The horse he took and rode away,   1005
nor dared to turn; but all that day
with heart as stone he hastened forth
and took the paths toward the North.

* * * * *

Once wide and smooth a plain was spread,
where King Fingolfin proudly led   1010
his silver armies on the green,
his horses white, his lances keen;
his helmets tall of steel were hewn,
his shields were shining as the moon.

    There trumpets sang both long and loud,   1015
and challenge rang unto the cloud
that lay on Morgoth's northern tower,
while Morgoth waited for his hour.

    Rivers of fire at dead of night
in winter lying cold and white   1020
upon the plain burst forth, and high
the red was mirrored in the sky.
From Hithlum's walls they saw the fire,
the steam and smoke in spire on spire
leap up, till in confusion vast   1025
the stars were choked. And so it passed,
the mighty field, and turned to dust,
to drifting sand and yellow rust,
to thirsty dunes where many bones
lay broken among barren stones.   1030
    Dor-na-Fauglith, Land of Thirst,
they after named it, waste accurst,
the raven-haunted roofless grave
of many fair and many brave.
Thereon the stony slopes look forth   1035
from Deadly Nightshade falling north,

from sombre pines with pinions vast,
black-plumed and drear, as many a mast
of sable-shrouded ships of death
slow wafted on a ghostly breath.   1040

    Thence Beren grim now gazes out
across the dunes and shifting drought,
and sees afar the frowning towers
where thunderous Thangorodrim lowers.
    The hungry horse there drooping stood,   1045
proud Gnomish steed; it feared the wood;
upon the haunted ghastly plain
no horse would ever stride again.
'Good steed of master ill,' he said,
'farewell now here! Lift up thy head,   1050
and get thee gone to Sirion's vale
back as we came, past island pale
where Thû once reigned, to waters sweet
and grasses long about thy feet.
And if Curufin no more thou find,   1055
grieve not! but free with hart and hind
go wander, leaving work and war,
and dream thee back in Valinor,
whence came of old thy mighty race
from Tavros' mountain-fencéd chase.'   1060
    There still sat Beren, and he sang,
and loud his lonely singing rang.
Though Orcs should hear, or wolf a-prowl,
or any of the creatures foul

within the shade that slunk and stared   1065
of Taur-na-Fuin, nought he cared,
who now took leave of light and day,
grim-hearted, bitter, fierce and fey.

   'Farewell now here, ye leaves of trees,
your music in the morning-breeze!   1070
Farewell now blade and bloom and grass
that see the changing seasons pass;
ye waters murmuring over stone,
and meres that silent stand alone!
Farewell now mountain, vale, and plain!   1075
Farewell now wind and frost and rain,
and mist and cloud, and heaven's air;
ye star and moon so blinding-fair
that still shall look down from the sky
on the wide earth, though Beren die –   1080
though Beren die not, and yet deep,
deep, whence comes of those that weep
no dreadful echo, lie and choke
in everlasting dark and smoke.
   'Farewell sweet earth and northern sky,   1085
for ever blest, since here did lie,
and here with lissom limbs did run
beneath the moon, beneath the sun,
Lúthien Tinúviel
more fair than mortal tongue can tell.   1090
Though all to ruin fell the world,
and were dissolved and backward hurled

unmade into the old abyss,
yet were its making good, for this –
the dawn, the dusk, the earth, the sea –   1095
that Lúthien on a time should be!'

His blade he lifted high in hand,
and challenging alone did stand
before the threat of Morgoth's power;
and dauntless cursed him, hall and tower,   1100
o'ershadowing hand and grinding foot,
beginning, end, and crown and root;
then turned to strike forth down the slope
abandoning fear, forsaking hope.

'A, Beren, Beren!' came a sound,   1105
'almost too late have I thee found!
O proud and fearless hand and heart,
not yet farewell, not yet we part!
Not thus do those of elven race
forsake the love that they embrace.   1110
A love is mine, as great a power
as thine, to shake the gate and tower
of death with challenge weak and frail
that yet endures, and will not fail
nor yield, unvanquished were it hurled   1115
beneath the foundations of the world.
Beloved fool! escape to seek
from such pursuit; in might so weak
to trust not, thinking it well to save

from love thy loved, who welcomes grave   1120
and torment sooner than in guard
of kind intent to languish, barred,
wingless and helpless him to aid
for whose support her love was made!'

    Thus back to him came Lúthien: 1125
they met beyond the ways of Men;
upon the brink of terror stood
between the desert and the wood.
    He looked on her, her lifted face
beneath his lips in sweet embrace: 1130
'Thrice now mine oath I curse,' he said,
'that under shadow thee hath led!
But where is Huan, where the hound
to whom I trusted, whom I bound
by love of thee to keep thee well   1135
from deadly wandering into hell?'

    'I know not! But good Huan's heart
is wiser, kinder, than thou art,
grim lord, more open unto prayer!
Yet long and long I pleaded there,   1140
until he brought me, as I would,
upon thy trail – a palfrey good
would Huan make, of flowing pace:
thou wouldst have laughed to see us race,
as Orc on werewolf ride like fire   1145

night after night through fen and mire,
through waste and wood! But when I heard
thy singing clear – (yea, every word
of Lúthien one rashly cried,
and listening evil fierce defied) –,   1150
he set me down, and sped away;
but what he would I cannot say.'

    Ere long they knew, for Huan came,
his great breath panting, eyes like flame,
in fear lest her whom he forsook   1155
to aid some hunting evil took
ere he was nigh. Now there he laid
before their feet, as dark as shade,
two grisly shapes that he had won
from that tall isle in Sirion: 1160
a wolfhame huge – its savage fell
was long and matted, dark the spell
that drenched the dreadful coat and skin,
the werewolf cloak of Draugluin;
the other was a batlike garb   1165
with mighty fingered wings, a barb
like iron nail at each joint's end –
such wings as their dark cloud extend
against the moon, when in the sky
from Deadly Nightshade screeching fly   1170
Thû's messengers.
                        'What hast thou brought,

good Huan? What thy hidden thought?
Of trophy of prowess and strong deed,
when Thû thou vanquishedst, what need
here in the waste?' Thus Beren spoke,   1175
and once more words in Huan woke:
his voice was like the deeptoned bells
that ring in Valmar's citadels:

  'Of one fair gem thou must be thief,
Morgoth's or Thingol's, loath or lief;   1180
thou must here choose twixt love and oath!
If vow to break is still thee loath,
then Lúthien must either die
alone, or death with thee defie
beside thee, marching on your fate   1185
that hidden before you lies in wait.
Hopeless the quest, but not yet mad,
unless thou, Beren, run thus clad
in mortal raiment, mortal hue,
witless and redeless, death to woo.   1190
  'Lo! good was Felagund's device,
but may be bettered, if advice
of Huan ye will dare to take,
and swift a hideous change will make
to forms most curséd, foul and vile,   1195
of werewolf of the Wizard's Isle,
of monstrous bat's envermined fell
with ghostly clawlike wings of hell.
  'To such dark straits, alas! now brought

are ye I love, for whom I fought.   1200
Nor further with you can I go –
whoever did a great hound know
in friendship at a werewolf's side
to Angband's grinning portals stride?
Yet my heart tells that at the gate   1205
what there ye find, 'twill be my fate
myself to see, though to that door
my feet shall bear me nevermore.
Darkened is hope and dimmed my eyes,
I see not clear what further lies;   1210
yet maybe backwards leads your path
beyond all hope to Doriath,
and thither, perchance, we three shall wend,
and meet again before the end.'

They stood and marvelled thus to hear   1215
his mighty tongue so deep and clear;
then sudden he vanished from their sight
even at the onset of the night.

His dreadful counsel then they took,
and their own gracious forms forsook;   1220
in werewolf fell and batlike wing
prepared to robe them, shuddering.
    With elvish magic Lúthien wrought,
lest raiment foul with evil fraught
to dreadful madness drive their hearts;   1225
and there she wrought with elvish arts

a strong defence, a binding power,
singing until the midnight hour.

Swift as the wolvish coat he wore,
Beren lay slavering on the floor,   1230
redtongued and hungry; but there lies
a pain and longing in his eyes,
a look of horror as he sees
a batlike form crawl to its knees
and drag its creased and creaking wings.   1235
Then howling under moon he springs
fourfooted, swift, from stone to stone
from hill to plain – but not alone:
a dark shape down the slope doth skim,
and wheeling flitters over him.   1240

Ashes and dust and thirsty dune
withered and dry beneath the moon,
under the cold and shifting air
sifting and sighing, bleak and bare;
of blistered stones and gasping sand,   1245
of splintered bones was built that land,
o'er which now slinks with powdered fell
and hanging tongue a shape of hell.
Many parching leagues lay still before
when sickly day crept back once more;   1250
many choking miles lay stretched ahead
when shivering night once more was spread
with doubtful shadow and ghostly sound

that hissed and passed o'er dune and mound.
    A second morning in cloud and reek   1255
struggled, when stumbling, blind and weak,
a wolvish shape came staggering forth
and reached the foothills of the North;
upon its back there folded lay
a crumpled thing that blinked at day.   1260

    The rocks were reared like bony teeth,
and claws that grasped from opened sheath,
on either side the mournful road
that onward led to that abode
far up within the Mountain dark   1265
with tunnels drear and portals stark.
    They crept within a scowling shade
and cowering darkly down them laid.
Long lurked they there beside the path,
and shivered, dreaming of Doriath,   1270
of laughter and music and clean air,
in fluttered leaves birds singing fair.
    They woke, and felt the trembling sound,
the beating echo far underground
shake beneath them, the rumour vast   1275
of Morgoth's forges; and aghast
they heard the stamp of stony feet
that shod with iron went down that street:
the Orcs went forth to rape and war,
and Balrog captains marched before.   1280

They stirred, and under cloud and shade
at eve stepped forth, and no more stayed;
as dark things on dark errand bent
up the long slopes in haste they went.
Ever the sheer cliffs rose beside,   1285
where birds of carrion sat and cried;
and chasms black and smoking yawned,
whence writhing serpent-shapes were spawned;
until at last in that huge gloom,
heavy as overhanging doom,   1290
that weighs on Thangorodrim's foot
like thunder at the mountain's root,
they came, as to a sombre court
walled with great towers, fort on fort
of cliffs embattled, to that last plain   1295
that opens, abysmal and inane
before the final topless wall
of Bauglir's immeasurable hall,
whereunder looming awful waits
the gigantic shadow of his gates.   1300

* * * * *

In that vast shadow once of yore
Fingolfin stood: his shield he bore
with field of heaven's blue and star
of crystal shining pale afar.
In overmastering wrath and hate   1305
desperate he smote upon that gate,

the Gnomish king, there standing lone,
while endless fortresses of stone
engulfed the thin clear ringing keen
of silver horn on baldric green.   1310
His hopeless challenge dauntless cried
Fingolfin there: 'Come, open wide,
dark king, your ghastly brazen doors!
Come forth, whom earth and heaven abhors!
Come forth, O monstrous craven lord,   1315
and fight with thine own hand and sword,
thou wielder of hosts of banded thralls,
thou tyrant leaguered with strong walls,
thou foe of Gods and elvish race!
I wait thee here. Come! Show thy face!'   1320

    Then Morgoth came. For the last time
in those great wars he dared to climb
from subterranean throne profound,
the rumour of his feet a sound
of rumbling earthquake underground.   1325
Black-armoured, towering, iron-crowned
he issued forth; his mighty shield
a vast unblazoned sable field
with shadow like a thundercloud;
and o'er the gleaming king it bowed,   1330
as huge aloft like mace he hurled
that hammer of the underworld,
Grond. Clanging to ground it tumbled
down like a thunder-bolt, and crumbled

the rocks beneath it; smoke up-started,   1335
a pit yawned, and a fire darted.

   Fingolfin like a shooting light
beneath a cloud, a stab of white,
sprang then aside, and Ringil drew
like ice that gleameth cold and blue,   1340
his sword devised of elvish skill
to pierce the flesh with deadly chill.
With seven wounds it rent his foe,
and seven mighty cries of woe
rang in the mountains, and the earth quook,   1345
and Angband's trembling armies shook.
   Yet Orcs would after laughing tell
of the duel at the gates of hell;
though elvish song thereof was made
ere this but one – when sad was laid   1350
the mighty king in barrow high,
and Thorondor, Eagle of the sky,
the dreadful tidings brought and told
to mourning Elfinesse of old.
Thrice was Fingolfin with great blows   1355
to his knees beaten, thrice he rose
still leaping up beneath the cloud
aloft to hold star-shining, proud,
his stricken shield, his sundered helm,
that dark nor might could overwhelm   1360
till all the earth was burst and rent
in pits about him. He was spent.

His feet stumbled. He fell to wreck
upon the ground, and on his neck
a foot like rooted hills was set,   1365
and he was crushed – not conquered yet;
one last despairing stroke he gave:
the mighty foot pale Ringil clave
about the heel, and black the blood
gushed as from smoking fount in flood.   1370
   Halt goes for ever from that stroke
great Morgoth; but the king he broke,
and would have hewn and mangled thrown
to wolves devouring. Lo! from throne
that Manwë bade him build on high,   1375
on peak unscaled beneath the sky,
Morgoth to watch, now down there swooped
Thorondor the King of Eagles, stooped,
and rending beak of gold he smote
in Bauglir's face, then up did float   1380
on pinions thirty fathoms wide
bearing away, though loud they cried,
the mighty corse, the Elven-king;
and where the mountains make a ring
far to the south about that plain   1385
where after Gondolin did reign,
embattled city, at great height
upon a dizzy snowcap white
in mounded cairn the mighty dead
he laid upon the mountain's head.   1390
Never Orc nor demon after dared

that pass to climb, o'er which there stared
Fingolfin's high and holy tomb,
till Gondolin's appointed doom.

Thus Bauglir earned the furrowed scar   1395
that his dark countenance doth mar,
and thus his limping gait he gained;
but afterward profound he reigned
darkling upon his hidden throne;
and thunderous paced his halls of stone,   1400
slow building there his vast design
the world in thraldom to confine.
Wielder of armies, lord of woe,
no rest now gave he slave or foe;
his watch and ward he thrice increased,   1405
his spies were sent from West to East
and tidings brought from all the North,
who fought, who fell; who ventured forth,
who wrought in secret; who had hoard;
if maid were fair or proud were lord;   1410
well nigh all things he knew, all hearts
well nigh enmeshed in evil arts.
Doriath only, beyond the veil
woven by Melian, no assail
could hurt or enter; only rumour dim   1415
of things there passing came to him.
A rumour loud and tidings clear
of other movements far and near
among his foes, and threat of war

from the seven sons of Fëanor,   1420
from Nargothrond, from Fingon still
gathering his armies under hill
and under tree in Hithlum's shade,
these daily came. He grew afraid
amidst his power once more; renown   1425
of Beren vexed his ears, and down
the aisléd forests there was heard
great Huan baying.

               Then came word
most passing strange of Lúthien
wild-wandering by wood and glen,   1430
and Thingol's purpose long he weighed,
and wondered, thinking of that maid
so fair, so frail. A captain dire,
Boldog, he sent with sword and fire
to Doriath's march; but battle fell   1435
sudden upon him: news to tell
never one returned of Boldog's host,
and Thingol humbled Morgoth's boast.
Then his heart with doubt and wrath was burned:
new tidings of dismay he learned,   1440
how Thû was o'erthrown and his strong isle
broken and plundered, how with guile
his foes now guile beset; and spies
he feared, till each Orc to his eyes
was half suspect. Still ever down   1445
the aisléd forests came renown

of Huan baying, hound of war
that Gods unleashed in Valinor.

Then Morgoth of Huan's fate bethought
long-rumoured, and in dark he wrought.　　1450
Fierce hunger-haunted packs he had
that in wolvish form and flesh were clad,
but demon spirits dire did hold;
and ever wild their voices rolled
in cave and mountain where they housed　　1455
and endless snarling echoes roused.
From these a whelp he chose and fed
with his own hand on bodies dead,
on fairest flesh of Elves and Men,
till huge he grew and in his den　　1460
no more could creep, but by the chair
of Morgoth's self would lie and glare,
nor suffer Balrog, Orc, nor beast
to touch him. Many a ghastly feast
he held beneath that awful throne　　1465
rending flesh and gnawing bone.
There deep enchantment on him fell,
the anguish and the power of hell;
more great and terrible he became
with fire-red eyes and jaws aflame,　　1470
with breath like vapours of the grave,
than any beast of wood or cave,
than any beast of earth or hell
that ever in any time befell,

surpassing all his race and kin,   1475
the ghastly tribe of Draugluin.

   Him Carcharoth, the Red Maw, name
the songs of Elves. Not yet he came
disastrous, ravening, from the gates
of Angband. There he sleepless waits;   1480
where those great portals threatening loom
his red eyes smoulder in the gloom,
his teeth are bare, his jaws are wide;
and none may walk, nor creep, nor glide,
nor thrust with power his menace past   1485
to enter Morgoth's dungeon vast.

   Now, lo! before his watchful eyes
a slinking shape he far descries
that crawls into the frowning plain
and halts at gaze, then on again   1490
comes stalking near, a wolvish shape
haggard, wayworn, with jaws agape;
and o'er it batlike in wide rings
a reeling shadow slowly wings.
Such shapes there oft were seen to roam,   1495
this land their native haunt and home;
and yet his mood with strange unease
is filled, and boding thoughts him seize.

   'What grievous terror, what dread guard
hath Morgoth set to wait, and barred   1500

his doors against all entering feet?
Long ways we have come at last to meet
the very maw of death that opes
between us and our quest! Yet hopes
we never had. No turning back!'   1505
Thus Beren speaks, as in his track
he halts and sees with werewolf eyes
afar the horror that there lies.
Then onward desperate he passed,
skirting the black pits yawning vast,   1510
where King Fingolfin ruinous fell
alone before the gates of hell.

   Before those gates alone they stood,
while Carcharoth in doubtful mood
glowered upon them, and snarling spoke, 1515
and echoes in the arches woke:
'Hail! Draugluin, my kindred's lord!
'Tis very long since hitherward
thou camest. Yea, 'tis passing strange
to see thee now: a grievous change   1520
is on thee, lord, who once so dire,
so dauntless, and as fleet as fire,
ran over wild and waste, but now
with weariness must bend and bow!
'Tis hard to find the struggling breath 1525
when Huan's teeth as sharp as death
have rent the throat? What fortune rare
brings thee back living here to fare –

if Draugluin thou art? come near!
I would know more, and see thee clear!'   1530

    'Who art thou, hungry upstart whelp,
to bar my ways whom thou shouldst help?
I fare with hasty tidings new
to Morgoth from forest-haunting Thû.
Aside! for I must in; or go   1535
and swift my coming tell below!'

    Then up that doorward slowly stood,
eyes shining grim with evil mood,
uneasy growling: 'Draugluin,
if such thou be, now enter in!   1540
But what is this that crawls beside
slinking as if 'twould neath thee hide?
Though wingéd creatures to and fro
unnumbered pass here, all I know.
I know not this. Stay, vampire, stay!   1545
I like not thy kin nor thee. Come, say
what sneaking errand thee doth bring,
thou wingéd vermin, to the king!
Small matter, I doubt not, if thou stay
or enter, or if in my play   1550
I crush thee like a fly on wall,
or bite thy wings and let thee crawl.'

    Huge-stalking, noisome, close he came.
In Beren's eyes there gleamed a flame;

the hair upon his neck uprose.   1555
Nought may the fragrance fair enclose,
the odour of immortal flowers
in everlasting spring neath showers
that glitter silver in the grass
in Valinor. Where'er did pass   1560
Tinúviel, such air there went.
From that foul devil-sharpened scent
its sudden sweetness no disguise
enchanted dark to cheat the eyes
could keep, if near those nostrils drew   1565
snuffling in doubt. This Beren knew
upon the brink of hell prepared
for battle and death. There threatening stared
those dreadful shapes, in hatred both,
false Draugluin and Carcharoth   1570
when, lo! a marvel to behold:
some power, descended from of old,
from race divine beyond the West,
sudden Tinúviel possessed
like inner fire. The vampire dark   1575
she flung aside, and like a lark
cleaving through night to dawn she sprang,
while sheer, heart-piercing silver, rang
her voice, as those long trumpets keen
thrilling, unbearable, unseen   1580
in the cold aisles of morn. Her cloak
by white hands woven, like a smoke,
like all-bewildering, all-enthralling,

all-enfolding evening, falling
from lifted arms, as forth she stepped   1585
across those awful eyes she swept,
a shadow and a mist of dreams
whereon entangled starlight gleams.

'Sleep, O unhappy, tortured thrall!
Thou woebegotten, fail and fall   1590
down, down from anguish, hatred, pain,
from lust, from hunger, bond and chain,
to that oblivion, dark and deep,
the well, the lightless pit of sleep!
For one brief hour escape the net,   1595
the dreadful doom of life forget!'

His eyes were quenched, his limbs were loosed;
he fell like running steer that noosed
and tripped goes crashing to the ground.
Deathlike, moveless, without a sound   1600
outstretched he lay, as lightning stroke
had felled a huge o'ershadowing oak.

*****

Into the vast and echoing gloom,
more dread than many-tunnelled tomb
in labyrinthine pyramid   1605
where everlasting death is hid,
down awful corridors that wind

down to a menace dark enshrined;
down to the mountain's roots profound,
devoured, tormented, bored and ground   1610
by seething vermin spawned of stone;
down to the depths they went alone.

   The arch behind of twilit shade
they saw recede and dwindling fade;
the thunderous forges' rumour grew,   1615
a burning wind there roaring blew
foul vapours up from gaping holes.
Huge shapes there stood like carven trolls
enormous hewn of blasted rock
to forms that mortal likeness mock;   1620
monstrous and menacing, entombed,
at every turn they silent loomed
in fitful glares that leaped and died.
There hammers clanged, and tongues there cried
with sound like smitten stone; there wailed   1625
faint from far under, called and failed
amid the iron clink of chain
voices of captives put to pain.

   Loud rose a din of laughter hoarse,
self-loathing yet without remorse;   1630
loud came a singing harsh and fierce
like swords of terror souls to pierce.
Red was the glare through open doors
of firelight mirrored on brazen floors,
and up the arches towering clomb   1635

to glooms unguessed, to vaulted dome
swathed in wavering smokes and steams
stabbed with flickering lightning-gleams.
To Morgoth's hall, where dreadful feast
he held, and drank the blood of beast   1640
and lives of Men, they stumbling came:
their eyes were dazed with smoke and flame.
The pillars, reared like monstrous shores
to bear earth's overwhelming floors,
were devil-carven, shaped with skill   1645
such as unholy dreams doth fill:
they towered like trees into the air,
whose trunks are rooted in despair,
whose shade is death, whose fruit is bane,
whose boughs like serpents writhe in pain.   1650

    Beneath them ranged with spear and sword
stood Morgoth's sable-armoured horde:
the fire on blade and boss of shield
was red as blood on stricken field.
Beneath a monstrous column loomed   1655
the throne of Morgoth, and the doomed
and dying gasped upon the floor:
his hideous footstool, rape of war.
About him sat his awful thanes,
the Balrog-lords with fiery manes,   1660
redhanded, mouthed with fangs of steel;
devouring wolves were crouched at heel.
And o'er the host of hell there shone
with a cold radiance, clear and wan,

the Silmarils, the gems of fate,   1665
emprisoned in the crown of hate.

Lo! through the grinning portals dread
sudden a shadow swooped and fled;
and Beren gasped – he lay alone,
with crawling belly on the stone: 1670
a form bat-wingéd, silent, flew
where the huge pillared branches grew,
amid the smokes and mounting steams.
And as on the margin of dark dreams
a dim-felt shadow unseen grows   1675
to cloud of vast unease, and woes
foreboded, nameless, roll like doom
upon the soul, so in that gloom
the voices fell, and laughter died
slow to silence many-eyed.   1680
A nameless doubt, a shapeless fear,
had entered in their caverns drear
and grew, and towered above them cowed,
hearing in heart the trumpets loud
of gods forgotten. Morgoth spoke,   1685
and thunderous the silence broke:
'Shadow, descend! And do not think
to cheat mine eyes! In vain to shrink
from thy Lord's gaze, or seek to hide.
My will by none may be defied.   1690
Hope nor escape doth here await
those that unbidden pass my gate.

Descend! ere anger blast thy wing,
thou foolish, frail, bat-shapen thing,
and yet not bat within! Come down!'   1695

Slow-wheeling o'er his iron crown,
reluctantly, shivering and small,
Beren there saw the shadow fall,
and droop before the hideous throne,
a weak and trembling thing, alone.   1700
And as thereon great Morgoth bent
his darkling gaze, he shuddering went,
belly to earth, the cold sweat dank
upon his fell, and crawling shrank
beneath the darkness of that seat,   1705
beneath the shadow of those feet.
Tinúviel spake, a shrill, thin, sound
piercing those silences profound:
'A lawful errand here me brought;
from Thû's dark mansions have I sought,   1710
from Taur-na-Fuin's shade I fare
to stand before thy mighty chair!'

'Thy name, thou shrieking waif, thy name!
Tidings enough from Thû there came
but short while since. What would he now?   1715
Why send such messenger as thou?'

'Thuringwethil I am, who cast
a shadow o'er the face aghast

of the sallow moon in the doomed land
of shivering Beleriand!'   1720

'Liar art thou, who shalt not weave
deceit before mine eyes. Now leave
thy form and raiment false, and stand
revealed, and delivered to my hand!'

There came a slow and shuddering change: 1725
the batlike raiment dark and strange
was loosed, and slowly shrank and fell
quivering. She stood revealed in hell.
About her slender shoulders hung
her shadowy hair, and round her clung   1730
her garment dark, where glimmered pale
the starlight caught in magic veil.
Dim dreams and faint oblivious sleep
fell softly thence, in dungeons deep
an odour stole of elven-flowers   1735
from elven-dells where silver showers
drip softly through the evening air;
and round there crawled with greedy stare
dark shapes of snuffling hunger dread.
    With arms upraised and drooping head   1740
then softly she began to sing
a theme of sleep and slumbering,
wandering, woven with deeper spell
than songs wherewith in ancient dell

Melian did once the twilight fill,   1745
profound and fathomless, and still.

   The fires of Angband flared and died,
smouldered into darkness; through the wide
and hollow halls there rolled unfurled
the shadows of the underworld.   1750
All movement stayed, and all sound ceased,
save vaporous breath of Orc and beast.
One fire in darkness still abode:
the lidless eyes of Morgoth glowed;
one sound the breathing silence broke: 1755
the mirthless voice of Morgoth spoke.

   'So Lúthien, so Lúthien,
a liar like all Elves and Men!
Yet welcome, welcome, to my hall!
I have a use for every thrall.   1760
What news of Thingol in his hole
shy lurking like a timid vole?
What folly fresh is in his mind
who cannot keep his offspring blind
from straying thus? or can devise   1765
no better counsel for his spies?'

   She wavered, and she stayed her song.
'The road,' she said, 'was wild and long,
but Thingol sent me not, nor knows

what way his rebellious daughter goes.   1770
Yet every road and path will lead
Northward at last, and here of need
I trembling come with humble brow,
and here before thy throne I bow;
for Lúthien hath many arts   1775
for solace sweet of kingly hearts.'

'And here of need thou shalt remain
now, Lúthien, in joy or pain –
or pain, the fitting doom for all,
for rebel, thief, and upstart thrall.   1780
Why should ye not in our fate share
of woe and travail? Or should I spare
to slender limb and body frail
breaking torment? Of what avail
here dost thou deem thy babbling song   1785
and foolish laughter? Minstrels strong
are at my call. Yet I will give
a respite brief, a while to live,
a little while, though purchased dear,
to Lúthien the fair and clear,   1790
a pretty toy for idle hour.
In slothful gardens many a flower
like thee the amorous gods are used
honey-sweet to kiss, and cast then bruised
their fragrance loosing, under feet.   1795
But here we seldom find such sweet
amid our labours long and hard,

from godlike idleness debarred.
And who would not taste the honey-sweet
lying to lips, or crush with feet   1800
the soft cool tissue of pale flowers,
easing like gods the dragging hours?
A! curse the Gods! O hunger dire,
O blinding thirst's unending fire!
One moment shall ye cease, and slake   1805
your sting with morsel I here take!'

   In his eyes the fire to flame was fanned,
and forth he stretched his brazen hand.
Lúthien as shadow shrank aside.
'Not thus, O king! Not thus!' she cried,   1810
'do great lords hark to humble boon!
For every minstrel hath his tune;
and some are strong and some are soft
and each would bear his song aloft,
and each a little while be heard,   1815
though rude the note, and light the word.
But Lúthien hath cunning arts
for solace sweet of kingly hearts.
Now hearken!' And her wings she caught
then deftly up, and swift as thought   1820
slipped from his grasp, and wheeling round,
fluttering before his eyes, she wound
a mazy-wingéd dance, and sped
about his iron-crownéd head.
Suddenly her song began anew;   1825

and soft came dropping like a dew
down from on high in that domed hall
her voice bewildering, magical,
and grew to silver-murmuring streams
pale falling in dark pools in dreams.   1830

She let her flying raiment sweep,
enmeshed with woven spells of sleep,
as round the dark void she ranged and reeled.
From wall to wall she turned and wheeled
in dance such as never Elf nor fay   1835
before devised, nor since that day;
than swallow swifter, than flittermouse
in dying light round darkened house
more silken-soft, more strange and fair
than sylphine maidens of the Air   1840
whose wings in Varda's heavenly hall
in rhythmic movement beat and fall.
Down crumpled Orc, and Balrog proud;
all eyes were quenched, all heads were bowed;
the fires of heart and maw were stilled,   1845
and ever like a bird she thrilled
above a lightless world forlorn
in ecstasy enchanted borne.
All eyes were quenched, save those that glared
in Morgoth's lowering brows, and stared   1850
in slowly wandering wonder round,
and slow were in enchantment bound.

Their will wavered, and their fire failed,
and as beneath his brows they paled,
the Silmarils like stars were kindled   1855
that in the reek of Earth had dwindled
escaping upwards clear to shine,
glistening marvellous in heaven's mine.

Then flaring suddenly they fell,
down, down upon the floors of hell.   1860
The dark and mighty head was bowed;
like mountain-top beneath a cloud
the shoulders foundered, the vast form
crashed, as in overwhelming storm
huge cliffs in ruin slide and fall;   1865
and prone lay Morgoth in his hall.
His crown there rolled upon the ground,
a wheel of thunder; then all sound
died, and a silence grew as deep
as were the heart of Earth asleep.   1870

Beneath the vast and empty throne
the adders lay like twisted stone,
the wolves like corpses foul were strewn;
and there lay Beren deep in swoon:
no thought, no dream nor shadow blind   1875
moved in the darkness of his mind.
   'Come forth, come forth! The hour hath knelled,
and Angband's mighty lord is felled!

Awake, awake! For we two meet
alone before the awful seat.'   1880
This voice came down into the deep
where he lay drowned in wells of sleep;
a hand flower-soft and flower-cool
passed o'er his face, and the still pool
of slumber quivered. Up then leaped   1885
his mind to waking; forth he crept.
The wolvish fell he flung aside
and sprang unto his feet, and wide
staring amid the soundless gloom
he gasped as one living shut in tomb.   1890
There to his side he felt her shrink,
felt Lúthien now shivering sink,
her strength and magic dimmed and spent,
and swift his arms about her went.

Before his feet he saw amazed   1895
the gems of Fëanor, that blazed
with white fire glistening in the crown
of Morgoth's might now fallen down.
To move that helm of iron vast
no strength he found, and thence aghast   1900
he strove with fingers mad to wrest
the guerdon of their hopeless quest,
till in his heart there fell the thought
of that cold morn whereon he fought
with Curufin; then from his belt   1905

the sheathless knife he drew, and knelt,
and tried its hard edge, bitter-cold,
o'er which in Nogrod songs had rolled
of dwarvish armourers singing slow
to hammer-music long ago.   1910
Iron as tender wood it clove
and mail as woof of loom it rove.
The claws of iron that held the gem,
it bit them through and sundered them;
a Silmaril he clasped and held,   1915
and the pure radiance slowly welled
red glowing through the clenching flesh.
Again he stooped and strove afresh
one more of the holy jewels three
that Fëanor wrought of yore to free.   1920
But round those fires was woven fate:
not yet should they leave the halls of hate.
The dwarvish steel of cunning blade
by treacherous smiths of Nogrod made
snapped; then ringing sharp and clear   1925
in twain it sprang, and like a spear
or errant shaft the brow it grazed
of Morgoth's sleeping head, and dazed
their hearts with fear. For Morgoth groaned
with voice entombed, like wind that moaned 1930
in hollow caverns penned and bound.
There came a breath; a gasping sound
moved through the halls, as Orc and beast

turned in their dreams of hideous feast;
in sleep uneasy Balrogs stirred,   1935
and far above was faintly heard
an echo that in tunnels rolled,
a wolvish howling long and cold.

* * * * *

Up through the dark and echoing gloom
as ghosts from many-tunnelled tomb,   1940
up from the mountains' roots profound
and the vast menace underground,
their limbs aquake with deadly fear,
terror in eyes, and dread in ear,
together fled they, by the beat   1945
affrighted of their flying feet.

   At last before them far away
they saw the glimmering wraith of day,
the mighty archway of the gate –
and there a horror new did wait.   1950
Upon the threshold, watchful, dire,
his eyes new-kindled with dull fire,
towered Carcharoth, a biding doom:
his jaws were gaping like a tomb,
his teeth were bare, his tongue aflame;   1955
aroused he watched that no one came,
no flitting shade nor hunted shape,
seeking from Angband to escape.

Now past that guard what guile or might
could thrust from death into the light?   1960

    He heard afar their hurrying feet,
he snuffed an odour strange and sweet;
he smelled their coming long before
they marked the waiting threat at door.
His limbs he stretched and shook off sleep,   1965
then stood at gaze. With sudden leap
upon them as they sped he sprang,
and his howling in the arches rang.
    Too swift for thought his onset came,
too swift for any spell to tame;   1970
and Beren desperate then aside
thrust Lúthien, and forth did stride
unarmed, defenceless to defend
Tinúviel until the end.
With left he caught at hairy throat,   1975
with right hand at the eyes he smote –
his right, from which the radiance welled
of the holy Silmaril he held.
As gleam of swords in fire there flashed
the fangs of Carcharoth, and crashed   1980
together like a trap, that tore
the hand about the wrist, and shore
through brittle bone and sinew nesh,
devouring the frail mortal flesh;
and in that cruel mouth unclean   1985
engulfed the jewel's holy sheen.

An isolated page gives five further lines in the process of composition:

> Against the wall then Beren reeled
> but still with his left he sought to shield
> fair Lúthien, who cried aloud
> to see his pain, and down she bowed
> in anguish sinking to the ground.

With the abandonment, towards the end of 1931, of *The Lay of Leithian* at this point in the tale of Beren and Lúthien my father had very largely reached the final form *in narrative structure* – as represented in the published *Silmarillion*. Although, after the completion of his work on *The Lord of the Rings*, he made some extensive revisions to *The Lay of Leithian* as it had lain since 1931 (see the Appendix, p. 257), it seems certain that he never extended the story any further in verse, save for this passage found on a separate sheet headed 'a piece from the end of the poem'.

> Where the forest-stream went through the wood,
> and silent all the stems there stood
> of tall trees, moveless, hanging dark
> with mottled shadows on their bark
> above the green and gleaming river,
> there came through leaves a sudden shiver,
> a windy whisper through the still
> cool silences; and down the hill,
> as faint as a deep sleeper's breath,

an echo came as cold as death:
'Long are the paths, of shadow made
where no foot's print is ever laid,
over the hills, across the seas!
Far, far away are the Lands of Ease,
but the Land of the Lost is further yet,
where the Dead wait, while ye forget.
No moon is there, no voice, no sound
of beating heart; a sigh profound
once in each age as each age dies
alone is heard. Far, far it lies,
the Land of Waiting where the Dead sit,
in their thought's shadow, by no moon lit.'

THE *QUENTA SILMARILLION*

In the years that followed, my father turned to a new prose version of the history of the Elder Days, and that is found in a manuscript bearing the title *Quenta Silmarillion*, which I will refer to as 'QS'. Of intermediate texts between this and its predecessor the *Quenta Noldorinwa* (p. 103) there is now no trace, though they must have existed; but from the point where the story of Beren and Lúthien enters the *Silmarillion* history there are several largely incomplete drafts, owing to my father's long hesitation between longer and shorter versions of the legend. A fuller version, which may be called for this purpose 'QS I', was abandoned, on account of its length, at the point where King Felagund in Nargothrond gave the crown to Orodreth his brother (p. 109, extract from the *Quenta Noldorinwa*).

This was followed by a very rough draft of the whole story; and that was the basis of a second, 'short' version, 'QS II', preserved in the same manuscript as QS I. It was very largely from these two versions that I derived the story of Beren and Lúthien as told in the published *Silmarillion*.

The making of QS II was a work still in progress in 1937; but in that year there entered considerations altogether aloof from the history of the Elder Days. On 21 September *The Hobbit* was published by Allen and Unwin, and was an immediate success; but it brought with it great pressure on my father to write a further book about hobbits. In October he said in a letter to Stanley Unwin, the chairman of Allen and Unwin, that he was 'a little perturbed. I cannot think of anything more to say about *hobbits*. Mr Baggins seems to have exhibited so fully both the Took and the Baggins side of their nature. But I have only too much to say, and much already written, about the world into which the hobbit intruded.' He said that he wanted an opinion on the value of these writings on the subject of 'the world into which the hobbit intruded'; and he put together a collection of manuscripts and sent them off to Stanley Unwin on 15 November 1937. Included in the collection was QS II, which had reached the moment when Beren took into his hand the Silmaril which he had cut from Morgoth's crown.

Long afterwards I learned that the list made out at Allen and Unwin of the manuscripts in my father's consignment contained, in addition to *Farmer Giles of Ham*, *Mr Bliss*, and *The Lost Road*, two elements referred to as *Long Poem* and *The Gnomes Material*, titles which carry a suggestion of despair. Obviously the unwelcome manuscripts landed on the desk at Allen and Unwin without adequate explanation.

I have told in detail the strange story of this consignment in an appendix to *The Lays of Beleriand* (1985), but to be brief, it is painfully clear that the *Quenta Silmarillion* (included in 'the Gnomes Material', together with whatever other texts may have been given this name) never reached the publishers' reader – save for a few pages that had been attached, independently (and in the circumstances very misleadingly) to *The Lay of Leithian*. He was utterly perplexed, and proposed a solution to the relationship between the Long Poem and this fragment (much approved) of the prose work (i.e. the *Quenta Silmarillion*) that was (very understandably) radically incorrect. He wrote a puzzled report conveying his opinion, across which a member of the staff wrote, also understandably, 'What are we to do?'

The outcome of a tissue of subsequent misunderstandings was that my father, wholly unaware that the *Quenta Silmarillion* had not in fact been read by anybody, told Stanley Unwin that he rejoiced that at least it had not been rejected 'with scorn', and that he now certainly hoped 'to be able, or to be able to afford, to publish the Silmarillion!'

While QS II was gone he continued the narrative in a further manuscript, which told of the death of Beren in *The Wolf-hunt of Carcharoth,* intending to copy the new writing into QS II when the texts were returned; but when they were, on 16 December 1937, he put *The Silmarillion* aside. He still asked, in a letter to Stanley Unwin of that date, 'And what more can hobbits do? They can be comic, but their comedy is suburban unless it is set against things more elemental.' But three days later, on 19 December 1937, he announced to

Allen and Unwin: 'I have written the first chapter of a new story about Hobbits – "A long expected party".'

It was at this point, as I wrote in the Appendix to *The Children of Húrin*, that the continuous and evolving tradition of *The Silmarillion* in the summarising, *Quenta* mode came to an end, brought down in full flight, at Túrin's departure from Doriath, becoming an outlaw. The further history from that point remained during the years that followed in the compressed and undeveloped form of the *Quenta* of 1930, frozen, as it were, while the great structures of the Second and Third Ages arose with the writing of *The Lord of the Rings*. But that further history was of cardinal importance in the ancient legends, for the concluding stories (deriving from the original *Book of Lost Tales*) told of the disastrous history of Húrin, father of Túrin, after Morgoth released him, and of the ruin of the Elvish kingdoms of Nargothrond, Doriath, and Gondolin of which Gimli chanted in the mines of Moria many thousands of years afterwards.

> *The world was fair, the mountains tall,*
> *in Elder Days before the fall*
> *of mighty kings in Nargothrond*
> *And Gondolin, who now beyond*
> *the Western Seas have passed away . . .*

And this was to be the crown and completion of the whole: the doom of the Noldorin Elves in their long struggle against the power of Morgoth, and the parts that Húrin and Túrin played in that history; ending with the *Tale of Eärendil*, who escaped from the burning ruin of Gondolin.

Many years later my father wrote in a letter (16 July 1964): 'I offered them the legends of the Elder Days, but their readers turned that down. They wanted a sequel. But I wanted heroic legends and high romance. The result was *The Lord of the Rings*.'

*

When *The Lay of Leithian* was abandoned there was no explicit account of what followed the moment when 'the fangs of Carcharoth crashed together like a trap' on Beren's hand in which he clutched the Silmaril; for this we must go back to the original *Tale of Tinúviel* (pp. 77–80), where there was a story of the desperate flight of Beren and Lúthien, of the hunt out of Angband pursuing them, and of Huan's finding them and guiding them back to Doriath. In the *Quenta Noldorinwa* (p. 138) my father said of this simply that 'there is little to tell'.

In the final story of the return of Beren and Lúthien to Doriath the chief (and radical) change to notice is the manner of their escape from the gates of Angband after the wounding of Beren by Carcharoth. This event, which *The Lay of Leithian* did not reach, is told in the words of *The Silmarillion*:

Thus the quest of the Silmaril was like to have ended in ruin and despair; but in that hour above the wall of the valley three mighty birds appeared, flying northward with wings swifter than the wind.

Among all birds and beasts the wandering and need of Beren had been noised, and Huan himself had bidden all things watch, that they might bring him aid. High above the realm of Morgoth Thorondor and his vassals soared, and seeing now the madness of the Wolf and Beren's fall they came swiftly down, even as the powers of Angband were released from the toils of sleep. Then they lifted up Beren and Lúthien from the earth, and bore them aloft into the clouds. . . .

(As they passed high over the lands) Lúthien wept, for she thought that Beren would surely die; he spoke no word, nor opened his eyes, and knew thereafter nothing of his flight. And at the last the eagles set them down upon the borders of Doriath; and they were come to that same dell whence Beren had stolen in despair and left Lúthien asleep.

There the eagles laid her at Beren's side and returned to the peaks of Crissaegrim and their high eyries; but Huan came to her, and together they tended Beren, even as before when she healed him of the wound that Curufin gave to him. But this wound was fell and poisonous. Long Beren lay, and his spirit wandered upon the dark borders of death, knowing ever an anguish that pursued him from dream to dream. Then suddenly, when her hope was almost spent, he woke again, and looked up, seeing leaves against the sky; and he heard beneath the leaves singing soft and slow beside him LúthienTinúviel. And it was spring again.

Thereafter Beren was named Erchamion, which is the One-handed; and suffering was graven in his face. But at last he was drawn back to life by the love of Lúthien, and he arose, and together they walked in the woods once more.

*

The story of Beren and Lúthien has now been told as it evolved in prose and verse over twenty years from the original *Tale of Tinúviel*. After initial hesitation Beren, whose father was at first Egnor the Forester, of the Elvish people called the Noldoli, translated into English as 'Gnomes', has become the son of Barahir, a chieftain of Men, and the leader of a band of rebels in hiding against the hateful tyranny of Morgoth. The memorable story has emerged (in 1925, in *The Lay of Leithian*) of the treachery of Gorlim and the slaying of Barahir (pp. 94 ff.); and while Vëannë who told the 'lost tale' knew nothing of what had brought Beren to Artanor, and surmised that it was a simple love of wandering (p. 41), he has become after the death of his father a far-famed enemy of Morgoth forced to flee to the South, where he opens the story of Beren and Tinúviel as he peers in the twilight through the trees of Thingol's forest.

Very remarkable is the story, as it was told in *The Tale of Tinúviel*, of the captivity of Beren, on his journey to Angband in quest of a Silmaril, by Tevildo Prince of Cats; so too is the total subsequent transformation of that story. But if we say that the castle of the cats 'is' the tower of Sauron on Tol-in-Gaurhoth 'Isle of Werewolves' it can only be, as I have remarked elsewhere, in the sense that it occupies the same 'space' in the narrative. Beyond this there is no point in seeking even shadowy resemblances between the two establishments. The monstrous gormandising cats, their kitchens and their sunning terraces, and their engagingly Elvish-feline names, *Miaugion*, *Miaulë*, *Meoita*, have all vanished without trace. But beyond their hatred of dogs (and the importance to the story of the mutual loathing of Huan and Tevildo) it is evident that the inhabitants of the castle are no ordinary cats: very notable is this passage from the *Tale* (p. 69) concerning 'the secret of the cats and the spell that Melko had entrusted to [Tevildo]':

and those were words of magic whereby the stones of his evil house were held together, and whereby he held all beasts of the catfolk under his sway, filling them with an evil power beyond their nature; for long has it been said that Tevildo was an evil fay in beastlike shape.

It is also interesting to observe in this passage, as elsewhere, the manner in which aspects and incidents of the original tale may reappear but in a wholly different guise, arising from a wholly altered narrative conception. In the old *Tale* Tevildo was forced by Huan to reveal the spell, and when Tinúviel uttered it 'the house of Tevildo shook; and there came therefrom a host of indwellers' (which was a host of cats). In the *Quenta Noldorinwa* (p. 135) when Huan overthrew the terrible werewolf-wizard Thû, the Necromancer, in Tol-in-Gaurhoth he 'won from him the keys and the spells that held together his enchanted walls and towers. So the stronghold was broken and the towers thrown down and the dungeons opened. Many captives were released . . .'

But here we move into the major shift in the story of Beren and Lúthien, when it was combined with the altogether distinct legend of Nargothrond. Through the oath of undying friendship and aid sworn to Barahir, the father of Beren, Felagund the founder of Nargothrond was drawn into Beren's quest of the Silmaril (p. 117, lines 157 ff.); and there entered the story of the Elves from Nargothrond who disguised as Orcs were taken by Thû and ended their days in the gruesome dungeons of Tol-in-Gaurhoth. The quest of the Silmaril involved also Celegorm and Curufin, sons of Fëanor and a powerful presence in Nargothrond, through the destructive oath sworn by the Fëanorians of vengeance against any 'who hold or take or keep a Silmaril against their will'. The captivity of Lúthien in Nargothrond, from which Huan rescued her, involved her in the plots and ambitions of Celegorm and Curufin: pp. 151–2, lines 247–72.

There remains the aspect of the story that is also the end of it, and of primary significance, as I believe, in the mind of its author. The earliest reference to the fates of Beren and Lúthien after Beren's death in the hunt of Carcharoth is in *The Tale of Tinúviel;* but at that time both Beren and Lúthien were Elves. There it was said (p. 87):

'Tinúviel crushed with sorrow and finding no comfort or light in all the world followed him swiftly down those dark ways that all must tread alone. Now her beauty and tender loveliness touched even the cold heart of Mandos, so that he suffered her to lead Beren forth once more into the world, nor has this ever been done since to Man or Elf . . . . Yet said Mandos to those twain: "Lo, O Elves, it is not to any life of perfect joy that I dismiss you, for such may no longer be found in all the world where sits Melko of the evil heart – and know that ye will become mortal even as Men, and when ye fare hither again it will be for ever . . . .""

That Beren and Lúthien had a further history in Middle-earth is made plain in this passage ('their deeds afterward were very great, and many tales are told thereof'), but no more is said there than that they are *i-Cuilwarthon*, the Dead that Live Again, and 'they became mighty fairies in the lands about the north of Sirion.'

In another of the *Lost Tales*, *The Coming of the Valar*, there is an account of those who came to Mandos (the name of his halls as well as that of the God, whose true name was Vê):

Thither in after days fared the Elves of all the clans who were by illhap slain with weapons or did die of grief for those that were slain – and only so might the Eldar die, and then it was only for a while. There Mandos spake their doom, and there they waited in the darkness, dreaming of their past deeds, until such time as he appointed when they might again be born into their children, and go forth to laugh and sing again.

With this may be compared the unplaced verses for *The Lay of Leithian* given on pp. 216–17, concerning 'the Land of the Lost . . . where the Dead wait, while ye forget':

> No moon is there, no voice, no sound
> of beating heart; a sigh profound
> once in each age as each age dies
> alone is heard. Far, far it lies,
> the Land of Waiting where the Dead sit,
> in their thought's shadow, by no moon lit.

The conception that the Elves died only from wounds of weapons, or from grief, endured, and appears in the published *Silmarillion*:

For the Elves die not till the world dies, unless they are slain or waste in grief (and to both these seeming deaths they are subject); neither does age subdue their strength, unless one grow weary of ten thousand centuries; and dying they are gathered to the halls of Mandos in Valinor, whence they may in time return. But the sons of Men die indeed, and leave the world; wherefore they are called the Guests, or the Strangers. Death is their fate, the gift of Ilúvatar, which as Time wears even the Powers shall envy.

It seems to me that the words of Mandos in *The Tale of Tinúviel* cited above, '*ye will become mortal even as Men*, and when ye fare hither again it will be for ever', imply that he was uprooting their destiny as Elves: having died as Elves could die, they would not be reborn, but be permitted – uniquely – to leave Mandos still in their own particular being. They would pay a price, nevertheless, for when they died a second time there would be no possibility of return, no 'seeming death', but the death that Men, of their nature, must suffer.

Later, in the *Quenta Noldorinwa* it is told (pp. 140–1) that 'Lúthien failed and faded swiftly and vanished from the earth . . . . And she came to the halls of Mandos, and she sang to him a tale of moving love so fair that he was moved to pity, as never has befallen since.'

Beren he summoned, and thus, as Lúthien had sworn as she kissed him at the hour of death, they met beyond the western sea. And Mandos suffered them to depart, but he said that Lúthien *should become mortal even as her lover*, and should leave the earth once more *in the manner of a mortal woman*, and her beauty become but a memory of song. So it was, but it is said that in recompense Mandos gave to Beren and to Lúthien thereafter a long span of life and joy, and they wandered knowing thirst nor cold in the fair land of Beleriand, and no mortal Man thereafter spoke to Beren or his spouse.

In the draft text of the story of Beren and Lúthien prepared for the *Quenta Silmarillion*, referred to on p. 218, there enters the idea of the 'choice of fate' proposed to Beren and Lúthien before Mandos:

And this was the choice that he decreed for Beren and Lúthien. They should dwell now in Valinor until the world's end in bliss, but in the end Beren and Lúthien must each go unto the fate appointed to their kind, when all things are changed: and of the mind of Ilúvatar concerning Men Manwë [Lord of the Valar] knows not. Or they might return unto Middle-earth without certitude of joy or life; then Lúthien should become mortal even as Beren, and subject to a second death, and in the end she should leave the earth for ever and her beauty become only a memory of song. And this doom they chose, that thus, whatsoever sorrow lay before them, their fates might be joined, and their paths lead together beyond the confines of the world. So it was that alone of the Eldalië Lúthien died and left the world long ago; yet by her have the Two Kindreds been joined, and she is the foremother of many.

This conception of the 'Choice of Fate' was retained, but in a different form, as seen in *The Silmarillion*: the choices were imposed on Lúthien alone, and they were changed. Lúthien may still leave Mandos and dwell until the end of the world in Valinor, because of her labours and her sorrow, and because she was the daughter of Melian; but thither Beren cannot come. Thus if she accepts the former, they must be separated now and for ever: because he cannot escape from his own destiny, cannot escape Death, which is the Gift of Ilúvatar and cannot be refused.

The second choice remained, and this she chose. Only so could Lúthien become united with Beren 'beyond the world': she herself must change the destiny of her being: she must become mortal, and die indeed.

As I have said, the story of Beren and Lúthien did not end with the judgement of Mandos, and some account of it, of its aftermath, and of the history of the Silmaril that Beren cut from the iron crown of Morgoth, must be given. There are difficulties in doing so in the form that I have chosen for this book, largely because the part played by Beren in his second life hinges on aspects of the history of the First Age that would cast the net too widely for the purpose of this book.

I have remarked (p. 103) of the *Quenta Noldorinwa* of 1930, which followed from and was much longer than the *Sketch of the Mythology*, that it remained 'a compression, a compendious account': it is said in the title of the work to be 'the brief history of the Noldoli or Gnomes, drawn from the *Book of Lost Tales*'. Of these 'summarising' texts I wrote in *The War of the Jewels* (1994): 'In these versions my father was drawing on (while also of course continually developing and extending) long works that already existed in prose and verse, and in the *Quenta Silmarillion* he perfected that characteristic tone, melodious, grave, elegiac, burdened with a sense of loss and distance in time, which resides partly, as I believe, in the literary fact that he was drawing down into a brief compendious history what he could also see in far more detailed, immediate, and dramatic form. With the completion of the great "intrusion" and departure of *The Lord of the Rings*, it seems that he returned to the Elder Days with a desire to take up again the far more ample scale with which he had begun long before, in *The Book of Lost Tales*. The completion of the *Quenta Silmarillion* remained an aim; but the "great tales", vastly developed from their original forms – from which its later chapters should be derived – were never achieved.'

We are here concerned with a story that goes back to the latest written of the *Lost Tales*, where it bore the title *The Tale of the Nauglafring*: that being the original name of the *Nauglamír*, the Necklace of the Dwarves. But we come here to the furthest point in my father's work on the Elder Days in the time following the completion of *The Lord of the Rings*: there is no new narrative. To cite my discussion in *The War of the Jewels* again, 'it is as if we come to the brink of a great cliff and look down from highlands raised in some later age onto an ancient plain far below. For the story of the Nauglamír and the destruction of Doriath . . . we must return through more than a quarter of a century to the *Quenta Noldorinwa* or beyond.' To the *Quenta Noldorinwa* (see p. 103) I will now turn, giving the relevant text in a very slightly shortened form.

The tale begins with the further history of the great treasure of Nargothrond that was taken by the evil dragon Glómund. After the death of Glómund, slain by Túrin Turambar, Húrin father of Túrin came with a few outlaws of the woods to Nargothrond, which as yet none, Orc, Elf, or Man, had dared to plunder, for dread of the spirit of Glómund and his very memory. But they found there one Mîm the Dwarf.

THE RETURN OF BEREN AND LÚTHIEN
ACCORDING TO THE *QUENTA NOLDORINWA*

Now Mîm had found the halls and treasure of Nargothrond unguarded; and he took possession of them, and sat there in joy fingering the gold and gems, and letting them run ever through his hands; and he bound them to himself with many spells. But the folk of Mîm were few, and the outlaws filled with the lust of the treasure slew them, though Húrin would have stayed them; and at his death Mîm cursed the gold.

[Húrin went to Thingol and sought his aid, and the folk of Thingol bore the treasure to the Thousand Caves; then Húrin departed.]

Then the enchantment of the accursed dragon gold began to fall even upon the king of Doriath, and long he sat and gazed upon it, and the seed of the love of gold that was in his heart was waked to growth. Wherefore he summoned the greatest of all craftsmen that now were in the western world, since Nargothrond was no more (and Gondolin was

233

not known), the Dwarves of Nogrod and Belegost, that they might fashion the gold and silver and the gems (for much was as yet unwrought) into countless vessels and fair things; and a marvellous necklace of great beauty they should make, whereon to hang the Silmaril.*

But the Dwarves coming were stricken at once with the lust and desire of the treasure, and they plotted treachery. They said one to another: 'Is not this wealth as much the right of the Dwarves as of the Elvish king, and was it not wrested evilly from Mîm?' Yet also they lusted for the Silmaril. And Thingol, falling deeper into the thraldom of the spell, for his part scanted his promised reward for their labour; and bitter words grew between them, and there was battle in Thingol's halls. There many Elves and Dwarves were slain, and the howe wherein they were lain in Doriath was named Cûm-nan-Arasaith, the Mound of Avarice. But the remainder of the Dwarves were driven forth without reward or fee.

Therefore gathering new forces in Nogrod and in Belegost they returned at length, and aided by the treachery of certain Elves on whom the lust of the accursed treasure had fallen they passed into Doriath secretly.

There they surprised Thingol upon a hunt with but small

---

* A later version of the story concerning the Nauglamír told that it had been made by craftsmen of the Dwarves long before for Felagund, and that it was the sole treasure that Húrin brought from Nargothrond and gave to Thingol. The task that Thingol then set the Dwarves was to *re-make* the Nauglamír and in it to set the Silmaril that was in his possession. This is the form of the story in the published *Silmarillion*.

company of arms; and Thingol was slain, and the fortress of the Thousand Caves taken at unawares and plundered; and so was brought well nigh to ruin the glory of Doriath, and but one stronghold of the Elves [Gondolin] against Morgoth now remained, and their twilight was nigh at hand.

Queen Melian the Dwarves could not seize or harm, and she went forth to seek Beren and Lúthien. Now the Dwarf-road to Nogrod and Belegost in the Blue Mountains passed through East Beleriand and the woods about the River Gelion, where aforetime were the hunting grounds of Damrod and Díriel, sons of Fëanor. To the south of those lands between the river Gelion and the mountains lay the land of Ossiriand, and there lived and wandered still in peace and bliss Beren and Lúthien, in that time of respite which Lúthien had won, ere both should die; and their folk were the Green Elves of the South. But Beren went no more to war, and his land was filled with loveliness and a wealth of flowers, and Men called it oft Cuilwarthien, the Land of the Dead that Live.

To the north of that region is a ford across the river Ascar, and that ford is named Sarn Athrad, the Ford of Stones. This ford the Dwarves must pass ere they reached the mountain passes that led unto their homes; and there Beren fought his last fight, warned of their approach by Melian. In that battle the Green Elves took the Dwarves unawares as they were in the midst of their passage, laden with their plunder; and the Dwarvish chiefs were slain, and well nigh all their host. But Beren took the Nauglamír, the Necklace of the Dwarves, whereon was hung the Silmaril; and it is said and sung that Lúthien wearing that necklace and that immortal jewel on her white breast was the vision of greatest beauty and glory that has ever been seen outside the realms of Valinor, and that for a while the Land of the Dead that Live became like a vision of the land of the Gods, and no places have been since so fair, so fruitful, or so filled with light.

Yet Melian warned them ever of the curse that lay upon the treasure and upon the Silmaril. The treasure they had drowned indeed in the river Ascar, and named it anew Rathlorion, Goldenbed, yet the Silmaril they retained. And in time the brief hour of loveliness of the land of Rathlorion departed. For Lúthien faded as Mandos had spoken, even as the Elves of later days faded and she vanished from the world;* and Beren died, and none know where their meeting shall be again.

Thereafter was Dior Thingol's heir, child of Beren and Lúthien, king in the woods: most fair of all the children of the world, for his race was threefold: of the fairest and goodliest of Men, and of the Elves, and of the spirits divine of Valinor; yet it shielded him not from the fate of the oath of the sons of Fëanor. For Dior went back to Doriath and for a time a part of its ancient glory was raised anew, though Melian no longer dwelt in that place, and she departed to the land of the Gods beyond the western sea, to muse on her sorrows in the gardens whence she came.

But Dior wore the Silmaril upon his breast and the fame

---

* The manner of Lúthien's death is marked for correction; subsequently my father wrote against it: 'Yet it hath been sung that Lúthien alone of Elves hath been numbered among our race, and goeth whither we go to a fate beyond the world.'

of that jewel went far and wide; and the deathless oath was waked once more from sleep.

For while Lúthien wore that peerless gem no Elf would dare assail her, and not even Maidros dared ponder such a thought. But now hearing of the renewal of Doriath and Dior's pride, the seven gathered again from wandering; and they sent unto Dior to claim their own. But he would not yield the jewel unto them, and they came upon him with all their host; and so befell the second slaying of Elf by Elf, and the most grievous. There fell Celegorm and Curufin and dark Cranthir, but Dior was slain, and Doriath was destroyed and never rose again.

Yet the sons of Fëanor gained not the Silmaril; for faithful servants fled before them and took with them Elwing the daughter of Dior, and she escaped, and they bore with them the Nauglafring, and came in time to the mouth of the river Sirion by the sea.

[In a text somewhat later than the *Quenta Noldorinwa,* the earliest form of *The Annals of Beleriand,* the story was changed, in that Dior returned to Doriath while Beren and Lúthien were still alive in Ossiriand; and what befell him there I will give in the words of *The Silmarillion*:

There came a night of autumn, and when it grew late, one came and smote upon the doors of Menegroth, demanding admittance to the King. He was a lord of the Green Elves hastening from Ossiriand, and the door-wards brought him to where Dior sat alone in his chamber; and there in silence he gave to the King a coffer, and took his leave. But in that coffer lay the Necklace of the Dwarves, wherein was set the Silmaril; and Dior looking upon it knew it for a sign that Beren Erchamion and Lúthien Tinúviel had died indeed, and gone where go the race of Men to a fate beyond the world.

Long did Dior gaze upon the Silmaril, which his father and mother had brought beyond hope out of the terror of Morgoth; and his grief was great that death had come upon them so soon.]

EXTRACT FROM THE *LOST TALE*
OF THE NAUGLAFRING

Here I will step back from the chronology of composition
and turn to the *Lost Tale* of the Nauglafring. The reason for
this is that the passage given here is a notable example of the
expansive mode, observant of visual and often dramatic detail,
adopted by my father in the early days of *The Silmarillion*; but
the *Lost Tale* as a whole extends into ramifications unneeded in
this book. A very brief summary of the battle at Sarn Athrad,
the Stony Ford, appears therefore in the text of the *Quenta*,
p. 235, while there follows here the much fuller account from
the *Lost Tale*, with the duel between Beren and Naugladur,
lord of the Dwarves of Nogrod in the Blue Mountains.

The passage begins with the approach of the Dwarves, led
by Naugladur, to Sarn Athrad, on their return from the sack
of the Thousand Caves.

Now came all that host [to the river Ascar], and their
array was thus: first a number of unladen Dwarves most fully

armed, and amidmost the great company of those that bore the treasury of Glómund, and many a fair thing beside that they had haled from Tinwelint's halls; and behind these was Naugladur, and he bestrode Tinwelint's horse, and a strange figure did he seem, for the legs of the Dwarves are short and crooked, but two Dwarves led that horse for it went not willingly and it was laden with spoil. But behind these came a mass of armed men but little laden; and in this array they sought to cross Sarn Athrad on their day of doom.

Morn was it when they reached the hither bank, and high noon saw them yet passing in long-strung lines and wading slowly the shallow places of the swift-running stream. Here doth it widen out and fare down narrow channels filled with boulders atween long spits of shingle and stones less great. Now did Naugladur slip from his burdened horse and pre- pare to get him over, for the armed host of the vanguard had climbed already the further bank, and it was great and sheer and thick with trees, and the bearers of the gold were some already stepped thereon and some amidmost of the stream, but the armed men of the rear were resting awhile.

Suddenly is all that place filled with the sound of elven horns, and one [? brays] with a clearer blast above the rest, and it is the horn of Beren, the huntsman of the woods. Then is the air thick with the slender arrows of the Eldar that err not neither doth the wind bear them aside, and lo, from every tree and boulder do the brown Elves and the green spring suddenly and loose unceasingly from full quivers. Then was there a panic and a noise in the host of Naugladur, and those that waded in the ford cast their golden burdens in the waters and sought affrighted to either bank, but many were stricken with those pitiless darts and fell with their gold into the currents of the Aros, staining its clear waters with their dark blood.

Now were the warriors on the far bank [? wrapped] in battle and rallying sought to come at their foes, but these fled nimbly before them, while [? others] poured still the hail of arrows upon them, and thus got the Eldar few hurts and the Dwarf-folk fell dead unceasingly. Now was that great fight of the Stony Ford . . . nigh to Naugladur, for even though Naugladur and his captains led their bands stoutly never might they grip their foe, and death fell like rain upon their ranks until the most part broke and fled, and a noise of clear laughter echoed from the Elves thereat, and they forbore to shoot more, for the illshapen figures of the Dwarves as they fled, their white beards torn by the wind, filled them with mirth. But now stood Naugladur and few were about him, and he remembered the words of Gwendelin,* for behold, Beren came towards him and he cast aside his bow, and drew a bright sword; and Beren was of great stature among the Eldar, albeit not of the girth and breadth of Naugladur of the Dwarves.

Then said Beren: 'Ward thy life if thou canst, O crook-legged murderer, else will I take it,' and Naugladur bid him even

---

* Earlier in the tale, when Naugladur was preparing to leave Menegroth, he declared that Gwendelin the queen of Artanor (Melian) must go with him to Nogrod: to which she replied: 'Thief and murderer, child of Melko, yet art thou a fool, for thou canst not see what hangs over thine own head.'

the Nauglafring, the necklace of wonder, that he be suffered to go unharmed; but Beren said: 'Nay, that may I still take when thou art slain,' and thereat he made alone upon Naugladur and his companions, and having slain the foremost of these the others fled away amid elven laughter, and so Beren came upon Naugladur, slayer of Tinwelint. Then did that aged one defend himself doughtily, and 'twas a bitter fight, and many of the Elves that watched for love and fear of their captain fingered their bow-strings, but Beren called even as he fought that all should stay their hands.

Now little doth the tale tell of wounds and blows of that affray, save that Beren got many hurts therein, and many of his shrewdest blows did little harm to Naugladur by reason of the [? skill] and magic of his dwarfen mail; and it is said that three hours they fought and Beren's arms grew weary, but not those of Naugladur accustomed to wield his mighty hammer at the forge, and it is more than like that otherwise would the issue have been but for the curse of Mîm; for marking how Beren grew faint Naugladur pressed him ever more nearly, and the arrogance that was of that grievous spell came into his heart, and he thought: 'I will slay this Elf, and his folk will flee in fear before me,' and grasping his sword he dealt a mighty blow and cried: 'Take here thy bane, O stripling of the woods,' and in that moment his foot found a jagged stone and he stumbled forward, but Beren slipped aside from that blow and catching at his beard his hand found the carcanet of gold, and therewith he swung Naugladur suddenly off his feet upon his face: and Naugladur's sword was shaken from his grasp, but Beren seized it and slew him therewith, for he said: 'I will not sully my bright blade with thy dark blood, since there is no need.' But the body of Naugladur was cast into the Aros.

Then did he unloose the necklace, and he gazed in wonder at it – and beheld the Silmaril, even the jewel he won from Angband and gained undying glory by his deed; and he said: 'Never have mine eyes beheld thee O Lamp of Faëry burn one half so fair as now thou dost, set in gold and gems and the magic of the Dwarves'; and that necklace he caused to be washed of its stains, and he cast it not away, knowing nought of its power, but bore it with him back into the woods of Hithlum.

To this passage from the *Tale of the Nauglafring* there corresponds only the few words of the *Quenta* cited in the extract cited on p. 235:

In that battle [Sarn Athrad] the Green Elves took the Dwarves unawares as they were in the midst of their passage, laden with their plunder; and the Dwarvish chiefs were slain, and well nigh all their host. But Beren took the Nauglamír, the Necklace of the Dwarves, whereon was hung the Silmaril . . .

This illustrates my observation on p. 231, that my father 'was drawing down into a brief compendious history what he could also see in far more detailed, immediate, and dramatic form.'

I will conclude this short excursion into the *Lost Tale* of the Necklace of the Dwarves with a further quotation, origin of the story as told in the *Quenta* (pp. 236–7) of the deaths of Beren and Lúthien, and the slaying of Dior, their son. I take up this extract with words between Beren and Gwendelin (Melian) when Lúthien first wore the Nauglafring. Beren declared that never had she appeared so beautiful; but Gwendelin said: 'Yet the Silmaril abode in the Crown of Melko, and that is the work of baleful smiths indeed.'

Then said Tinúviel that she desired not things of worth or precious stones, but the elven gladness of the forest, and to pleasure Gwendelin she cast it from her neck; but Beren was little pleased and he would not suffer it to be flung away, but warded it in his [? treasury].

Thereafter did Gwendelin abide a while in the woods among them and was healed [of her overwhelming grief for Tinwelint]; and in the end she fared wistfully back to the land of Lórien and came never again into the tales of the dwellers of Earth; but upon Beren and Lúthien fell swiftly that doom of mortality that Mandos had spoken when he sped them from his halls – and in this perhaps did the curse of Mîm have [? potency] in that it came more soon upon them; nor this time did those twain fare the road together, but when yet was their child, Dior the Fair, a little one, did Tinúviel slowly fade, even as the Elves of later days have done throughout the world, and she vanished in the woods, and none have seen her dancing ever there again. But Beren searched all the lands of Hithlum and of Artanor ranging after her; and never has any of the Elves had more loneliness than his, or ever he too faded from life, and Dior his son was left ruler of the brown Elves and the green, and Lord of the Nauglafring.

Mayhap what all Elves say is true, that those twain hunt now in the forest of Oromë in Valinor, and Tinúviel dances on the green swards of Nessa and Vána daughters of the Gods for ever more; yet great was the grief of the Elves when the Guilwarthon went from among them, and being leaderless and lessened of magic their numbers minished; and many fared away to Gondolin, the rumour of whose growing power and glory ran in secret whispers among all the Elves.

Still did Dior when come to manhood rule a numerous folk, and he loved the woods even as Beren had done; and songs name him mostly Ausir the Wealthy for his possession of that wondrous gem set in the Necklace of the Dwarves. Now the tales of Beren and Tinúviel grew dim in his heart, and he took to wearing it about his neck and to love its loveliness most dearly; and the fame of that jewel spread like fire through all the regions of the North, and the Elves said one to another: 'A Silmaril burns in the woods of Hisilómë.'

The *Tale of the Nauglafring* told in greater detail of the assault on Dior and his death at the hands of the sons of Fëanor, and this last of the *Lost Tales* to receive consecutive form ends with the escape of Elwing:

She wandered in the woods, and of the brown Elves and the green a few gathered to her, and they departed for ever from the glades of Hithlum and got them to the south towards Sirion's deep waters, and the pleasant lands.

And thus did all the fates of the fairies weave then to one strand, and that strand is the great tale of Eärendel; and to that tale's true beginning are we now come.

*

There follow in the *Quenta Noldorinwa* passages concerned with the history of Gondolin and its fall, and the history of Tuor, who was wedded to Idril Celebrindal daughter of Turgon king of Gondolin; their son was Eärendel, who with them escaped from the destruction of the city and came to the Mouths of Sirion. The *Quenta* continues, following from the flight of Elwing daughter of Dior from Doriath to the mouths of Sirion (pp. 236–7):

By Sirion there grew up an elven folk, the gleanings of Doriath and Gondolin, and they took to the sea and to the making of fair ships, and they dwelt nigh unto its shores and under the shadow of Ulmo's hand. . . .

In those days Tuor felt old age creep upon him, and he could not forbear the longing that possessed him for the sea; wherefore he built a great ship Eärámë, Eagle's Pinion, and with Idril he set sail into the sunset and the West, and came no more into any tale. But Eärendel the shining became the lord of the folk of Sirion and took to wife fair Elwing, the daughter of Dior; and yet he could not rest. Two thoughts were in his heart blended as one: the longing for the wide sea; and he thought to sail thereon following after Tuor and Idril Celebrindal who returned not, and he thought to find perhaps the last shore and bring ere he died a message to the Gods and Elves of the West that should move their hearts to pity on the world and the sorrows of Mankind.

Wingelot he built, fairest of the ships of song, the Foam-flower; white were its timbers as the argent moon, golden were its oars, silver were its shrouds, its masts were crowned with jewels like stars. In *The Lay of Eärendel* is many a thing sung of his adventures in the deep and in lands untrod, and in many seas and many isles. . . But Elwing sat sorrowing at home.

Eärendel found not Tuor, nor came he ever on that journey to the shores of Valinor; and at last he was driven by the winds back East, and he came at a time of night to the havens of Sirion, unlooked for, unwelcomed, for they were desolate. . . .

The dwelling of Elwing at Sirion's mouth, where still she possessed the Nauglamír and the glorious Silmaril, became known to the sons of Fëanor; and they gathered together from their wandering hunting-paths.

But the folk of Sirion would not yield that jewel which Beren had won and Lúthien had worn, and for which fair Dior had been slain. And so befell the last and cruellest slaying of Elf by Elf, the third woe achieved by the accursed oath; for the sons of Fëanor came down upon the exiles of Gondolin and the remnant of Doriath, and though some of their folk stood aside and some few rebelled and were slain upon the other part aiding Elwing against their own lords, yet they won the day. Damrod was slain and Díriel, and Maidros and Maglor alone now remained of the Seven; but the last of the folk of Gondolin were destroyed or forced to depart and join them to the people of Maidros. And yet the sons of Fëanor gained not the Silmaril; for Elwing cast the Nauglamír into the sea, whence it shall not return until the End; and she leapt herself into the waves, and took the form of a white sea-bird, and flew away lamenting and seeking for Eärendel about all the shores of the world.

But Maidros took pity upon her child Elrond, and took him with him, and harboured and nurtured him, for his heart was sick and weary with the burden of the dreadful oath.

Learning these things Eärendel was overcome with sorrow; and he set sail once more in search of Elwing and of Valinor. And it is told in the Lay of Eärendel that he came at last unto the Magic Isles, and hardly escaped their enchantment, and found again the Lonely Isle, and the Shadowy Seas, and the Bay of Faërie on the borders of the world. There he landed on the immortal shore alone of living Men, and his feet climbed the marvellous hill of Kôr; and he walked in the deserted ways of Tûn, where the dust upon his raiment and his shoes was a dust of diamonds and gems. But he ventured not into Valinor.

He built a tower in the Northern Seas to which all the sea-birds of the world might at times repair, and ever he grieved for fair Elwing, looking for her return to him. And Wingelot was lifted on their wings and sailed now even in the airs searching for Elwing; marvellous and magical was that ship, a starlit flower in the sky. But the Sun scorched it and the Moon hunted it in heaven, and long Eärendel wandered over Earth, glimmering as a fugitive star.

Here the tale of Eärendel and Elwing ends in the *Quenta Noldorinwa* as originally composed; but at a later time a rewriting of this last passage altered profoundly the idea that the Silmaril of Beren and Lúthien was lost for ever in the sea. As rewritten it reads:

And yet Maidros gained not the Silmaril, for Elwing seeing that all was lost and her children Elros and Elrond taken captive, eluded the host of Maidros, and with the Nauglamír upon her breast she cast herself into the sea, and perished, as folk thought. But Ulmo bore her up, and upon her breast there shone as a star the shining Silmaril, as she flew over the water to seek Eärendel her beloved. And on a time of night Eärendel at the helm saw her come towards him, as a white cloud under moon exceeding swift, as a star over the sea moving in strange course, a pale flame on wings of storm.

And it is sung that she fell from the air upon the timbers of Wingelot, in a swoon, nigh unto death for the urgency of her speed, and Eärendel took her into his bosom. And in the morn with marvelling eyes he beheld his wife in her own form beside him with her hair upon his face; and she slept.

From here onwards the tale told in the *Quenta Noldorinwa*, largely rewritten, reached in essentials that in *The Silmarillion*, and I will end the story in this book with citation of that work.

THE MORNING
AND EVENING STAR

Great was the sorrow of Eärendil and Elwing for the ruin of the havens of Sirion, and the captivity of their sons, and they feared that they would be slain; but it was not so. For Maglor took pity upon Elros and Elrond, and he cherished them, and love grew after between them, as little might be thought; but Maglor's heart was sick and weary with the burden of the dreadful oath.

Yet Eärendil saw now no hope left in the lands of Middle-earth, and he turned again in despair and came not home, but sought back once more to Valinor with Elwing at his side. He stood now most often at the prow of Vingilot, and the Silmaril was bound upon his brow; and ever its light grew greater as they drew into the West. ...

Then Eärendil, first of living Men, landed on the immortal shores; and he spoke there to Elwing and to those that were with him, and they were three mariners who had sailed all the seas beside him: Falathar, Erellont, and Aerandir were their names. And Eärendil said to them: 'Here none but myself shall set foot, lest you fall under the wrath of the Valar. But that peril I will take on myself alone, for the sake of the Two Kindreds.'

But Elwing answered: 'Then would our paths be sundered for ever, but all thy perils I will take on myself also.' And she leaped into the white foam and ran towards him; but Eärendil was sorrowful, for he feared the anger of the Lords of the West upon any of Middle-earth that should dare to pass the leaguer of Aman. And there they bade farewell to the companions of their voyage, and were taken from them for ever.

Then Eärendil said to Elwing: 'Await me here; for one only may bring the message that it is my fate to bear.' And he went up alone into the land, and came into the Calacirya, and it seemed to him empty and silent; for even as Morgoth and Ungoliant came in ages past, so now Eärendil had come at a time of festival, and wellnigh all the Elvenfolk were gone to Valimar, or were gathered in the halls of Manwë upon Taniquetil, and few were left to keep watch upon the walls of Tirion.

But some there were who saw him from afar, and the great light that he bore; and they went in haste to Valimar. But Eärendil climbed the green hill of Túna and found it bare; and he entered into the streets of Tirion, and they were empty; and his heart was heavy, for he feared that some evil had come even to the Blessed Realm. He walked in the deserted ways of Tirion, and the dust upon his raiment and his shoes was a dust of diamonds, and he shone and glistened as he climbed the long white stairs. And he called aloud in many tongues, both of Elves and Men, but there were none to answer him. Therefore he turned back at last towards the sea; but even as he took the shoreward road one stood upon the hill and called to him in a great voice, crying:

'Hail Eärendil, of mariners most renowned, the looked for that cometh at unawares, the longed for that cometh beyond hope! Hail Eärendil, bearer of light before the Sun and Moon! Splendour of the Children of Earth, star in the darkness, jewel in the sunset, radiant in the morning!'

That voice was the voice of Eönwë, herald of Manwë, and he came from Valimar, and summoned Eärendil to come before the Powers of Arda. And Eärendil went into Valinor and to the halls of Valimar, and never again set foot upon the lands of Men. Then the Valar took counsel together, and they summoned Ulmo from the deeps of the sea; and Eärendil stood before their faces, and delivered the errand of the Two Kindreds. Pardon he asked for the Noldor and pity for their great sorrows, and mercy upon Men and Elves and succour in their need. And his prayer was granted.

It is told among the Elves that after Eärendil had departed, seeking Elwing his wife, Mandos spoke concerning his fate; and he said: 'Shall mortal man step living upon the undying lands, and yet live?' But Ulmo said: 'For this he was born into the world. And say unto me: whether is he Eärendil Tuor's son of the line of Hador, or the son of Idril, Turgon's daughter, of the Elven-house of Finwë?' And Mandos answered: 'Equally the Noldor, who went wilfully into exile, may not return hither.'

But when all was spoken, Manwë gave judgement, and he

said: 'In this matter the power of doom is given to me. The peril that he ventured for love of the Two Kindreds shall not fall upon Eärendil, nor shall it fall upon Elwing his wife, who entered into peril for love of him; but they shall not walk again ever among Elves or Men in the Outer Lands. And this is my decree concerning them: to Eärendil and Elwing, and to their sons, shall be given leave each to choose freely to which kindred their fates shall be joined, and under which kindred they shall be judged.'

[Now when Eärendil was long time gone Elwing became lonely and afraid; but as she wandered by the margin of the sea he found her.] Ere long they were summoned to Valimar; and there the decree of the Elder King was declared to them.

Then Eärendil said to Elwing: 'Choose thou, for now I am weary of the world.' And Elwing chose to be judged among the Firstborn Children of Ilúvatar, because of Lúthien; and for her sake Eärendil chose alike, though his heart was rather with the kindred of Men and the people of his father.

Then at the bidding of the Valar Eönwë went to the shore of Aman, where the companions of Eärendil still remained, awaiting tidings; and he took a boat, and the three mariners were set therein, and the Valar drove them away into the East with a great wind. But they took Vingilot, and hallowed it, and bore it away through Valinor to the uttermost rim of the world; and there it passed through the Door of Night and was lifted up even into the oceans of heaven.

Now fair and marvellous was that vessel made, and it was filled with a wavering flame, pure and bright; and Eärendil the Mariner sat at the helm, glistening with dust of elven-gems, and the Silmaril was bound upon his brow. Far he journeyed in that ship, even into the starless voids; but most often was he seen at morning or at evening, glimmering at sunrise or at sunset, as he came back to Valinor from voyages beyond the confines of the world.

On those journeys Elwing did not go, for she might not endure the cold and the pathless voids, and she loved rather the earth and the sweet winds that blow on sea and hill. Therefore there was built for her a white tower northward upon the borders of the Sundering Seas; and thither at times all the sea-birds of the earth repaired. And it is said that Elwing learned the tongues of birds, who herself had once worn their shape; and they taught her the craft of flight, and her wings were of white and of silver-grey. And at times, when Eärendil returning drew near again to Arda, she would fly to meet him, even as she had flown long ago, when she was rescued from the sea. Then the far-sighted among the Elves that dwelt in the Lonely Isle would see her like a white bird, shining, rose-stained in the sunset, as she soared in joy to greet the coming of Vingilot to haven.

Now when first Vingilot was set to sail in the seas of heaven it rose unlooked for, glittering and bright; and the people of Middle-earth beheld it from afar and wondered, and they took it for a sign, and called it Gil-Estel, the Star of High Hope. And when this new star was seen at evening, Maedhros spoke to Maglor his brother, and he said: 'Surely that is a Silmaril that shines now in the West?'

And of the final departure of Beren and Lúthien? In the words of the *Quenta Silmarillion*: None saw Beren and Lúthien leave the world or marked where at last their bodies lay.

APPENDIX

REVISIONS TO
THE LAY OF LEITHIAN

Among the first, perhaps even the very first, of the literary tasks that attracted my father after the completion of *The Lord of the Rings* was a return to *The Lay of Leithian*: not (needless to say) to continue the narrative from the point reached in 1931 (the attack on Beren by Carcharoth at the gates of Angband), but from the beginning of the poem. The textual history of the writing is very complex, and no more need be said of it here beyond remarking that whereas at first my father seems to have embarked on a radical rewriting of the *Lay* as a whole, the impulse soon died away, or was overtaken, and was reduced to short and scattered passages. I give here, however, as a substantial example of the new verse after the lapse of a quarter of a century, the passage of the *Lay* concerning the treachery of Gorlim the Unhappy that led to the slaying of Barahir, the father of Beren, and all his companions, save Beren alone. This is by far the longest of the new passages; and – conveniently – it may be compared with the original text that has been given on pp. 94–102. It will be seen that Sauron (Thû), ridden here from 'Gaurhoth Isle', has replaced Morgoth; and that in the quality of the verse this is a new poem.

I begin the new text with a short passage entitled *Of Tarn Aeluin the Blessed* which has no counterpart in the original version: these verses are numbered 1–26.

> Such deeds of daring there they wrought
> that soon the hunters that them sought
> at rumour of their coming fled.
> Though price was set upon each head
> to match the weregild of a king,   5
> no soldier could to Morgoth bring
> news even of their hidden lair;
> for where the highland brown and bare
> above the darkling pines arose
> of steep Dorthonion to the snows   10
> and barren mountain-winds, there lay
> a tarn of water, blue by day,
> by night a mirror of dark glass
> for stars of Elbereth that pass
> above the world into the West.   15
> Once hallowed, still that place was blest:
> no shadow of Morgoth, and no evil thing
> yet thither came; a whispering ring
> of slender birches silver-grey
> stooped on its margin, round it lay   20
> a lonely moor, and the bare bones

of ancient Earth like standing stones
thrust through the heather and the whin;
and there by houseless Aeluin
the hunted lord and faithful men   25
under the grey stones made their den.

OF GORLIM UNHAPPY

Gorlim Unhappy, Angrim's son,
as the tale tells, of these was one,
most fierce and hopeless. He to wife,
while fair was the fortune of his life,   30
took the white maiden Eilinel:
dear love they had ere evil fell.
To war he rode; from war returned
to find his fields and homestead burned,
his house forsaken roofless stood,   35
empty amid the leafless wood;
and Eilinel, white Eilinel,
was taken whither none could tell,
to death or thraldom far away.
Black was the shadow of that day   40
for ever on his heart, and doubt
still gnawed him as he went about
in wilderness wandring, or at night
oft sleepless, thinking that she might
ere evil came have timely fled   45
into the woods: she was not dead,

she lived, she would return again
to seek him, and would deem him slain.
Therefore at whiles he left the lair,
and secretly, alone, would peril dare,   50
and come to his old house at night,
broken and cold, without fire or light,
and naught but grief renewed would gain,
watching and waiting there in vain.

    In vain, or worse – for many spies   55
had Morgoth, many lurking eyes
well used to pierce the deepest dark;
and Gorlim's coming they would mark
and would report. There came a day
when once more Gorlim crept that way,   60
down the deserted weedy lane
at dusk of autumn sad with rain
and cold wind whining. Lo! a light
at window fluttering in the night
amazed he saw; and drawing near,   65
between faint hope and sudden fear,
he looked within. 'Twas Eilinel!
Though changed she was, he knew her well.
With grief and hunger she was worn,
her tresses tangled, raiment torn;   70
her gentle eyes with tears were dim,
as soft she wept: 'Gorlim, Gorlim!
Thou canst not have forsaken me.
Then slain, alas! thou slain must be!

And I must linger cold, alone,   75
and loveless as a barren stone!'

    One cry he gave – and then the light
blew out, and in the wind of night
wolves howled; and on his shoulder fell
suddenly the griping hands of hell.   80
There Morgoth's servants fast him caught
and he was cruelly bound, and brought
to Sauron captain of the host,
the lord of werewolf and of ghost,
most foul and fell of all who knelt   85
at Morgoth's throne. In might he dwelt
on Gaurhoth Isle; but now had ridden
with strength abroad, by Morgoth bidden
to find the rebel Barahir.
He sat in dark encampment near,   90
and thither his butchers dragged their prey.
There now in anguish Gorlim lay:
with bond on neck, on hand and foot,
to bitter torment he was put,
to break his will and him constrain   95
to buy with treason end of pain.
But naught to them would he reveal
of Barahir, nor break the seal
of faith that on his tongue was laid;
until at last a pause was made,   100
and one came softly to his stake,
a darkling form that stooped, and spake

to him of Eilinel his wife.

    'Wouldst thou,' he said, 'forsake thy life,
who with few words might win release   105
for her, and thee, and go in peace,
and dwell together far from war,
friends of the King? What wouldst thou more?'
And Gorlim, now long worn with pain,
yearning to see his wife again   110
(whom well he weened was also caught
in Sauron's net), allowed the thought
to grow, and faltered in his troth.
Then straight, half willing and half loath,
they brought him to the seat of stone   115
where Sauron sat. He stood alone
before that dark and dreadful face,
and Sauron said: 'Come, mortal base!
What do I hear? That thou wouldst dare
to barter with me? Well, speak fair!   120
What is thy price?' And Gorlim low
bowed down his head, and with great woe,
word on slow word, at last implored
that merciless and faithless lord
that he might free depart, and might   125
again find Eilinel the white,
and dwell with her, and cease from war
against the King. He craved no more.

    Then Sauron smiled, and said: 'Thou thrall!
The price thou askest is but small   130

for treachery and shame so great!
I grant it surely! Well, I wait:
Come! Speak now swiftly and speak true!'
Then Gorlim wavered, and he drew
half back; but Sauron's daunting eye   135
there held him, and he dared not lie:
as he began, so must he wend
from first false step to faithless end:
he all must answer as he could,
betray his lord and brotherhood,   140
and cease, and fall upon his face.

Then Sauron laughed aloud. 'Thou base,
thou cringing worm! Stand up,
and hear me! And now drink the cup
that I have sweetly blent for thee!   145
Thou fool: a phantom thou didst see
that I, I Sauron, made to snare
thy lovesick wits. Naught else was there.
Cold 'tis with Sauron's wraiths to wed!
Thy Eilinel! She is long since dead,   150
dead, food of worms less low than thou.
And yet thy boon I grant thee now:
to Eilinel thou soon shalt go,
and lie in her bed, no more to know
of war – or manhood. Have thy pay!'   155

And Gorlim then they dragged away,
and cruelly slew him; and at last

in the dank mould his body cast,
where Eilinel long since had lain
in the burned woods by butchers slain.   160
    Thus Gorlim died an evil death,
and cursed himself with dying breath,
and Barahir at last was caught
in Morgoth's snare; for set at naught
by treason was the ancient grace   165
that guarded long that lonely place,
Tarn Aeluin: now all laid bare
were secret paths and hidden lair.

OF BEREN SON OF BARAHIR & HIS ESCAPE

Dark from the North now blew the cloud;
the winds of autumn cold and loud   170
hissed in the heather; sad and grey
Aeluin's mournful water lay.
'Son Beren', then said Barahir,
'Thou knowst the rumour that we hear
of strength from the Gaurhoth that is sent   175
against us; and our food nigh spent.
On thee the lot falls by our law
to go forth now alone to draw
what help thou canst from the hidden few
that feed us still, and what is new   180
to learn. Good fortune go with thee!
In speed return, for grudgingly

we spare thee from our brotherhood
so small: and Gorlim in the wood
is long astray or dead. Farewell!'   185
As Beren went, still like a knell
resounded in his heart that word,
the last of his father that he heard.

    Through moor and fen, by tree and briar
he wandered far: he saw the fire   190
of Sauron's camp, he heard the howl
of hunting Orc and wolf a-prowl,
and turning back, for long the way,
benighted in the forest lay.
In weariness he then must sleep,   195
fain in a badger-hole to creep,
and yet he heard (or dreamed it so)
nearby a marching legion go
with clink of mail and clash of shields
up towards the stony mountain-fields.   200
He slipped then into darkness down,
until, as man that waters drown
strives upwards gasping, it seemed to him
he rose through slime beside the brim
of sullen pool beneath dead trees.   205
Their livid boughs in a cold breeze
trembled, and all their black leaves stirred:
each leaf a black and croaking bird,
whose neb a gout of blood let fall.
He shuddered, struggling thence to crawl   210

through winding weeds, when far away
he saw a shadow faint and grey
gliding across the dreary lake.
Slowly it came, and softly spake:
'Gorlim I was, but now a wraith   215
of will defeated, broken faith,
traitor betrayed. Go! Stay not here!
Awaken, son of Barahir,
and haste! For Morgoth's fingers close
upon thy father's throat; he knows   220
your trysts, your paths, your secret lair.'
    Then he revealed the devil's snare
in which he fell, and failed; and last
begging forgiveness, wept, and passed
out into darkness. Beren woke,   225
leapt up as one by sudden stroke
with fire of anger filled. His bow
and sword he seized, and like the roe
hotfoot o'er rock and heath he sped
before the dawn. Ere day was dead   230
to Aeluin at last he came,
as the red sun westward sank in flame;
but Aeluin was red with blood,
red were the stones and trampled mud.
Black in the birches sat a-row   235
the raven and the carrion crow;
wet were their nebs, and dark the meat
that dripped beneath their griping feet.
One croaked: 'Ha, ha, he comes too late!'

'Ha, ha!' they answered, 'ha! too late!'   240
   There Beren laid his father's bones
in haste beneath a cairn of stones;
no graven rune nor word he wrote
o'er Barahir, but thrice he smote
the topmost stone, and thrice aloud   245
he cried his name. 'Thy death', he vowed,
'I will avenge. Yea, though my fate
should lead at last to Angband's gate.'
And then he turned, and did not weep:
too dark his heart, the wound too deep.   250
Out into night, as cold as stone,
loveless, friendless, he strode alone.

   Of hunter's lore he had no need
the trail to find. With little heed
his ruthless foe, secure and proud,   255
marched north away with blowing loud
of brazen horns their lord to greet,
trampling the earth with grinding feet.
Behind them bold but wary went
now Beren, swift as hound on scent,   260
until beside a darkling well,
where Rivil rises from the fell
down into Serech's reeds to flow,
he found the slayers, found his foe.
From hiding on the hillside near   265
he marked them all: though less than fear,
too many for his sword and bow

to slay alone. Then, crawling low
as snake in heath, he nearer crept.
There many weary with marching slept,   270
but captains, sprawling on the grass,
drank and from hand to hand let pass
their booty, grudging each small thing
raped from dead bodies. One a ring
held up, and laughed: 'Now, mates,' he cried,   275
'here's mine! And I'll not be denied,
though few be like it in the land.
For I 'twas wrenched it from the hand
of that same Barahir I slew,
the robber-knave. If tales be true,   280
he had it of some elvish lord,
for the rogue-service of his sword.
No help it gave him – he's dead.
They're parlous, elvish rings, 'tis said;
still for the gold I'll keep it, yea   285
and so eke out my niggard pay.
Old Sauron bade me bring it back,
and yet, methinks, he has no lack
of weightier treasures in his hoard:
the greater the greedier the lord!   290
So mark ye, mates, ye all shall swear
the hand of Barahir was bare!'
And as he spoke an arrow sped
from tree behind, and forward dead
choking he fell with barb in throat;   295
with leering face the earth he smote.

Forth then as wolfhound grim there leapt
Beren among them. Two he swept
aside with sword; caught up the ring;
slew one who grasped him; with a spring   300
back into shadow passed, and fled
before their yells of wrath and dread
of ambush in the valley rang.
Then after him like wolves they sprang,
howling and cursing, gnashing teeth,   305
hewing and bursting through the heath,
shooting wild arrows, sheaf on sheaf,
at trembling shade or shaken leaf.

In fateful hour was Beren born:
he laughed at dart and wailing horn;   310
fleetest of foot of living men,
tireless on fell and light on fen,
elf-wise in wood, he passed away,
defended by his hauberk grey,
of dwarvish craft in Nogrod made,   315
where hammers rang in cavern's shade.

As fearless Beren was renowned:
when men most hardy upon ground
were reckoned folk would speak his name,
foretelling that his after-fame   320
would even golden Hador pass
or Barahir and Bregolas;
but sorrow now his heart had wrought
to fierce despair, no more he fought

in hope of life or joy or praise,   325
but seeking so to use his days
only that Morgoth deep should feel
the sting of his avenging steel,
ere death he found and end of pain:
his only fear was thraldom's chain.   330
Danger he sought and death pursued,
and thus escaped the doom he wooed,
and deeds of breathless daring wrought
alone, of which the rumour brought
new hope to many a broken man.   335
They whispered 'Beren', and began
in secret swords to whet, and soft
by shrouded hearths at evening oft
songs they would sing of Beren's bow,
of Dagmor his sword: how he would go   340
silent to camps and slay the chief,
or trapped in his hiding past belief
would slip away, and under night
by mist or moon, or by the light
of open day would come again.   345
Of hunters hunted, slayers slain
they sang, of Gorgol the Butcher hewn,
of ambush in Ladros, fire in Drûn,
of thirty in one battle dead,
of wolves that yelped like curs and fled,   350
yea, Sauron himself with wound in hand.
Thus one alone filled all that land

with fear and death for Morgoth's folk;
his comrades were the beech and oak
who failed him not, and wary things   355
with fur and fell and feathered wings
that silent wander, or dwell alone
in hill and wild and waste of stone
watched o'er his ways, his faithful friends.

　　Yet seldom well an outlaw ends;   360
and Morgoth was a king more strong
than all the world has since in song
recorded: dark athwart the land
reached out the shadow of his hand,
at each recoil returned again;   365
two more were sent for one foe slain.
New hope was cowed, all rebels killed;
quenched were the fires, the songs were stilled,
tree felled, hearth burned, and through the waste
marched the black host of Orcs in haste.   370
　　Almost they closed their ring of steel
round Beren; hard upon his heel
now trod their spies; within their hedge
of all aid shorn, upon the edge
of death at bay he stood aghast   375
and knew that he must die at last,
or flee the land of Barahir,
his land beloved. Beside the mere
beneath a heap of nameless stones

must crumble those once mighty bones,   380
forsaken by both son and kin,
bewailed by reeds of Aeluin.

In winter's night the houseless North
he left behind, and stealing forth
the leaguer of his watchful foe   385
he passed – a shadow on the snow,
a swirl of wind, and he was gone,
the ruin of Dorthonion,
Tarn Aeluin and its water wan,
never again to look upon.   390
No more shall hidden bowstring sing,
no more his shaven arrows wing,
no more his hunted head shall lie
upon the heath beneath the sky.
The Northern stars, whose silver fire   395
of old Men named the Burning Briar,
were set behind his back, and shone
o'er land forsaken; he was gone.

Southward he turned, and south away
his long and lonely journey lay,   400
while ever loomed before his path
the dreadful peaks of Gorgorath.
Never had foot of man most bold
yet trod those mountains steep and cold,
nor climbed upon their sudden brink,   405
whence, sickened, eyes must turn and shrink

to see their southward cliffs fall sheer
in rocky pinnacle and pier
down into shadows that were laid
before the sun and moon were made.   410
In valleys woven with deceit
and washed with waters bitter-sweet
dark magic lurked in gulf and glen;
but out away beyond the ken
of mortal sight the eagle's eye   415
from dizzy towers that pierced the sky
might grey and gleaming see afar,
as sheen on water under star,
Beleriand, Beleriand,
the borders of the Elven-land.   420

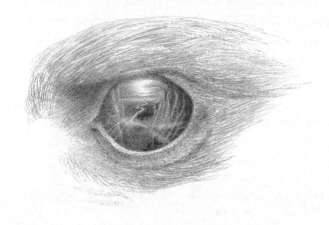

LIST OF NAMES IN THE
ORIGINAL TEXTS

I have made this *List of Names* (restricted to names that occur
in the passages of my father's writing), which is obviously not
an index, with two purposes in mind.

Neither of them is in any way essential to the book. In the
first place, it is intended to assist a reader who cannot recall,
among the mass of names (and forms of names), the reference
of one that may be of significance in the narrative. In the second
place, certain names, especially those that occur rarely or only
once in the texts, are provided with a slightly fuller explanation. For example, while this is obviously of no significance
in the tale, one may nonetheless want to know why the Eldar
would not touch spiders 'because of Ungweliantë' (p. 41).

Aeluin   A lake in the northeast of Dorthonion where Barahir and
his companions made their lair.
Aglon   A narrow pass between Taur-na-Fuin and the Hill of
Himring, held by sons of Fëanor.
Ainur   (singular *Ainu*) 'The Holy Ones': the Valar and the Maiar.

[The name *Maiar* was a late introduction of an earlier conception: 'With the great ones came many lesser spirits, beings of their own kind but of smaller might' (such as Melian).]

Aman The Land in the West beyond the Great Sea in which the Valar dwelt ('the Blessed Realm').

Anfauglith 'The Gasping Dust'. See *Dor-na-Fauglith, The Thirsty Plain*.

Angainu The great chain, made by the Vala Aulë, in which Morgoth was bound (later *Angainor*).

Angamandi (plural) 'The Hells of Iron'. See *Angband*.

Angband The great dungeon-fortress of Morgoth in the north-west of Middle-earth.

Angrim Father of Gorlim the Unhappy.

Angrod Son of Finrod (later Finarfin).

Arda The Earth.

Artanor 'The Land Beyond'; region subsequently named Doriath, the kingdom of Tinwelint (Thingol).

Aryador 'Land of Shadow', a name of Hisilómë (Dor-lómin) among Men. See *Hisilómë*.

Ascar River in Ossiriand, renamed *Rathlorion* 'Goldenbed' when the treasure of Doriath was sunk in it.

Aulë The great Vala known as Aulë the Smith; he is 'a master of all crafts', and 'his lordship is over all the substances of which Arda is made.'

Ausir A name of Dior.

Balrogs [In the *Lost Tales* the Balrogs are conceived as existing 'in hundreds'. They are called 'demons of power'; they wear iron armour, and they have claws of steel and whips of flame.]

Barahir A chieftain of Men, the father of Beren.

Bauglir 'The Constrainer', a name of Morgoth among the Noldor.

Beleg Elf of Doriath, a great archer, called *Cúthalion*, 'Strongbow'; close companion and friend of Túrin Turambar, by whom he was tragically slain.

Belegost One of the two great cities of the Dwarves in the Blue Mountains.

Beleriand   (earlier name *Broseliand*) The great region of Middle-earth, largely drowned and destroyed at the end of the First Age, extending from the Blue Mountains in the East to the Mountains of Shadow in the North (see *Iron Mountains*) and the western coasts.

Bëor   Leader of the first Men to enter Beleriand. See *Edain*.

Bitter Hills   See *Iron Mountains*.

Blessed Realm   See *Aman*.

Blue Mountains   The great range forming the eastern bounds of Beleriand.

Boldog   A captain of Orcs.

Bregolas   Brother of Barahir.

Burning Briar   The constellation of the Great Bear.

Calacirya   A pass in the Mountains of Valinor in which was the city of the Elves.

Carcharoth   See *Karkaras*.

Celegorm   Son of Fëanor, called 'the Fair'.

Cranthir   Son of Fëanor, called 'the Dark'.

i-Cuilwarthon   'The Dead that Live Again', Beren and Lúthien after their return from Mandos; *Cuilwarthien*: The land where they dwelt. (Later form *Guilwarthon*.)

Cuiviénen   The Water of Awakening: the lake in Middle-earth where the Elves awoke.

Cûm-nan-Arasaith   The Mound of Avarice, raised over the slain in Menegroth.

Curufin   Son of Fëanor, called 'the Crafty'.

Dagmor   Beren's sword.

Dairon   A minstrel of Artanor, numbered among 'the three most magic players of the Elves'; originally the brother of Lúthien.

Damrod and *Díriel*   The youngest sons of Fëanor. (Later names *Amrod* and *Amras*.)

Deadly Nightshade   A translation of *Taur-na-Fuin*; see *Mountains of Night*.

Dior   Son of Beren and Lúthien; father of Elwing, the mother of Elrond and Elros.

Doriath   The later name of Artanor, the great forested region ruled by Thingol (Tinwelint) and Melian (Gwendeling).

Dor-lómin   See *Hisilómë*.

Dor-na-Fauglith   The great grassy plain of Ard-galen north of the Mountains of Night (*Dorthonion*) that was transformed into a desert (see *Anfauglith*, *The Thirsty Plain*).

Dorthonion   'Land of Pines'; vast region of pinewoods on the northern borders of Beleriand; afterwards called *Taur-na-Fuin*, 'the Forest under Night'.

Drûn   A region to the north of Lake Aeluin; not named elsewhere.

Draugluin   Greatest of the werewolves of Thû (Sauron).

Eärámë   'Eagle's Pinion', Tuor's ship.

Eärendel   (later form *Eärendil*) Son of Tuor and Idril daughter of Turgon King of Gondolin; wedded Elwing.

Edain   'The Second People', Men, but used chiefly of the three Houses of the Elf-friends who came earliest to Beleriand.

Egnor bo-Rimion   'The huntsman of the Elves': the father of Beren, replaced by Barahir.

Egnor   Son of Finrod (later Finarfin).

Eilinel   Wife of Gorlim.

Elbereth   'Queen of the Stars'; see *Varda*.

Eldalië   (The people of the Elves), the Eldar.

Eldar   The Elves of the Great Journey from the place of their awakening; sometimes used in early texts to mean all Elves.

Elfinesse   An inclusive name for all the lands of the Elves.

Elrond of Rivendell   Son of Elwing and Eärendel.

Elros   Son of Elwing and Eärendel; first King of Númenor.

Elwing   Daughter of Dior, wedded Eärendel, mother of Elrond and Elros.

Eönwë   Herald of Manwë.

Erchamion   'One-handed', name given to Beren; other forms *Ermabwed*, *Elmavoitë*.

Esgalduin   River of Doriath, passing Menegroth (the halls of Thingol), and flowing into Sirion.

Fëanor   Eldest son of Finwë; maker of the Silmarils.

Felagund   Noldorin Elf, founder of Nargothrond and sworn friend of Barahir father of Beren. [On the relation of the names *Felagund* and *Finrod* see p. 104.]

Fingolfin   The second son of Finwë; slain in single combat with Morgoth.

Fingon   Eldest son of Fingolfin; king of the Noldor after the death of his father.

Finrod   The third son of Finwë. [Name replaced by *Finarfin*, when *Finrod* became the name of his son, *Finrod Felagund*.]

Finwë   Leader of the second host of the Elves, the Noldor (Noldoli), on the Great Journey.

Foamriders   The kindred of the Eldar named the *Solosimpi*, later the *Teleri*; the third and last host on the Great Journey.

Gaurhoth   The werewolves of Thû (Sauron); *Gaurhoth Isle*, see *Tol-in-Gaurhoth*.

Gelion   The great river of East Beleriand fed by rivers flowing from the Blue Mountains in the region of Ossiriand.

Gilim   A giant, named by Lúthien in her 'lengthening' spell sung over her hair (p. 55), unknown save for the corresponding passage in *The Lay of Leithian*, where he is called 'the giant of Eruman' [a region on the coast of Aman 'where the shadows were deepest and thickest in the world'].

Gimli   A very old and blind Noldorin Elf, long a captive slave in the stronghold of Tevildo, possessed of an extraordinary power of hearing. He plays no part in *The Tale of Tinúviel* or in any other tale, and never reappears.

Ginglith   River flowing into the Narog above Nargothrond.

Glómund, Glorund   Earlier names of Glaurung, 'Father of Dragons', the great dragon of Morgoth.

Gnomes   Early translation of *Noldoli*, *Noldor*: See pp. 32–3.

Gods   See *Valar*.

Gondolin   The hidden city founded by Turgon the second son of Fingolfin.

Gorgol   the Butcher   An Orc slain by Beren.

Gorgorath (Also *Gorgoroth*) The Mountains of Terror; the precipices in which Dorthonion fell southwards.

Gorlim One of the companions of Barahir, the father of Beren; he revealed their hiding place to Morgoth (later Sauron). Called *Gorlim the Unhappy.*

Great Lands The lands east of the Great Sea: Middle-earth [a term never used in the *Lost Tales*].

Great Sea of the West *Belegaer*, extending from Middle-earth to Aman.

Green Elves The Elves of Ossiriand, called *Laiquendi.*

Grinding Ice *Helkaraxë*: the strait in the far North between Middle-earth and the Western Land.

Grond Weapon of Morgoth, a great club known as the Hammer of the Underworld.

Guarded Plain The great plain between the rivers Narog and Teiglin, north of Nargothrond.

Guilwarthon See *i-Cuilwarthon*.

Gwendeling Earlier name of Melian.

Hador A great chieftain of Men, called 'the Goldenhaired', grandfather of Húrin father of Túrin, and of Huor father of Tuor father of Eärendel.

Haven of the Swans See *Notes on the Elder Days*, p. 23.

Hills of the Hunters (also *The Hunters' Wold*) The highlands west of the river Narog.

Himling A great hill in the north of East Beleriand, a stronghold of the sons of Fëanor.

Hirilorn 'Queen of Trees', a great beech-tree near Menegroth (Thingol's halls); in its branches was the house in which Lúthien was imprisoned.

Hisilómë Hithlum. [In a list of names of the period of the *Lost Tales* it is said: '*Dor-lómin* or the "Land of Shadow" was that region named of the Eldar *Hisilómë* (and this means "shadowy twilights") . . . and it is so called by reason of the scanty sun which peeps little over the Iron Mountains to the east and south of it.']

Hithlum See *Hisilómë*.

Huan The mighty wolfhound of Valinor, who became the friend and saviour of Beren and Lúthien.

Húrin Father of Túrin Turambar and Niënor.

Idril Called *Celebrindal* 'Silverfoot', daughter of Turgon King of Gondolin; wedded to Tuor, mother of Eärendel.

Ilkorins, Ilkorindi Elves not of Kôr, city of the Elves in Aman (see *Kôr*).

Indravangs (also *Indrafangs*) 'Long Beards', the Dwarves of Belegost.

Ingwil River flowing into the Narog at Nargothrond (later form *Ringwil*).

Iron Mountains Also called the *Bitter Hills*. A great range corresponding to the later *Ered Wethrin, the Mountains of Shadow*, forming the southern and eastern borders of Hisilómë (Hithlum). See *Hisilómë*.

Ivárë A renowned minstrel of the Elves, 'who plays beside the sea'.

Ivrin The lake below the Mountains of Shadow where the Narog rose.

Karkaras The huge wolf that guarded the gates of Angband (later *Carcharoth*), its tail named in Lúthien's 'lengthening spell'; translated 'Knife-fang'.

Kôr City of the Elves in Aman, and the hill on which it was built; later the city became *Tûn* and the hill alone was *Kôr*. [Finally the city became *Tirion* and the hill *Túna*.]

Ladros A region to the northeast of Dorthonion.

Lay of Leithian, The See p. 88.

Lonely Isle *Tol Eressëa*: a large island in the Great Sea near the coasts of Aman; the most easterly of the Undying Lands, where many Elves dwelt.

Lórien The Valar Mandos and Lórien were called brothers, and named the *Fanturi*: Mandos was *Néfantur* and Lórien was *Olofantur*. In the words of the *Quenta* Lórien was the 'maker of visions and of dreams; and his gardens in the land of the Gods were the fairest of all places in the world and filled with many spirits of beauty and power.'

Mablung   'Heavy hand', Elf of Doriath, chief captain of Thingol; present at the death of Beren in the hunt of Karkaras.

Magic Isles   Isles in the Great Sea.

Maglor   The second son of Fëanor, a celebrated singer and minstrel.

Maiar   See *Ainur*.

Maidros   Eldest son of Fëanor, called 'the Tall' (later form *Maedhros*).

Mandos   A Vala of great power. He is the Judge; and he is the keeper of the Houses of the Dead, and the summoner of the spirits of the slain [the *Quenta*]. See *Lórien*.

Manwë   The chief and most mighty of the Valar, the spouse of Varda.

Melian   The Queen of Artanor (Doriath), earlier name *Gwendeling*; a Maia, who came to Middle-earth from the realm of the Vala Lórien.

Melko   The great evil Vala, Morgoth (later form *Melkor*).

Menegroth   See *The Thousand Caves*.

Miaulë   A cat, cook in the kitchen of Tevildo.

Mîm   A dwarf, who settled in Nargothrond after the departure of the Dragon and laid a curse on the treasure.

Mindeb   A river flowing into Sirion in the region of Doriath.

Mountains of Night   The great heights (*Dorthonion*, 'Land of Pines') that came to be called *The Forest of Night* (*Taurfuin*, later *Taur-na-[-nu-]fuin*).

Mountains of Shadow, Shadowy Mountains   See *Iron Mountains*.

Nan   The only thing known of Nan seems to be the name of his sword, *Glend*, named in Lúthien's 'lengthening spell' (see *Gilim*).

Nan Dumgorthin   'The land of the dark idols' where Huan came upon Beren and Lúthien in their flight from Angband. In the alliterative poem the *Lay of the Children of Húrin* (see p. 78) occur these lines:

in Nan Dungorthin   where nameless gods
have shrouded shrines   in shadows secret,
more old than Morgoth   or the ancient lords
the golden Gods   of the guarded West.

Nargothrond The great cavernous city and fortress founded by Felagund on the river Narog in West Beleriand.

Narog River in West Beleriand; see *Nargothrond*. Often used in the sense 'realm', i.e. 'of Nargothrond'.

Naugladur Lord of the Dwarves of Nogrod.

Nauglamír The Necklace of the Dwarves, in which was set the Silmaril of Beren and Lúthien.

Nessa The sister of Oromë and spouse of Tulkas. See *Valier*.

Nogrod One of the two great cities of the Dwarves in the Blue Mountains.

Noldoli, later *Noldor* The second host of the Eldar on the Great Journey, led by Finwë.

Oikeroi A fierce warrior-cat in the service of Tevildo, slain by Huan.

Orodreth Brother of Felagund; King of Nargothrond after the death of Felagund.

Oromë The Vala called the Hunter; led on his horse the hosts of the Eldar on the Great Journey.

Ossiriand 'The Land of Seven Rivers', Gelion and its tributaries from the Blue Mountains.

Outer Lands Middle-earth.

Palisor The region of the Great Lands where the Elves awoke.

Rathlorion River in Ossiriand. See *Ascar*.

Ringil The sword of Fingolfin.

Rivil River rising in the west of Dorthonion and flowing into Sirion at the fens of Serech, north of Tol Sirion.

Sarn Athrad The Ford of Stones, where the river Ascar in Ossiriand was crossed by the road to the cities of the Dwarves in the Blue Mountains.

Serech Great fens where the Rivil flowed into the Sirion; see *Rivil*.

Shadowy Mountains, *Mountains of Shadow* See *Iron Mountains*.

Shadowy Seas A region of the Great Sea of the West.

Sickle of the Gods   The constellation of the Great Bear [which Varda set above the North as a threat to Morgoth and an omen of his fall.]

Silmarils   The three great jewels filled with the light of the Two Trees of Valinor, made by Fëanor. See pp. 36–7.

Silpion   The White Tree of Valinor, from whose flowers there fell a dew of silver light; also called *Telperion*.

Sirion   The great river of Beleriand, rising in the Mountains of Shadow and flowing southward, dividing East from West Beleriand.

Taniquetil   The highest Mountain of Aman, the abode of Manwë and Varda.

Taurfuin, *Taur-na-fuin*, (later -*nu*-)   The Forest of Night; see *Mountains of Night*.

Tavros   Gnomish name of the Vala Oromë: 'Lord of Forests'; later form *Tauros*.

Tevildo   The Prince of Cats, mightiest of all cats, 'possessed of an evil spirit' (see pp. 49, 69); a close companion of Morgoth.

Thangorodrim   The mountains above Angband.

Thingol   King of Artanor (Doriath); earlier name *Tinwelint*. [His name was *Elwë*: he was a leader of the third host of the Eldar, the Teleri, on the Great Journey, but in Beleriand he was known as 'Greycloak' (the meaning of *Thingol*).]

Thirsty Plain   See *Dor-na-Fauglith*.

Thorondor   King of Eagles.

Thousand Caves   *Menegroth*: The hidden halls of Tinwelint (Thingol) on the river Esgalduin in Artanor.

Thû   The Necromancer, greatest of the servants of Morgoth, dwelling in the Elvish watchtower on Tol Sirion; later name *Sauron*.

Thuringwethil   Name taken by Lúthien in bat-form before Morgoth.

Timbrenting   Old English name of Taniquetil.

Tinfang Warble   A famous minstrel [*Tinfang* = Quenya *timpinen* 'fluter'.]

Tinúviel   'Daughter of Twilight', nightingale: name given to Lúthien by Beren.

Tinwelint King of Artanor; see *Thingol*, the later name.

Tirion City of the Elves in Aman; see *Kôr*.

Tol-in-Gaurhoth Isle of Werewolves, the name of Tol Sirion after its capture by Morgoth.

Tol Sirion The island in the river Sirion on which there was an Elvish fortress; see *Tol-in-Gaurhoth*.

Tulkas The Vala described in the *Quenta* as 'the strongest of all the Gods in limbs (IV.79) and greatest in all feats of valour and prowess'.

Tuor Cousin of Túrin and father of Eärendil.

Túrin Son of Húrin and Morwen; named *Turambar* 'Master of Doom'.

Uinen A Maia (see *Ainur*). 'The Lady of the Seas', 'whose hair lies spread through all the waters under sky'; named in Lúthien's 'lengthening spell'.

Ulmo 'Lord of Waters', the great Vala of the Seas.

Umboth-Muilin The *Twilight Meres*, where Aros, the southern river of Doriath, flowed into Sirion.

Umuiyan An old cat, the doorkeeper of Tevildo.

Ungweliantë The monstrous spider, dwelling in Eruman (see *Gilim*), who with Morgoth destroyed the Two Trees of Valinor; (later form *Ungoliant*).

Valar (singular Vala) 'The Powers'; in early texts referred to as the *Gods*. They are the great beings who entered the World at the beginning of Time. [In the *Lost Tale of the Music of the Ainur* Eriol said: 'I would fain know who be these Valar; are they the Gods?' He received this reply: 'So be they, though concerning them Men tell many strange and garbled tales that are far from the truth, and many strange names they call them that you will not hear here.']

Valier (singular *Valië*) The 'Queens of the Valar'; in this book are named only Varda, Vána and Nessa.

Valinor The land of the Valar in Aman.

Valmar, Valimar   City of the Valar in Valinor.

Vána   The spouse of Oromë. See *Valier.*

Varda   Greatest of the Valier; the spouse of Manwë; maker of the stars [hence her name *Elbereth*, 'Queen of the Stars'].

Vëannë   The teller of *The Tale of Tinúviel.*

Wingelot   'Foamflower', Eärendel's ship.

Wizard's Isle   Tol Sirion.

Wood-elves   Elves of Artanor.

GLOSSARY

This glossary contains words (including forms and meanings of words differing from modern usage) that seemed to me liable to give difficulty. The content of such a list as this cannot of course be systematic, deriving from some external standard.

an   if, 45, 48, 52, 59, 80, 82, etc.
bent   open place covered with grass, 144
bid   offered, 241
chase   hunting ground, 181
clomb   old past tense of *climb*, 202
corse   corpse, 193
croft   small plot of land, 122
drouth   dryness, 125
entreat   treat, 60, 65; [modern sense] 61, 83
envermined   full of noxious creatures, 186. This word seems not to be otherwise recorded.
fell   hide, 72, 101, 146, 153–4, 185–8, etc.
flittermouse   bat, 210

forhungered   starved, 173
frith   wood, woodland, 143
frore   very cold, 113
glamoury   magic, enchantment, 125
haggard   (of hills) wild, 177
haply   perhaps, 45, 96, 118
hem and hedge   enclose and fence off, 101
howe   burial mound, barrow, 234
inane   empty, 190
lave   wash, 55
leeches   physicians, 173, 176
let   hinder, 124: *their going let* 'hinder their passing'
like   please, 88 (in *doth it like thee?*)
limber   supple, 143
march   borderland, 178, 195
neb   beak, bill, 97, 265–6
nesh   soft, tender, 215
opes   opens, 198
parlous   dangerous, 268
pled   old past tense of *plead*, 170
quook   old past tense of *quake*, 192
rede   counsel, 48, 59
rove   past tense of *rive* 'rend, tear apart, cleave', 213
ruel-bone   ivory, 143
runagate   deserter, renegade, 48
scullion   kitchen drudge, 51
shores   supports, 203
sigaldry   sorcery, 125
slot   track of an animal, 83–4
spoor   the same as *slot*, 84
sprite   spirit, 49
sylphine   of the nature of a sylph (a spirit inhabiting the air), 210.
   This adjective is not recorded.
swath   (space left after passage of a mower) track, trace, 127
tarn   a small mountain lake, 258

thews   bodily strength, 76

thrall   a slave, one who is in bondage (thraldom), 20, 47–9, 59, 69, 73, etc.

trammelled   hampered, impeded, 151

unkempt   uncombed, 51

viol   a stringed instrument played with a bow, 158, 176

weft   woven fabric, 173

weird   fate, 144, 177

weregild   (Old English) the price set upon a man in accordance with his rank, 258

whin   gorse, 259

wolfhame   wolfskin, 185

woof   woven fabric, 213

would   wished, 184–5, 205